ARCHANGEL ONE

ALSO BY EVAN CURRIE

Odyssey One Series

Into the Black

The Heart of Matter

Homeworld

Out of the Black

Warrior King

Odysseus Awakening

Odysseus Ascendant

Odyssey One: Star Rogue Series

King of Thieves

Warrior's Wings Series

On Silver Wings

Valkyrie Rising

Valkyrie Burning

The Valhalla Call

By Other Means

De Oppresso Liber

Open Arms

The Scourwind Legacy

Heirs of Empire

An Empire Asunder

The Atlantis Rising Series

The Knighthood

The Demon City

The Superhuman Series

Superhuman

Superhuman: Countdown to Apocalypse

Other Works

SEAL Team 13

Steam Legion

Thermals

ARCHANGEL ONE

ONE

EVAN CURRIE

47NORTH

This is a work of fiction. Names, characters, organizations, places, events, and incidents are either products of the author's imagination or are used fictitiously. Any resemblance to actual persons, living or dead, or actual events is purely coincidental.

Published by 47North, Seattle

www.apub.com

Amazon, the Amazon logo, and 47North are trademarks of Amazon.com, Inc., or its affiliates.

ISBN-13: 9781542004862
ISBN-10: 1542004861

Cover design by Mike Heath | Shannon Associates

Printed in the United States of America

ARCHANGEL ONE

Prologue

Commander Stephen "Stephanos" Michaels walked the long curving corridors of the new stellar base, rather enjoying the feel of the first human-built platform that had the advantages of Priminae technology behind it. He liked human construction—or "Terran construction" to be precise, he supposed—as a rule.

The Priminae were fond of ceramics as their primary work material, and in fairness they had access to some exceptional variations of that material. For Steph, however, steel was king.

Luckily, metals were cheap once you had access to the solar system. Even more so when you had even the beginnings of a Kardashev Class Two Network propagating itself through the system. The replicating machines that consisted of the admiral's first line of defense for Sol were also exceptional miners.

Steph glanced at the camera as he approached the security door, letting it scan his biometrics, and didn't pause or slow his pace as the door locks disengaged. It slid smoothly open in time for him to pass from the transit corridor into the main flight hangar.

Life had changed since the showdown with the Empire; it had gotten a lot less exciting in some ways, but a lot more fun from his perspective.

"Commander." Alexandra Black nodded in his direction as he approached. "Morning."

"Good morning, Alex." Steph smiled. "It's a fine one, isn't it?"

She smirked. "I doubt you'd be as chipper if you weren't on the flight schedule today."

"Chipper? Really?" he asked, amused. "How rather British of you, Commander Black."

Alexandra rolled her eyes, shifting the subject. "Any idea what this one is going to be?"

Steph shook his head. "Afraid not. We've been running through so many design concepts in the last few months that I've lost track, but this one is coming down the pipe from Gracen's office, so I'm looking forward to it."

Alex frowned. "Don't know the admiral that well."

"She's good people," Steph said. "And effective."

"That's always a good sign," Black said, rising up from her position as her eyes looked over Steph's shoulder.

Steph noticed her stiffening to attention and automatically did the same himself, not turning around.

"It is, isn't it?" Admiral Amanda Gracen said crisply as she stepped into view, nodding to Steph. "And for what it's worth, Steph, the word is that you're good people too. Effective? Well, we'll have to see about that."

"Yes ma'am," he said curtly.

What else was there to say?

"It's a pleasure to see you." Gracen smoothly shifted to business. "As you both know, we've been testing new high-mobility platforms since the standoff at Luna."

They nodded. The pair of them had been testing new designs for manned and unmanned combat craft and delivering reports on the weaknesses and strengths of the new platform designs for some time. The new projects had been ongoing since shortly after the military standoff was ended by the deployment of Earth's captured heliocannon against Imperial targets, in fact. It wasn't the same as a deep-space deployment, but it was work that both pilots were enthusiastic about, enjoyed intensely, and knew would be absolutely vital to Earth's continued defense.

Prior to the last few battles that led to the standoff, light high-mobility craft had been considered obsolete compared to the sheer power of an Odysseus Class battle cruiser. Both Steph and Alex had been integral to proving that manned and unmanned fighters still had a place in modern doctrine. That had bought them their new jobs while many of their compatriots enjoyed extended leave. Since the two would either have been flying anyway while on leave or bored to tears, neither was complaining about the work.

"Your reports on the new designs have been invaluable," Gracen told them. "And, in fact, your findings were all funneled into the design specifications for the project you'll be testing today. The project lead has been most appreciative of your hard work."

"Thank you, ma'am," the two said as one.

"At ease, both of you," Gracen ordered, gesturing past them toward the secure hangar. "Shall we?"

With Gracen leading the way, Steph and Alex followed along while most of the admiral's staff remained behind. At the secure hangar access, Gracen let the system scan her biometrics but then followed it up with a code that unlocked the doors and let them through.

Inside the secure zone, a lot of work was in progress, and the frenetic energy of the hangar had multiple areas competing for attention. Both pilots' gazes locked onto an object in the center of the hangar, eyes widening as they took it in.

The design was unlike anything either had seen, let alone flown. It looked too sleek to be Terran or Priminae space design, and it certainly wasn't anything remotely like what the Imperials had fielded during the conflict.

Steph recognized the telltale sheen of cam-plate armor, but that was about all the design had in common with anything he'd ever encountered. The craft was gorgeous.

A sleek needlepoint design bulged out toward the aft, and no signs of external hard points were evident anywhere. The wings were stubby but clearly designed to operate as airfoils, and as they got closer, Steph realized that he couldn't see any sign of a cockpit canopy.

"Is it a drone?" he asked the admiral.

"No, it's a functional prototype that's almost ready to go to full production," she answered. "Operated by small crews with a primary function as a fighter/bomber, but with extended operational ability."

"Never seen anything like it," Steph said. "Priminae design from the archives?"

"Negative." Gracen shook her head. "And the uniqueness of the design is intentional. We're pairing this design with a small logistics vessel to outfit a squadron for deep-black runs."

Steph frowned pensively for a moment as he considered that, but Alex got it first.

"You're setting up a . . . privateer force?" she asked, uncertain.

"Not precisely, but close," Gracen confirmed. "More a covert operations group . . . a *well-equipped* covert operations group. I want you two to run this prototype through the final testing phase. Everything should be in order, but there are a few new systems incorporated that require a top-to-bottom test before I give the final production clearance."

"How long do we have?"

"Not long," Gracen told Steph with a serious purse of her lips. "Admiralty does not believe that the Empire will stay cowed for long. They aren't the type."

Steph nodded, knowing that was the truth. He walked around the fighter, examining it from all directions before finally giving up.

"How the hell do we get *into* this thing?"

4

"That, Stephan," a new voice sounded from around them, "is all in a twist of the mind."

Steph jumped back as a section of the fighter wavered, then flowed apart to reform into a ramp. He smiled a moment later as he recognized the person stepping out of the dark interior.

"Milla!" Steph hugged the smaller form as she alighted on the deck. "I thought you were back on Ranquil!"

"Non." Milla shook her head. "The admiral asked me to help with the designs for the new class of ships. It was not something I could turn down."

Gracen snorted softly. "Lieutenant Commander Chans led the project, turning your test results into what you see before you. This is her baby."

Milla shrugged, a little self-conscious as she turned back to the ship. "It was a pleasure. Stephan, I believe you will like this."

"You're bringing fighters back, Milla," Steph said lightly. "I already *love* it."

"It is . . . not the same as your fighter, Stephan, but I believe it will be what is needed now," she told him as she gestured to the interior of the craft. "Please, after you both."

Alex and Steph exchanged glances before moving toward the lowered ramp. Steph walked up first into the interior and found himself looking at an almost featureless space. He paused, confused, forcing Alex to step out around him to see for herself.

"Where are the controls?" he asked. "Recessed somewhere?"

"Yes and no," Milla told him, gesturing in front of her.

An image appeared in the air, displaying an interface that she deftly manipulated.

"It is what your people called 'quantum locked photons,'" she said. "Or, as I've been told, hard light. Somewhat of a misnomer, I'm afraid, but it does provide tactile feedback from the projection system."

"Holographic controls?" Alex winced. "Last I checked, those weren't cleared for mil-spec use in field combat."

"They still aren't," Gracen said from the entry to the craft. "The control system here is something . . . else. Lieutenant Commander, see them through it, yes?"

"Of course, Admiral," Milla responded quickly.

"I'll leave you to it, then," Gracen said, nodding at the salutes she received before stepping out.

Steph refocused on the interior of the craft, an eagerness in his gaze as he looked it over.

"Alright then, Milla . . . show us what's under the hood."

Imperial Capital, World Garisk

Jesan Mich stood silently in the midst of the gathered nobles, enduring the scowls and disdain thrown in his direction without outward emotion.

Inwardly, however, was a different matter entirely. He noted several who he knew to be fitting their weapons for a shot at his undefended flank, both literally and figuratively. He would have to deal with them when he got a chance.

If he got a chance.

The empress was not looking in his direction, listening instead to the words and accusations being flung at him while he was bound not to respond.

He had known this would happen when he ordered the retreat from the unknown race's homeworld. But dishonor was the lesser evil in his mind compared to the stupidity of risking vital resources against whatever superweapon the Terrans had deployed against his forces.

His mind still wracked itself over what he had seen out there at that alien star.

Pure energy, barely formed into a coherent mass, had torched a ship under his command from *nowhere*.

He'd lost more than his share of ships and men in the past, but to lose too much to such an unknown factor, well, that ate at him.

Where did that beam come from? A stealth vessel?

It didn't make sense. Nothing could hide while unleashing that much power. By nature that level of pure force was the very antithesis of stealth.

And then there was the military facility destroyed here, in the Empire, at the same time.

He'd confirmed that as soon as he returned to Imperial space, of course, half-afraid until then that he had been manipulated by the Terrans. But the conflagration had been real, an entire set of slips burned in fire from sources unknown.

The Empire *had* to have that weapon.

"An example must be made!"

Jesan brought his attention back to the situation at hand, forcing himself to focus on the byplay between the nobles. There would be consequences, he knew. No Imperial Fleet retreated without consequence, not in the entire long history of the Empire. He just hoped that his cause would be enough to forestall the ultimate consequences, at least for now.

Anything short of summary execution could be risen from, with the appropriate level of work and daring and luck.

"Execute the man for rank cowardice!"

There it was. Jesan felt a chill in his blood.

Lord Gith Ver, an old . . . *friend* . . . had been the first to voice such an opinion. Jesan made note of that, but it was hardly the first time he'd had to mark Ver as a foe. Once the words had been spoken, however, the murmurs began and started to build. There was nothing he could do but endure the talk, as any attempt to defend himself would only be adding oxygen to the flames.

Instead he looked to the empress, trying to get a feel for her mood. An exercise in futility. Her Highness had not survived the highest levels of the Imperial Court as long as she had by revealing even the slightest hint of her emotions without damned good cause.

Cause, it seemed, she did not have at this point.

So he listened to the demands for his life, exercising his own control to keep his expression stoic and as free of care as he could while his guts churned and threatened to eat him up from the inside.

"Enough."

Jesan started, as did most of the others in the room, as the empress made herself known, ending the debate. He looked to see her turning her focus on him as he froze in place, the deep, churning anxiety dying in him as it was replaced by an icy pit.

"*Former* Lord Jesan will not be executed," she said, both relieving him and causing his stomach to drop. "We have reviewed the mission recordings, and none of you have offered a better solution than the former lord decided upon. Asking for his execution in a situation that you would have failed at, at least in equal portion as he, is an act of *weakness.*"

Jesan winced slightly, almost feeling bad for the men and women clamoring for his life.

In other levels of Imperial culture, the empress' words might be overlooked, but in the Imperial Court, calling out the nobility for weakness was an insult worthy of challenge. He didn't envy any who sought to challenge the empress, however. There were reasons she had long held her title against all comers, her father's blood running in her veins least among them.

Silence fell as he locked his eyes on the throne behind Her Highness, waiting for the pronouncement he knew was coming.

"Former Lord Jesan will be stripped of his noble responsibilities," the empress intoned, "but will remain in rank."

Jesan's eyes widened a hair, as soft murmurs started again around him. Her Highness ignored both as she went on.

"This discussion has ended," Her Highness decreed, rising to her feet. "And court is closed. Former Lord Jesan, remain. You will be given your new assignment."

Jesan bowed his head and remained in place as the room emptied.

———

Imperial Court, Inner Chambers

Jesan walked into the inner chamber of Her Highness at court, dropping to one knee in the center of the room automatically, though he was alone. He waited there, motionless, for several long moments before the door opened to reveal the empress' bodyguards.

They secured the room with care while he remained in place until finally the bodyguards cleared the empress to enter.

"Former Lord Jesan," she said softly. "How the mighty have fallen."

"I failed, Your Majesty," Jesan replied, head bowed. "Nothing less could be expected."

"I still recall the young buck who told my father, in all confidence, that he would succeed where all others had failed . . . and then went on to do exactly that against the Pierman warlords. Father had made a note to have you killed when you failed then, did you know that?"

Jesan shook his head. "No, I did not, but in retrospect it is not something that surprises me."

The empress sighed, taking a seat before him. "I find myself in a difficult position. I rather like you, Jesan. I always have; after all, any who had the nerve . . . or the lack of intelligence, I suppose, to challenge my father while he sat on his own throne, is sure to be entertaining. In that, I must say, you have never failed me. Still, this entertainment is hardly worth the cost to the Empire."

"No, Your Highness, I know this. The shipyard slips . . ."

"Bah!" she spat, waving her hand impatiently to silence him. "A minor loss, at most. Antiquated, costing almost as much in maintenance by this point as they would to replace. The loss of actual production is a security concern, I suppose, as that sector will be light on replacement vessels for some time, but the *real* cost is to the Imperial reputation. Spies have already delivered the news of your defeat, and the manner of it, to every adversary we have in all galactic vectors. Predators have smelled a touch of blood now, Jesan. Not enough to make them believe we are weak, but enough that the *thought* will be entertained."

"The Empire is as strong today as it has ever been. We are at the *peak* of our power."

"Exactly," she practically whispered. "Once you are at your peak, there is nowhere to go but down . . . and many of our enemies know this and are watching for the signs of decline."

"They must be taught the error of misconception, then."

The empress smiled slowly. "Exactly right. Your fleet will not be reinforced, Jesan, but it remains your own. Take it and *instruct* the more belligerent of our neighbors in the errors of their ways."

Jesan nodded. "Including the . . . Priminae?"

"No. They and their allies are now off-limits to you." The empress' tone was sharp and left no room for interpretation. "Others have been assigned to that task, specifically the Eighth Fleet."

Jesan looked up sharply, forgetting himself in his surprise, before ducking his head again.

The Eighth Fleet was the only Imperial Navy organization that was *not* specifically a combat group. They certainly could wage war if forced into a corner, but their task was generally in-depth intelligence gathering on an order rarely required by the Empire.

It left the Eighth with a reputation of being near worthless, and from his experience, Jesan knew that they were often underequipped for their job because of that. If the empress was sending them, she was making a point to the court and sector governors. Jesan suspected that the Eighth would not be looked upon in the same way for long, not if those in positions of influence had any brains.

He could see the gravity well changing.

I wonder how many will be foolish enough to miss Her Highness' point on this? And how many will live to regret their mistake?

"Dismissed," the empress said, a gleam in her eye as she saw the expression on Jesan's face and expected that he had seen what others might overlook. "Before you go, however . . ."

"Yes, Your Highness?" Jesan hadn't budged from his position.

"Cooperate with the Eighth when they come to you."

"With zero hesitation, Your Highness, on my oath of service."

Chapter 1

Eric Weston looked down on the round of the Earth, hands clasped behind his back as he stood in front of the observation deck of the *Odysseus*. The blue-white ball still looked better from orbit than it ever did from the battlefield, in his opinion at least, but the black of space didn't seem so pure any longer either.

Only a few light-seconds from where he stood, he'd called down the fire of the gods . . . in a very literal sense of the word . . . and torched an alien warship in seconds. It had been a strange moment in time, one he still regarded almost as though he had been standing in front of a blackboard, lecturing a particularly stubborn student.

I hope the lesson sunk in.

Eric smiled, amused.

"Do you believe that is likely?"

Eric glanced sideways, now used to the particular nuances of the entity that existed as part of his ship.

"Honestly?" he asked the young armored entity. "No, I rather doubt it did. The Imperials we've met don't strike me as particularly good students."

"How can you tell?"

"Don't you know?" Eric asked. "Being in our heads, after all?"

"I don't live that way, Captain," Odysseus told him. "I'm not surprised you thought that, but it's more complicated. I cannot access everything you know, only those things you actively think while in my presence."

"Your presence is the entire ship," Eric said.

"Plus a significant volume surrounding the vessel, yes. However"— Odysseus frowned—"just because you think something doesn't mean you reflect on the full context of what makes that thought meaningful to you. Sometimes I know only that you believe something, not why you believe it."

Eric nodded. "I suppose that makes sense. The reason I don't believe they learned their lesson is because I'm familiar with how these sorts think. I've fought against, and served with, more than a few who thought just like them."

"I don't understand."

"Some people believe that there's no such thing as overkill, that all problems can be solved by power," Eric said. "A common belief that stems from people who aren't capable of adjusting their preconceptions as the job changes. A grunt on the ground sees only the problem in front of him, and those sorts of problems can almost always be solved by a greater application of force. As you get to see the bigger picture, though, force becomes less ideal. Small-picture people try to solve every problem with a bigger hammer, but it never works out the way they think."

"How? As long as the problem is eliminated . . ."

"There, that's the issue," Eric said. "It's not about *eliminating* problems. It's about *solving* them. Violence is spectacular at eliminating problems, but it is entirely incapable of solving them on any level. When you employ violence, there are inevitably collateral issues."

Odysseus frowned, looking puzzled and disturbed. "How so?"

"You have a terrorist, about to destroy a building," Eric said, unconsciously dropping into a lecturing tone. "To stop him, you kill the man. Problem eliminated, correct?"

The entity nodded slowly.

"But by killing the man you've now angered his family and friends, maybe motivated them to action, or possibly done the same for strangers who were previously uncommitted to the terrorist's cause. So in the future, you now have two or three or more terrorists whose direct call to action was the violence you committed to stop one terrorist."

"Does that mean one shouldn't stop a terror act with violence?" Odysseus asked in puzzlement.

"Of course not. If you have someone threatening lives, you *must* take action," Eric said. "However, you need to be cognizant of the results of that action beyond the immediate good. If you ignore the consequences, you *will* make things worse."

"I . . . I don't know how to handle or process that," Odysseus admitted. "I am . . . In a very real way, I am a warship. I am equipped to deliver violence by nature. I thought that we were solving problems facing my crew."

"Sadly, no," Eric said, shaking his head. "Violence doesn't solve problems; it just isn't a solution."

"Then why do I exist?"

"That's a weighty question," Eric said and smiled softly. "Why do any of us? But that isn't the question you really mean to ask. It's not why you exist, but why do we do what we do if violence isn't a solution, right?"

Odysseus was silent, processing.

"Perhaps," the entity finally said.

"Violence may not be a solution, but it *is* an important currency," Eric said. "Ideally, we employ violence to buy *time* for real solutions to be put into action."

Odysseus frowned. "If we're not the problem solvers, but only buy time for them . . . who solves the problems?"

Eric laughed cynically. "The way the system is currently set up? Politicians, diplomats . . ."

"I . . . am not encouraged by that answer," Odysseus admitted.

"Yeah, well, if the system worked, we wouldn't have a job," Eric joked, though he quickly sobered. "Nothing is perfect, not when humans are involved. The diplomats and politicians sure as hell aren't, but neither are we. We do our jobs, buy them time, and we trust them to do theirs and hunt for real solutions."

"This feels like something worse than merely imperfect," Odysseus said. "It is also very inefficient."

"That's not a bug, 'Diss," Eric said firmly. "That's the feature."

Odysseus stared at him. "And again I do not understand the context needed to process that."

"Efficient governments and systems *are* possible," Eric said with a shrug. "They've been done in the past. They can accomplish amazing things in short times, but they also, inevitably, do horrifying things as well. The inefficiency is the check that gives sane people time to put a stop to growing power before it can be concentrated in too few hands. Beware an efficient government, or any such organization. People in groups give up their morality in exchange for the goals of the group, so if the group is efficient, you would be horrified by how quickly you can become mired in an absolutely immoral situation."

Odysseus looked down on the planet below, considering that, before he finally spoke again.

"What do we do if that happens here?"

"We're soldiers, Odysseus," Eric said softly. "We follow orders as long as they are legal. If you wear the uniform, you follow the chain of command for any and all lawful orders."

"Lawful does not mean moral."

"No," Eric said, his voice dropping more. "No, it does not. But you do it anyway as long as you wear the uniform."

"I . . . I cannot process that," Odysseus admitted. "How can you do what is wrong, even if it's legal?"

"Every man has a line, son," Eric said. "One they will not cross. My government has never ordered me into disgrace, though there have been times I felt I was closer to that line than I ever wanted to be. If they do order me to cross it, then I hope I have the strength to take the uniform off. I'll march into hell for my world, 'Diss—I'll march anywhere for my allegiance, even hell—anywhere except into disgrace."

The entity fell silent, having nothing more to say as he considered the words. Eric decided that he had said his piece and fell silent as well. The pair remained that way, looking out on the quiet of the black beyond the observation bubble, meditating on the blue-white pearl floating in its midst.

———

Miram Heath examined the status board on the bridge, mostly out of habit, since the ship had been essentially at anchor or station-keeping while much of the crew were on leave. The *Odysseus* had completed primary repairs in a relatively short time, but now they were in the queue for major refits through the Star Forge, and that was taking longer than projected.

Because of course it is.

With major refits on the board, they were officially off the rotation for new missions, and that meant Miram was willing to take any duty shift she could in a failing attempt to avoid her paperwork.

The *Odysseus* was spooky with only a couple skeleton shifts on board, all the more so since she was well aware that the ship was, in fact, *haunted*.

"I am not a ghost, Commander."

Miram barely managed to keep from uttering a decidedly unprofessional squeak of surprise as she jumped and twisted around.

"Don't *do* that!"

"I apologize, Commander. I did not mean to surprise you."

"The hell you didn't." Miram scowled at the armored teen. "You do it too often for it not to be intentional."

The entity shrugged slightly in his armor but said nothing.

Miram rolled her eyes. "If you were enlisted, I'd put you on report. As it is, I'm telling the captain on you."

The teen's eyes widened and he took a step back. "I would prefer if you did not."

"I have no doubt you would," she said, "but you still keep this nonsense up."

The boy looked abashed, an amusing look for someone dressed in ancient Greek combat armor, Miram had to note. She sighed. "Why are you here, Odysseus?"

"You were bored," the entity said with simple honesty, "and you fed me a good entry line."

Miram scowled. "You spent far too much time with Commander Michaels."

Odysseus perked up. "When will the commander be back?"

She gestured uncertainly but with little concern. "He's on detached assignment. Nothing new has come over the reports. But, of course, you know that. I don't know why you insist on asking."

Odysseus turned slowly around, walking away from her to stand in the central command station.

"The captain told me that speaking with the crew is vital," he said, obviously quoting. "Without communication, confusion reigns . . . and communication is a two-way street."

Miram nodded. "That does sound like something the captain would say, and it's true enough too. So why are you sneaking up on me?"

"Commander Michaels said it would be funny."

Miram could only groan.

Sol System, Inside the Orbit of Mercury

Two sleek vessels accelerated hard past the dull gray orb of a planet, blue flashes of Cerenkov radiation visible as they sped past light-speed. The lead decelerated sharply and arced hard into Mercury's orbit, dipping deep enough into thin atmosphere for the heat of friction to ignite the hydrogen and oxygen present, sending flickering flames in their wake.

"Angel Lead, *Angel One.*"

"Go for Angel Lead, *Angel One.*"

"Back off, Stephanos, you're pushing the system too hard," Black said as she eased up slightly on the follow craft and lifted the nose to get a bit more minimum safe altitude from Mercury's surface.

"I need to know what it can do, Noire," Steph replied easily, increasing speed and dropping closer to the surface. "The new system is a quantum leap over NICS, but there are differences I need to map out."

"You can do that in space, where there's more margin for error."

"Negative," Steph said with a bit of a smirk in his voice. "I need to see the difference between the system's readings and what my eyes see."

He floated in the middle of a vista of the world around him, the enhanced view of Mercury lit up like an iridescent digital dream as he flew through it. He glanced over his shoulder, past the full-surround imagery that made him feel like he was flying through space under his own power.

"You okay back there?"

Milla Chans was rather pale as she gripped tightly to the straps holding her in place. "I . . . I am fine."

Steph chuckled. "You sure? You look like you've seen a ghost."

"I wish I had," Milla said sourly. "Odysseus would be a safer pilot."

"Hey! That hurts," Steph said.

"Not so much as that mountain will! Look where we are going!"

Steph glanced back to the front, noting the approach of the mountain in question.

A little small for a mountain, but it would do a job on us if we hit it, I suppose.

He adjusted his approach, climbing the incline up the range and angling through a low pass. Cliff faces flashed by, only meters away from either side of the craft, before it blew out past the mountain into the open space beyond.

"This new interface you built is a work of art, Milla," Steph said. "It's like I'm flying under my own power through open space."

He glanced up and over his shoulder, noting that Lieutenant Commander Black was holding above and just behind his position, keeping pace with his lead ship.

"You holding up okay there, Noire?" he radioed back.

"Har har, Commander," Black responded. "Are you done showboating?"

"Almost," Steph replied before pulling back sharply and putting his fighter into a steep climb, accelerating as the craft clawed for altitude.

A deep whine reverberated through the interior as the inertial compensation was pushed to the limit. The imagery flickered at the forward edge of the fighter's screens as the heat dissipation capacity of the system was overloaded by the sudden increase in friction.

"Need to work on this, Milla," Steph said. "Can't have my visibility compromised by accelerated maneuvers."

"This is not a mere accelerated maneuver!" Milla objected, white faced as she was pushed back hard into her bolstered seat by the acceleration that had overwhelmed the compensators. "You are exposing the forward sensors to extreme heat from friction!"

"This is a thin atmosphere, Milla," Steph said as the red haze cleared, the heat burning out as the ship exploded out into Mercury's orbit. "If it can't take friction here, then what happens when we take her into a habitable world's atmosphere, like Earth's?"

"Perhaps you shouldn't be approaching significant percentages of light-speed inside *any* planetary atmosphere, Stephan!"

"I need to know the limits," he said, his tone becoming serious. He ran through the diagnostics as Commander Black's fighter caught up with them and settled into a tight formation by space standards, holding off a little over a hundred kilometers from his position and course. Steph checked her course on reflex, though it was hardly necessary. "Did you get the telemetry on that, Noire?"

Black's response took a moment. "Yeah, I got it, and I also get why you guys had a rep for being insane during the war."

Steph laughed openly as he finished the diagnostics, getting green results across every category.

"Yeah, I've heard that before," he said, his focus now on the computers. "But everything looks good on this side, so I'm inclined to give my stamp of approval pending an outer hull teardown."

Black sighed audibly over the network. "Agreed. Lieutenant Commander Chans, my compliments. I've never flown anything as responsive, and this new interface is intuitive on a level I've never experienced. We do need to war-game these against realistic foes, however, because I'm not certain about reaction times in combat."

"We have been simulating that so far, and there have been issues," Milla admitted. "Primarily, it is extremely difficult to react quickly enough in the event of near-contact combat."

Steph snorted. "No kidding. When your weapons travel at light-speed, anything less than a few tens of thousands of kilometers is point-blank—and anything more than that, you *still* won't get any warning before a shot lands. I don't suppose we could use swarm drones, the way the *Odysseus* did in the battle of Sol?"

"Unfortunately not," Milla said. "The cargo space is too limited, even if we completely emptied all consumables, including weapons—"

"We won't be doing that," Steph interrupted hastily.

"Even if we did," Milla went on, giving him a sour look, "we could not deploy more than a tiny handful of useful drones. The *Odysseus* requires *hundreds* to create a reasonable detection grid along even a nominal firing arc. Thousands would be required to defend the entire vessel, and even with those numbers there would be a significant number of potential holes in the detection grid. It simply isn't possible to do the same with fighters of this size."

"Pity," Black offered over the open channel as the two ships headed back toward the Star Forge at a more moderate cruise.

"Yeah, no kidding," Steph sighed. "But I suppose our strengths are the same as they've always been: small, fast, and nimble. Sure, we could be taken out easy enough if you can hit us—but good luck meeting that requirement."

"That is more or less what I was told when I presented the issues with drones, yes," Milla answered. "Defensively, this class of fighter is quite impressive by older standards . . . but against a warship? No, there is no armor or defense we could mount that would guarantee survival in that scenario."

"Never has been," Black said. "So can't miss what we never had."

"Ain't that the truth," Steph said before he grinned. "Besides, as fast and maneuverable as these are, hitting us just got *magnitudes* more difficult. Float like a photon, sting like antihydrogen."

Milla scrunched up her face. "What?"

"Never mind," Black cut in. "That one would take too long to explain, and it's not particularly clever anyway."

Steph pouted the rest of the way back to the Star Forge.

———

Star Forge Alpha

"How are they looking?"

Commodore Beckett glanced back over his shoulder, nodding to the admiral, before looking back down to the telemetry they were receiving from the two prototype fighters. Gracen was not one to stand on ceremony when there was no reason for it, so he just gestured down to the screens before answering.

"Aside from Michaels being insane? Looking good," he admitted dryly.

"During the war, the Archangels were known for accomplishing missions no one thought were possible. Crazy comes with the territory," Gracen replied as she walked up to the display and glanced over the numbers herself. "What did he do that was crazy?"

"See these velocity readings here?"

Gracen nodded. "Right. What about them?"

"He was inside the atmosphere of Mercury at the time."

The admiral was silent for a long moment, then merely nodded again. "Ah, yes, that would qualify, I suppose."

She jotted down a note into the system without further comment, attracting the commodore's curiosity.

"What was that?" he asked.

"Just making sure that the engineering team knows to strip his fighter down to the bare fuselage and measure *everything* before they let him back out in it," Gracen told him, wryly amused. "No sense wasting the research possibilities. I dare say he set a new record?"

"Highest velocity inside a planetary atmosphere? Yes ma'am, I checked . . . not that I really needed to."

"No, I suppose you wouldn't. One more under his belt, I suppose."

"One more? How many does the man hold?"

"I'd have to look up the records," Gracen said, "but off the top of my head, I think at least twenty. Commodore Weston holds twice that, if I recall. Most of the high-performance aeronautical records are held by Double A pilots these days, and probably will be forever, since no one is building high-performance aircraft any longer."

She gestured idly. "Maybe in fifty years a civilian engineering team will put something together that beats the platform just to say they did it, but the Archangels are the last of the high-performance aeronautical pioneers, I think. It's a starship galaxy now."

"End of an era?" Beckett asked, amused that the admiral knew even the general stats from memory.

"Some would say so." Gracen nodded. "Though others would say it's just the continuation of the old into the new. Records get retired all the time as technical skills march on. Does anyone keep track of who holds steam engine speed records anymore?"

"Actually, they have yearly trials for those at a set of tracks just outside London," Beckett answered without thinking.

Gracen looked at him, surprised. "Really?"

"Oh yes, it's a small community but it's still around," he confirmed. "I grew up in a borough nearby and used to visit to watch the trains race the clock. Of course, they do steam car races on salt flats in the States, so that's a different set of records."

Gracen laughed lightly, shaking her head. "Maybe it's not the end of an era, then, so much as just shifting gears. I can see Commander Michaels consulting in thirty years on some civilian attempt to break his records."

"Hopefully not the one he just broke, by my preference," Beckett said.

"Not in Earth's atmosphere, at least, though with the use of the counter-mass systems, the Double A platform was quite capable of coming closer than I'm comfortable with."

"Agreed."

"Well, inform the commanders and lieutenant that I want reports on my desk as soon as possible," she said as she straightened up. "We need the fighters in full production as quickly as we can manage."

"Yes ma'am," the commodore said before looking around to see if anyone was in earshot. "Ma'am?"

"Yes, Commodore?"

"What are the odds the Empire makes another play soon?"

Gracen shook her head. "I would be shocked to my core if they hadn't already set their plans in motion, Commodore."

Beckett nodded slowly. "Aye ma'am, I was afraid you were going to say that."

"That is why, if the teardown of the commander's fighter doesn't show anything unexpected, I'm ordering the system into full production," Gracen said firmly. "We have a need, and we have the strong political backing of both Earth and the Priminae. I'm pushing *everything* I can through, as fast as possible."

"Interesting times," the commodore said tiredly. "But it's nice to see things moving quickly. For a while there, after the war, all I could see was the world sinking back into old patterns. Maybe we can avoid that this time?"

"Those who don't know history are doomed to repeat it," Gracen said with a cynical tone. "Those who do? We're doomed to watch others repeat it around us while we try to hold things together. So no, I doubt we can avoid the repeating pattern, but maybe we can push it off to another generation."

"With the new life-extension therapies being made available?" Beckett asked, amused.

"Give me a couple decades, and I'll take my own ship and find some quiet planet ten thousand light-years from here to retire on," Gracen said. "Until then, I have a job to do—and so do you."

"Aye, aye, Admiral."

Chapter 2

Imperial Capital, World Garisk

"Lord Mich!"

Jesan half turned, barely looking at the person approaching him. "I am a lord no longer."

He turned to continue on his way, but the woman had caught up to him by that point and fell into step at his side.

"My apologies, Fleet Commander," she said. "I hadn't been informed of your loss."

"The council meeting was only a few days ago," he said. "I suppose it has not filtered down."

"Interesting," she said, something in her tone catching his attention.

"How so?" Jesan asked, glancing at her long enough to get her rank in mind. "Fleet Commander."

"Fleet Commander Helena Birch, Fleet Commander Mich." She nodded curtly to him as they walked. "And I merely find it interesting that Her Majesty did not mention your loss in her orders to me."

That almost made Jesan miss a step. He didn't recognize the name, and a fleet commander shouldn't be receiving orders directly from Her Imperial Highness in the first place. An untitled military commander would receive orders from a noble of equal or higher military rank.

"You must be with the Eighth," he said finally, as there was no other real possibility he could imagine. No one else would have met with the empress and then chased him down.

"I must, mustn't I?" Birch asked with a very slight smile. "I want to speak with you concerning your experiences with the Oathers and their new allies."

"Her Highness ordered me to your service on this matter." Jesan gestured ahead of them. "We are nearly to my offices here, or you may choose a place."

"Your offices would be fine, Fleet Commander."

Jesan nodded and led the way forward to the newly assigned, and much lesser, offices he had been given in the capital.

Lord Mich's Office

Helena Birch watched the man who had fallen from grace yet somehow managed to snag a limb on the way down. Few, in her experience, survived such a fall.

Fewer still managed to keep their command, albeit with a rather ugly assignment lined up for the foreseeable future.

She'd read Mich's file when the empress had given her the assignment, and she hadn't been lying when she said there had been no mention of his loss of title. Her Highness had not mentioned the change, nor was it in his file, yet as she looked around the offices he had led her to, she knew she was not in a nobleman's suite.

Curious.

"What would you like to know?" the man asked tiredly as he settled in behind an old desk that was dented and scraped from years of service. He gestured to the equally battered seat that sat across from him.

"I've read your analysis of the enemy weapons," Helena said as she shifted to business, taking the offered seat. "However, there are a great number of holes in the data."

"Don't I know it? That is the problem, Fleet Commander. Our intelligence on the Oathers is ten thousand years out of date—not a particular problem with those people, I admit, but their allies? With them, it's completely nonexistent."

Helena shook her head, resisting the urge to rant.

It was an ongoing problem, in her opinion, that the Empire didn't take the time to do proper—if *any*—intelligence gathering. While groups like her Eighth Fleet did exist, both in the military and within the government, few bothered to listen to what they learned, and even fewer bothered to let people like herself know what they were planning so that she could get the information they might need.

The Empire was the biggest gun in the galaxy, as best they could tell so far, and that had left a great deal of people with the impression that nothing more was required to accomplish Imperial goals than bringing that gun to bear.

It was a costly quirk, but so far had been proven more or less correct.

Now, however, the Empire had been visited with an extremely rare defeat, but far more than that, they'd been struck within their own borders for the first time in centuries. It had been so long, in fact, that Helena had been forced to delve into the archives upon receiving her assignment just to determine if such an act had *ever* happened.

"I've examined all the ship logs and recordings of your encounters," she said. "The majority of the contacts fit within expected parameters pulled from the archives."

"I am aware, yes," Jesan said. "The anomaly, however, first encountered by the Drasin and recorded by my predecessor, should have been a warning to us that something very different was going on."

Helena nodded. "Indeed. The power curve on that vessel was essentially nonexistent. Were you ever able to determine how they were masking it?"

"If I had, the details would be in the reports," Jesan assured her dryly. "At best I have guesses, but even those make little sense."

"I'll take a guess at this point, Fleet Commander."

"Call me Jesan," he said and sighed, settling back as he considered his thoughts. "As to a guess . . . to be honest, there is only one thing that remotely seems reasonable: they're generating power as they need it and are highly efficient in its use."

"Generating . . . You mean fusion? That's antiquated," Helena objected.

"Possibly fusion, possibly something else." He nodded. "Whatever technology they use doesn't register as a power curve to our systems, however, which leaves us with only two options. First, they're somehow masking their signature, which is impossible, or they're generating power as needed from base constituents rather than storing it in singularities."

"The second is certainly possible, but no one *does* that," Helena said. "It's too limited. A singularity core can store entire planetary masses worth of power and be efficiently converted back to useable power at need. There's simply no way a vessel could match that with any type of old-style reactor."

"I didn't say that they did," Jesan pointed out. "That brings us to the second part of their technical prowess: they're simply more efficient in power use than we are. I can point to their beam weapons as the perfect example—weapons, I might add, that have affected Imperial designs based on our guesses about their functionality."

Helena frowned, thinking about that.

He was right, she realized. What little they did know about the anomalous species indicated that they were hyperefficient in power use. The beam weapons they used were noted as being capable of frequency shifts in order to more efficiently vaporize the material they were targeting.

If that were not merely a simple example of their technology, but rather indicative of their philosophy as a species, the fleet commander might well be correct, she realized.

"So possibly a lower technology species, or one with a divergent development," she said. "But with extreme skill in using what they have? Interesting."

"That was my conclusion, yes," Jesan said carefully.

One word caught her ear.

"Was?" Helena asked.

"Their superweapon, what their fleet commander referred to as a 'strategic weapon'"—Jesan scowled angrily—"that was not old technology, nor particularly efficient. It was brute force unlike anything I've ever seen."

Helena sighed, but had to concede the point.

The enemy superweapon was like nothing any of the archives could boast knowledge of.

Jesan had a haunted look in his eyes, and she could almost see the memories playing out behind them. He sighed after a moment, slumping in his place.

"I still have occasional flashes of that horrendous rage of pure unadulterated power," he admitted tiredly. "It just appeared from nowhere to flash ships and infrastructure into plasma in an instant. No sign of what cast that power out into the universe, just . . . a raging pillar of flame from nowhere."

Jesan sounded even more weary, as though each word was almost being torn from him against his will. When he finally fell silent again, Helena leaned in closer.

"The enemy fleet commander—did you notice anything when he spoke to you?"

Jesan shrugged. "Very little of use I expect. He was well disciplined, despite holding fear and anger in check . . ."

Jesan frowned, thinking back. "And disdain. A lot of disdain."

Helena's eyes widened almost imperceptibly. It wasn't uncommon, in her experience, for a non-Imperial to hold the Empire in disdain, but it was rare that an Imperial lord would deign to notice it.

"How so?"

Jesan laughed bitterly. "He informed me that he was conducting a lesson in the proper application of strategic weapons, right before he annihilated our bases. His tone was such as I might use when instructing a junior officer in how to properly cleanse his quarters before an inspection. As though he knew I was too stupid to understand what he was uttering, but it was his duty to impart the lesson either way."

Helena managed to bury her amusement. It wouldn't do to show such emotions; doing so would likely irritate her source, which was counterproductive, and of course it would also be in rather bad taste given how many people and resources that "lesson" had wiped out.

Even so, she couldn't help but ask, "Did you learn the lesson he was teaching?"

Jesan stared at her for a moment before barking with self-deprecating laughter. "I rather doubt I did, Fleet Commander. I hadn't even thought much on it until now."

Helena nodded silently but didn't comment further.

His words did not surprise her.

Imperial Palace, Empress' Private Reception

"You were correct in your assessment of the man," Helena said some time later, casually lounging in a comfortable settee as the empress stood across the room, examining herself in the mirror.

"I normally am," Her Highness said simply. "Do you have anything to add?"

"Not particularly," Helena said. "He's competent, better than most of the imbeciles who are elevated to lordship. Why didn't you mention that he'd been demoted, by the way?"

Her Highness, Emilia Starsbane, chuckled softly as she looked over her shoulder. "Because a little reminder of his fall was due the man, my mercy on his case notwithstanding. Besides, I expect that he won't be a fallen lord for long. Either he'll regain his position or he will die in the attempt."

"Set that up already, did you?" Helena asked her old friend, the girl she'd grown up with until the day she had gone to join the Imperial Fleets.

"Of course," Emilia said, scoffing. "But I'm more concerned about these unknown people who've allied with the Oathers."

"There's nothing on the records that matches anything close to what they've fielded," Helena said, "which implies a separate genesis."

Emilia hissed, her lips curling in a mixture of disgust and anger. "You speak of heresy."

"Truth supplants all things, Your Majesty, even faith," Helena said. "We would need to take biological samples to be sure, but at this point that isn't truly what concerns me."

"What could possibly be more concerning than a clear affront to our place in the universe?" Emilia demanded, her tone having shifted to a low-burning anger.

Helena didn't flinch, as nearly every other person in the Empire might. If her old friend wanted her execution and was willing to order it, then there was nothing left for her anyway.

"They're, at the very least, an entirely lost colony. In that case, they would have to be Oathers who escaped the Empire without an archive core," she said. "They've clearly *not* followed any technical development we might project from the archives. I stand by my assessment that they are likely a separate genus, however, no matter how Imperial they might appear at a glance. I would bet that once we acquire samples, we'll discover that they aren't human at all."

"Xeno." Emilia spat the word.

Helena gestured noncommittally. "In so much as one might be, I suppose. They clearly came from the same seed as Imperials, of course, as only the directed evolution of our seeding could explain the development we've seen."

Emilia turned away, glaring at her reflection in the mirrored image on the wall. "There hasn't been a mock-human culture discovered since the Sundering. You know that, don't you?"

"I didn't," Helena admitted. "Not my field, but I suppose it's not a surprise. Is that what the Oathers left over, then?"

Emilia nodded slowly. "Those heretical filth refused to see how necessary it was to cleanse the universe of that *mockery*."

Helena nodded, pretending agreement. Personally, she didn't feel as strongly about such matters as the empress, but then it wasn't her responsibility to see to those issues. Her job was much simpler and didn't require nearly the same conviction.

"Well, whether they are or not," she said, "they propose a particular problem for our operations because of their large degree of unknown and unpredictable assets and strategies. Getting appropriate intelligence will not be easy."

"If it were easy, I would not have summoned you, Helena. Can it be done?"

"Anything can be done, Your Majesty. This case will simply take longer and be more expensive than average."

"Cost does not interest me. Time, however, is not so simply set aside."

"There is no option there," Helena insisted. "Not until we identify and develop a countermeasure for that superweapon of theirs, at least, or figure out how they target it, perhaps. If we push them too hard, too quickly, they may torch the capital itself. We simply don't know their capability at this time."

Emilia walked over to the balcony and looked out over the massive metropolis that was her capital city, the lights illuminating it against the falling night. Spires reached so far into the sky that they, like her personal balcony, required enhanced conditioning to provide breathable air. Far below, through wispy clouds, she could see the lights of the lower city wavering up through atmospheric distortion. Emilia leaned on the rail, hands tightening around the metal until her knuckles turned white as she thought about the raging column of fire striking down from nowhere as described in the reports.

"As quickly as you can," she said finally, looking back. "Swear that to me, my friend."

"I swear," Helena said, getting to her feet and saluting formally. "I will push as hard as I dare."

"Good." The empress looked back out to the city arrayed below her. "You may leave."

Helena didn't speak. As much as she was willing to push her old friend more than most, she knew when it was time to do as told. She took two steps back, twisted on her heel, and strode out of the chambers.

Emilia looked out on the city for a long time in silence.

"Xeno filth and Xeno lovers," she spat angrily after a long time. "We seem doomed to forever be plagued by them, Father."

An older man's voice echoed in the room as a figure stepped out of the shadows across the space. "There comes an end to all things, Daughter. Even the evils that have plagued our people for all time are not immune to that universal truth."

Emilia nodded and turned around, smiling very slightly at the tall, broad-shouldered figure.

"You look good today, Father."

"It is a good day," he said. "We know what happened to our plans now, and we have a strategy to move our interests forward as they should."

She nodded. "The galaxy will be cleansed."

"And then the universe beyond."

Chapter 3

The darkened halls of the ship at rest felt empty as Eric walked them in silence. Knowing that the ship did in fact have a ghost of sorts in the machine just added to the feeling, a sensation he reveled in rather than feared.

He was making his way to the primary landing bay. The admiral's shuttle had been on final approach a few moments earlier and should be through the lock cycle at about the time he arrived.

From nowhere, one set of footsteps became two in a pattern that Eric was becoming used to.

"She doesn't like me," Odysseus said as he marched one half step behind Eric's own pace.

"The admiral doesn't much like me either, so I'm not sure what your point is."

"She respects you."

"Respect is earned," Eric said. "At least in these circles. You'll acquire it, in time. You're just a . . ."

He chuckled, pausing at the thought.

"Midshipman?" Odysseus asked, picking the thought out of Eric's mind. "I'm not familiar with that rank."

"We don't use it any longer, but it's as close to what you are as anything I can think of," Eric said after a moment. "And admirals never respect midshipmen."

"If you say so." Odysseus seemed to pout slightly under his Grecian helmet.

"Don't pout!" Eric snapped. "It's unbecoming."

"Yes sir!" The entity straightened his stance, his expression becoming neutral as they reached the entrance to the shuttle bay.

—

Terran shuttles hadn't changed much since after the war, Eric thought as they watched the admiral's personal transport get pulled into position and locked away.

It was a massive delta-wing shuttle that had a lifting body design and big aero-spike engines that gave it a distinct profile. They were hardly the most efficient or effective drive mechanism available anymore, but for close-range transport, the performance difference current models offered was insignificant and the cost was considerably cheaper, since the shuttles had already been commissioned.

The smaller Priminae transports certainly had their uses, of course, being faster and more efficient.

Maybe I'm getting old, but give me the sense of presence of a shuttle over one of those small flying boxes.

Eric laughed internally.

In all likelihood, he supposed he *was* in fact getting old. He missed his fighter, he liked the way things were done in the past, and he didn't much care for the future he saw unfolding. Of course, he didn't have to like any of it. He just had to make sure that what did come their way wasn't able to destroy what humanity had built and would continue to build.

A simple job, but it suited him.

The shuttle's belly hatch hissed as pressure stabilized, and then began to open. Admiral Gracen was already moving as soon as the craft cleared enough space, casually dropping to the deck without waiting for her befuddled aides. Eric smiled as they scrambled to catch up to the stern woman who was already walking in his direction.

"Admiral," he said as he saluted.

"As you were, Commodore," Gracen said as she marched up to and then past him. "Walk with me."

Eric then found himself being the one scrambling to catch up, though he hoped that he managed to pull it off a little more smoothly than the admiral's aides.

"In a hurry, Admiral?" he asked as he fell into step beside her.

"After a fashion," Gracen replied. "Are you familiar with the Star Forge?"

"Of course, ma'am," Eric said. "I read the brief before it came online."

"Good. I'm sure you're aware that we're building new Odysseus Class vessels," she went on, pausing only to catch his nod before she continued. "I've also been working on several pet projects as the facility winds up."

That didn't shock Eric, knowing what he did about the admiral. Gracen was a workaholic and had a near-obsessive drive to push Earth's defenses forward. He could hardly blame her for it. Any officer worth their oxygen had at least a little of that in their blood after the Drasin invasion.

All he had to do was look down on some of the scars that could still be seen from orbit to fire up his emotions, drive away any sense or need for sleep, and set him to working on some new idea or another. Unlike the admiral, however, Eric knew that he tended to work better under immediate pressure.

Give him an enemy to fight, and he'd start pulling rabbits out of his ass like a magician on the Vegas strip. The admiral worked better when she had time to think, to plan. In his personal opinion, it was what made the two of them effective when working on a problem together. Given that the admiral consistently deployed him to hot spots she was tasked with, Eric was confident that she felt much the same.

"One of those pet projects is a resurrection of Project Double A," Gracen said.

Eric faltered a step, eyes widening as he snapped his head over to look at her. "I'm surprised you didn't inform me sooner."

"We're giving the project the green light for full production."

"A *lot* sooner," Eric growled. "With all due respect, Admiral, what the hell?"

"You had more important things to take care of," Gracen said without pausing in her walk, again forcing Eric to scramble a bit to catch up. "Not the least of which was needing time off once you completed your after-action report on the last mission."

"I would have thought that I could have provided useful input all the same. I did help design the previous project," Eric said, unable to keep from letting a little testiness creep into his voice.

"And we used your project requirements as the baseline going in," Gracen said, unconcerned. "I wanted an outside view on the project, however, so I left it to Lieutenant Chans."

"Milla? She's an . . . unusual choice." Eric felt like he was being pushed off-balance intentionally and refocused his mind, trying to figure out what he was being set up for. "Weapon specialist for the Priminae, true, but not the first to come to mind for this sort of project."

"She also worked on their transport systems in her early career," Gracen said. "Plus I gave her some of our best aeronautical engineers. A short while ago, I turned over the prototypes to Commanders Black and Michaels for final proofing. They passed."

"You have my attention," Eric admitted. "Since you're informing me about it now, I assume there's something I can bring to the table?"

"You know tactics and strategies for independent long-range fighter combat better than anyone alive," Gracen said. "These new craft are going to vastly extend those capabilities, and we're going to need a new doctrine."

"Mission profile?"

"Long-range extended reconnaissance," she answered instantly, "with an emphasis on plausible deniability."

Eric looked sharply over at her, gesturing ahead. "My office is just this way. Technical specifications?"

Gracen produced a small crystal holographic chip, the sort used to transport ultrasecure intelligence when one couldn't trust transmission methods.

"I don't need to tell you to secure that, I hope."

Eric snorted as he accepted the holo-chip. "Not if I'm reading you right. You're talking Q-Ships, not fighters."

"Q-Ships with teeth, but yes," Gracen confirmed. "Standard air and space superiority fighters are extremely limited in application. We're keeping the Vorpals for the moment. Oh, and the *Odysseus* will get a few squadrons to augment your force projection capability, but we need the black version of what the Archangels were on Earth. The scales involved mean enhancing their capacities significantly."

Eric fell silent as they entered his office, immediately crossing to his desk so he could examine the specs on the chip, his mind running a light-year per second.

Q-Ships, under various names, had a long history in naval warfare and military intelligence. The name itself sourced to the Second World War, when various factions would refit merchant vessels for different tasks—sometimes for combat, often for spying, or for some other special service need.

They weren't particularly good in a fight, traditionally, because most were barely refit with whatever weapons could be bolted to the decks, but in recent years, Eric had heard that wasn't always the case.

Purpose-built special service vessels had been used in several wars since, up to and including the Block War, by all sides of the conflicts.

In the right hands, tasked with the right job, a lot could be accomplished with such a vessel.

Eric looked over the files, getting a feel for the new generation of Archangel as his brain tried to catch up with what the admiral was proposing.

"Q-Ships are subtle as a rule. These aren't . . ."

"They aren't a match for any profile in our forces, or the Priminae's either."

Eric nodded as he examined the files. "True enough. Third faction?"

"That's the plan, Eric."

The new-generation fighters were massively larger than the original Archangel fighters, which had been retrofitted from air superiority airframes in a rush to take advantage of the newly acquired counter-mass technology stolen from China. They hadn't had time, back then, to really capitalize on the capabilities the technology offered, so he had made the call to take a bunch of surplus Raptor airframes out of an Airforce boneyard and turn them into something viable.

What he was looking at here was a completely different animal.

"These are more like cutters than fighters," he said, examining the mass and designs. "Or maybe PT boats."

Gracen shrugged. "Different environment, different specifications. They can outmaneuver your generation Archangel, outrace even the Odysseus in both acceleration and top end, and pack enough firepower to make a Rogue think twice about engaging them."

"I can see that," Eric admitted. "Not saying it's a bad design. I like what I'm seeing, just having trouble parsing it with the idea of these being a new-generation Archangel. You're thinking a long-term mission, largely independent of NACOM?"

"That's correct, yes."

"Age-of-sail rules, then," Eric mumbled. "Privateers, though a little more official. They'll be out of contact for long periods. Even with FTL comms you're not going to be able to maintain the sort of command structure we're used to. That means giving the commander of the unit a *lot* of leeway in their orders and authority."

Gracen nodded. "That was my expectation."

"Who's on tap for the job?" Eric asked, delving deeper into the fighter specs as he did.

"Michaels."

Eric looked up, staring at her seriously for a moment before he shook his head. "You're stealing my chief helmsman, and I'm assuming my tactical officer too?"

"Don't feel too bad. We're also raiding the other ships," she told him with a slight smile.

"Yeah, the other ships under *my* command, so that's not making me feel better." Eric laughed openly now. "I'm assuming these are NICS equipped, then?"

"Next generation, far more efficient interface."

"Damn. I'm jealous."

And he was. The sort of mission profile she was talking about—flying under a false flag, answering to your own authority, and spending months or possibly even years away from official contact—was something no one had done in hundreds of years.

It was an assignment that would take a certain sort of personality to do, or want to do, but for that type it was a dream assignment. Some thrived in the chain of command; for some, however, freedom called to their blood. It had been a long time since the sort of freedom the admiral was talking about had truly been available to explore.

"It's going to take a lot of work to write up a rough doctrine," he said seriously. "But I'll get it done. Just remember, the nature of the beast is going to mean that a lot of it will be rewritten on the fly in the field. You're talking about sending people out into unknowns that we can't even guess at."

"I know," Gracen acknowledged. "But a framework will help."

Eric nodded. "I'll get it done."

Star Forge Alpha

Milla groaned slightly as she pulled herself out of the cramped access port to the power conduits that fed the primary systems in Commander Michaels' fighter, irritated with herself and Steph in equal portion.

How is it even possible for him to have stressed those particular conduits?

She understood that the point of the test flights was to do just that, if it were possible, but she couldn't work out how it was possible in the first place.

"I swear, that man generates a field of entropy aimed directly at any machine he operates," she grumbled as she brushed grease and dust off her hands as best she could before rubbing her palms on the thighs of her work suit.

"That's pilots for you."

Milla squeaked as she jumped, pivoting around to see Commander Black leaning against the deactivated wall of the cockpit.

"Please do not do that." Milla breathed as she clutched at her chest, her heart racing. "Odysseus was quite bad enough. I do not need real people doing the same to me."

Alexandra Black raised her eyebrow. "I've heard about Odysseus, of course, but never met . . . him?"

Milla nodded. "He seems male, yes . . . for the most part?"

Alex raised an eyebrow at the general uncertainty that the other woman seemed to project as she thought about the entity that had made the *Odysseus* his . . . her . . . its? . . . home.

"Strange. A living ship is some weird-level stuff," Alex said, shaking her head. "But I guess that's the time we live in."

Milla stifled a laugh. "How so?"

"Well, space travel and all," Alex said. "I guess the weird stuff is to be expected."

"I have been in a starship, in one way or another, for most of my life at this point," Milla said with an amused tone. "And my people have been spacefaring for longer than we teach in our histories, and never have I encountered anything like Odysseus. I will be quite honest, Commander Black, I do not believe it to be a 'space' thing. I believe it is a Terran thing."

Black laughed. "Touché, and call me Alex."

"Milla, then."

"Milla." Alex smiled. "I suppose you might be right. I grew up on science fiction, and this is just the sort of thing that would make it into some of those old stories. Usually in those, though, Odysseus would go crazy and murder everyone in gory ways."

Milla raised an eyebrow. "I do not think that will happen."

"Hope not, but that's how it would go in the vids."

"You people have strange entertainment," Milla said, shaking her head. "I went to the . . . theater, is it? I went with Stephan a few times, but the violence was unreal."

"You let him pick the movies, didn't you?"

"Of course." Milla looked puzzled. "I didn't know anything about any of them."

"Never let the guy pick all the movies," Alex said. "At least not if you want to avoid all action and horror flicks."

"I do not understand?"

"Just trust me on this. Look up the movie description and pick out ones that you think you'll like," Alex told her. "Don't trust anyone else to pick for you, especially a *fighter jock*."

"Are you not a 'fighter jock'?" Milla asked.

"Sure," Alex agreed with a grin. "And I'd probably have picked the same movies Stephanos did."

Milla looked perplexed, her face screwed up as she seemed to think that through.

"But you said—" she started to ask, only to be cut off by Alex.

"I'm not exactly your stereotypical lady-in-waiting, Milla." She laughed, waving off the lieutenant's confusion. "So how did the systems hold up?"

Milla put aside the confusing topic and glanced back over her shoulder to the open hatch that allowed access to the fighter's inner workings.

"Well enough, I believe," she said, "considering the velocity the commander pushed them to inside the planet's atmosphere."

"That could have been worse," Alex said dryly. "The Archangels were known for pushing their counter-mass generators beyond all sane limits during the war. I wasn't flying then, but I've seen records of those nuts limping a plane back into the barn, armor plating ablated by atmospheric friction—or, once, with literal *fish* clogging intakes."

Milla frowned. "I am not sure I want to know how they managed that."

"Apparently counter-mass gets more efficient in thicker 'atmosphere,'" Alex said. "And even more efficient, again apparently, in liquid. They used counter-mass to push a bubble around their fighters and approached the target from below sea level."

Milla gaped slightly, doing the math in her head. She was well aware that the Terran counter-mass systems were a cruder version of Priminae space-time manipulation, but no one had ever tried what Alex just indicated the Terrans played around with.

"But . . ." she said slowly. "Efficiency, yes I can see that, but that doesn't mean that it would be able to push aside that much liquid. There are limits to effectiveness, even if efficiency increases. There would be a point of, what is the expression? Diminishing returns, I believe, yes?"

"That's the expression, yes. However, it obviously worked somehow, otherwise the fish wouldn't have gotten sucked into their intakes," Alex replied.

"But"—Milla was aware she was repeating herself, but there didn't seem to be any better word to use—"the Archangels were *reaction-thrust* craft! How . . . but . . ."

"I never said it made sense, just that I saw the reports," Alex said.

"The Double A platform isn't a mere reaction-thrust system." A new voice startled them, causing the pair to turn to see Steph crouched on the cockpit's top access point. "It's a modified SCRAMJet reactor, capable of burning stored oxygen at lower speeds in order to build up to hypersonic velocity. Eric ordered us to run full power through the intakes, flash-electrolyzing water into hydrogen and oxygen and using vapor filtration to keep the water out."

He hopped down into the rather expansive space that was the cockpit of the new fighter. "Shouldn't have worked, frankly, but with counter-mass running full power, it was really more like water vapor than water to start with. The fish were just unlucky to be sucked up as we flew through the space they'd been swimming in a second earlier."

He paused. "Okay, maybe 'flying' isn't the right word, but it worked. That Block supercarrier never saw us coming."

"They didn't see you coming because they weren't *insane*, Stephanos." Alex rolled her eyes. "Who expects a raid from air superiority fighters to come from *underwater?*"

Steph just waved idly. "It worked."

"Broken clocks 'work' twice a day, Stephanos," Alex responded archly. "That doesn't make them functional in any sense of the word."

"Ouch." Steph put a hand over his heart. "Don't go telling a guy he's not functional, Black. That's hitting . . . well, below the belt."

Alex rolled her eyes, an action she was becoming all too accustomed to since she had begun working with the commander.

Milla, for her part, was mostly puzzled by the exchange but remained focused on the information presented.

"I have not examined the exact specifications of your space-time manipulation technology," she admitted. "However, it should not have functioned in the way you describe. I believe I will need to familiarize myself more with the technology."

"Find a Block engineer," Alex advised her. "Eric stole the tech from them, but even today they're the most knowledgeable in its operation."

Milla nodded slowly. "I will do so at the earliest opportunity, thank you."

"I'm sure it'll be riveting information," Steph said, dropping into the interior of the pilot's pit and landing easily on the substrate that made up the floor when the fighter's interface wasn't in operation. "I've been looking over the mission specifications the admiral left with me. If we're to meet the schedule she wants, we need to have a squadron sucking vacuum within the month. How close are we on that?"

"Another six platforms are currently in construction," Milla responded, "four of which will be ready within the timeframe the admiral has laid out. I'm informed that recruiting for their crews has officially begun as of two days ago."

"Six boats," Steph said. "That'll mean at least a dozen NICS-qualified pilots."

"I would prefer eighteen," Alex said.

Steph nodded. "So would I, but when Congress defunded the squadron after the war, they put a recruitment freeze on pilots for the system. After our losses with the Drasin conflict, I'm not even sure we'll be able to scrounge up a dozen who are fully space and system qualified, let alone eighteen."

Alex scowled, seemingly particularly irritated by that point. "Since I was one of the people hit by that same recruitment freeze, I have an idea of how tough that job is going to be. Sure, I pushed on and scored a slot with the Vorpals eventually, but that was no easy row to hoe.

Most of the people I knew, well, they dropped out to look for other opportunities."

Steph nodded soberly. "Yeah, I knew a handful as well; people on the waiting list who'd been training with us for months before they got axed. I might be able to pull up some of their contact information, though."

"I might have a few names in my contact list too," Alex said after a moment. "The admiral would know of them, of course, but they'd be low on her list, since they dropped out of the program when it became clear there were no openings."

"Can they fly?" Steph asked the only question that mattered.

Alex smirked. "Better than you."

"I'll take that bet. Fire up your contact list, Black. Let's find us some more pilots. I have a couple to add to the list myself, people who aren't on the official list, come to think of it."

"The Admiralty might object to bringing nonmilitary personnel into the mix," Alex reminded him.

"Let them blow it out their collective ass," Steph said. "I've read the mission specifications, and military is the last thing we need. Yo-ho, yo-ho, Black . . . beard?"

"Oh God, you're really going to make me regret signing on with this, aren't you?"

Chapter 4

Vindict Morow, *Imperial Eighth Fleet Command Vessel*

"Attend the commander's presence!"

"Be as you were," Helena ordered crisply, stepping into the ship's command and control center, eyes darting to the various displays that showed repeater feeds from her squadrons.

"Yes milady. All return to your duties!"

Helena ignored the commotion on the deck, taking her place with a practiced ease. Her Eighth Fleet was the smallest and, by far, least powerful of the Empire's fleets, but that had never overly bothered her. Fleets like the Third were a sword, a useful tool to be sure, but sometimes they were too unwieldy to truly achieve the best results.

That normally didn't matter, given that Imperial Fleets generally employed more than enough force to annihilate anything that gave them pause. But this time it had been made clear that power alone would not suffice.

"New heading has been sent to the navigation computers," Helena said firmly. "Signal all vessels to prepare for departure at the earliest opportunity."

"Yes milady," Sub-Commander Steppen responded instantly even as he dispatched the orders.

Helena ignored him, continuing to put mission parameters into the squadron-wide servers. By the time the fleet was ready to move, she intended that every commander would be fully cognizant of the mission profile facing them, along with every known issue she could cover.

Of course, the known issues were never the problem.

These anomalous ships and the race they belong to are more of an issue than the Empire realizes, she thought as she worked.

Worse, they seemed to grow *more* anomalous even as they were clearly incorporating Imperial technology, no doubt acquired from the Oathers. That made no sense. They should be conforming to Imperial thinking and tactics as they were constricted by the capabilities of Imperial technology.

Instead, they seemed to have leveraged Imperial technology to make themselves even *more* unpredictable.

Helena smiled.

I'm going to enjoy this.

"All squadrons report ready to depart, on your order, milady."

Helena looked up and nodded curtly. "Secure all stations for maneuvering, and order the Eighth into motion."

She looked around calmly.

"It's time to go hunting."

Imperial Third Fleet Command Vessel

"Welcome back, Commander."

Jesan nodded briefly, hearing the slight undercurrent of censure from his second in command, but he ignored it. It was more respectful than what he heard from most of the people he had to deal with.

He passed a secure holographic crystal chip across. "Our orders. Prepare the fleet to depart."

"As you will it."

The response was textbook but the tone brittle, leaving Jesan to wonder whether the empress' stay of execution was more a cruelty than a mercy. If his command of the fleet were compromised by his fall from grace, then his death might well be assured anyway—and his crew's along with him.

Is she intending to wipe the Third out entirely? he wondered. Eliminate the stain of their failure by washing it away in blood and fire?

It was well within Her Majesty's mind, he knew. She was much like her father in that regard. Cool and measured, even when sliding the dagger home.

He wasn't certain, however, because she could also be pragmatic and merciful, leading men to redeem their failures and then bringing them back into the fold. The uncertainty that resulted among the nobility was one of the more impressive methods the Imperial Court had of keeping them all in check.

Worse, he was well aware of it, and yet he still could not avoid the trap he could see right in front of him.

"All vessels report ready to depart, Commander."

Jesan nodded, mind focused on the task that had been set for him and his crew.

"Understood," he said. "Order all ships out."

"We cannot. The Eighth Fleet has secured local space and are departing orbit," his second in command said.

Jesan scowled. "Very well. Depart as soon as orbit has cleared."

"As you will it, Commander."

Jesan waved casually, dismissing the man as he opened the files on the systems the empress had assigned him.

Pocket empires, he thought as he examined the data.

Mostly early Imperial colonies from long before the Oather Sundering. Small colonial governments had moved for independence and, by the time the Empire had established enough general control, became strong enough to make reclaiming them a costly measure. The Empire also tended to benefit from having the occasional visible "threat" to parade in front of its people, keeping them nicely distracted from issues at home.

Still, pocket empires had ambitions like any other group, and occasionally they had to be reminded who the big power was in the region.

That was his mission this time around. Dirty work, but necessary.

It would even be considered routine if his squadrons hadn't just been through a vicious set of battles that cost them over thirty percent of their number and left much of the remaining vessels at less than a hundred-percent efficiency.

Thankfully, the empress had deigned to permit them time to do repairs, though he suspected that was as much to keep him in the area while the court deliberated on his fate. But proper slip repairs for much of his cohort would give them a little better than a fighting chance in combat, if nothing else.

Jesan looked up as the Eighth Fleet began to move out of their position in orbit, their numbers still smaller than his own squadron despite the damages he'd suffered. He wondered how many people watching understood that they were seeing a shift in political power here on Garisk as they watched the Empire's smallest fleet leave orbit in an orderly fashion.

He doubted most had a clue.

More the fool are they, then, Jesan thought as he closed the files and settled down into the command position.

"Orbital Plot will be clear in a few moments, Commander."

"Power all drives and follow the Eighth out of orbit."

"Milady," Steppen said softly, catching Helena's attention.

"What is it?" she asked, looking up from where she was studying the scanner records of the Third's fight with the anomalous vessels.

"The Third is powering their drives and following our path out of orbit."

Helena nodded absently. "Ignore them. They're being dispatched to Riegal before heading outward."

"Ah," Steppen said.

She didn't need to say anything else. There was really only one thing the Empire ever did immediately outward from Riegal, and that was slap down the oft-warring pocket empires that populated that region of space.

Barring extraordinary circumstances, being assigned to that region was known to be a reprimand for *something*. Steppen waved a hand, banishing the Third Fleet from his console and mind as he went on to other business.

"Squadron Commanders are examining the mission brief. I've had requests for consultation with you from three already," he went on.

"I'll speak with them all once we're out of the system," Helena replied. "I'm still familiarizing myself with the objective and want to have it all fresh from my own perspective before anyone else offers opinions."

"Understood, milady."

They had time, Helena knew. The enemy wasn't interested in pursuing a shooting war at the moment, and that meant that the Empire could handle things on its own schedule. She'd normally be suspicious, as it seemed to be bad tactics, but given the anomalous nature of the enemy, Helena wasn't willing to invest much effort in trying to puzzle them out. Yet.

Time enough for that once I've gathered intelligence of my own.

Besides, in her opinion, the most likely explanation was that they simply didn't have enough forces to project them into Imperial space. Extrastellar force projection was no simple matter, and every bit of data currently available on the anomalous group indicated that they occupied very few star systems and had few ships, or they wanted to appear as such.

In either case, that would make logistics a nightmare in the persecution of long-range warfare.

All I need to figure out is which is which, she thought with a wry tilt to her lips as she read over the data. *That and what their superweapon is, where it is based, and whether the Empire can capture the device or if we will have to destroy it. Just a simple assignment from Her Imperial Majesty.*

She glanced to one side, eyes drifting to the system telemetry plot. The Eighth Fleet were moving quickly toward the edge of the system, preparing to accelerate past the speed of light. Behind them, the Third was now angling off and heading on a different course as they too continued to increase their speed to the maximum in system velocity.

Good luck, Commander. I will be very interested in seeing how you handle yourself if we meet again.

Imperial Palace

"Your Highness, the Eighth and Third Fleets have departed orbit."

Emilia tilted her head regally. "Thank you, Geral. You may go."

The man bowed slightly and departed, leaving her alone with her thoughts as she looked up at the night sky.

There was too much illumination from the local city for her to see the dim, reflected light of even a pair of significant fleets as they left orbit, but she imagined that she could see them all the same. When she was younger, Emilia had wanted to captain one of those vessels and see the majesty of the Imperial Domain from the point of view of one of her guardians.

Those were the thoughts of someone with fewer responsibilities, however, and they had died when . . . well, they were not thoughts she had kept long for herself.

Shepherding the Empire was not a job for dreamers.

Too many evils existed in the universe, evils that would tear apart everything built by the Empire at the slightest provocation. Xeno came in many forms. Some, she had discovered early, were a far cry from the monstrosity of the Drasin.

The truly insidious evils were masked in the appearance of humanity.

Emilia's eyes lit with an inner fire as she turned from the balcony and made her way back into the royal chambers, ignoring the baths and attendants to instead cross to the copy of the local Imperial command and control center; it was smaller than the actual center but equally powerful.

The holographic image of the galaxy floated placidly at the center of the room, deceptive in its peaceful appearance. She reached out her hands and casually caused the image to move, to focus in on the arm of the galaxy that held Imperial space. As she did, the white light of the galactic stellar furnaces changed to the strategic map of the Empire and its neighbors.

Imperial purple, Her Majesty's color, covered hundreds of stars, thousands truly, but only a fraction of those counted, of course. The pocket empires she had set Jesan Mich after glowed a sickly yellow in dotted spaces around the periphery of Imperial space. Just worlds that the Empire had not bothered to take firmly under its control.

Emilia hated those pocket *empires*. The very word itself was insulting to the power and majesty of the *true* Empire, but they were too useful to do away with. Her father had known this, and his father before him, as did all her line back to very nearly the beginning. The existence of humanity that was nonaffiliated with Imperial control gave the Starsbane Empire a useful lever with which to control people.

It was amazing how easily convinced the people were that some minor star system a thousand light-years away was the true source of their problems. It would make her sad for the state of human intelligence but for the fact that such beliefs were so very useful.

Useful fools, she thought. *Waving flags and chanting Imperial propaganda.*

Emilia took a breath.

The pocket empires were not her concern at the moment.

Instead she cast her gaze to the green and red lights that sparsely dotted a section of space she'd come to know better than she had ever wished.

Oather space.

The Oather green disgusted her in a different way than the nonaffiliated yellow. The pocket empires were a useful tool, but really they were Imperial in all ways that truly mattered. Born of Imperial colonies unfortunately cut off during early periods, they'd grown somewhat independently, but at their cores they were still as much Imperial as they had been when their ships were dispatched by the young and growing politic of the day.

The Oathers, the *traitors*, were another matter.

"Show me the Oather space," she said softly, her expression darkening as the stars shifted abruptly, now centered around the world the Oathers called Ranquil.

Treason.

"Calmly now, Daughter."

Emilia twisted, surprised by the voice despite all the years and experience she had dealing with the source. She settled quickly and smiled. "Father."

The large, broad-shouldered man smiled down at her with a paternal air as he stepped up from behind, looking over her head to the floating map.

"You must be calm," he said again, repeating an old remonstration. "Anger must serve you. You must never serve anger."

"I know, Father," she said softly, feeling small in the shadow of the former emperor. "It is hard, though. I wish you had not left all of this in my hands."

"I gifted the Empire to you precisely because I knew you could handle the responsibilities that it would require," he told her warmly.

His eyes drifted to the green lights that connoted the positions of known Oather worlds and the red that indicated the areas where their patrols had spotted Drasin activity.

"Great though those responsibilities may be . . ."

Emilia's eyes followed his to the red lights, and she shivered. "We should have left them buried in their graves."

"Possibly," he conceded. "However, they are generation limited, and that makes them a minor threat. I am more concerned with *them*."

Emilia didn't need to follow his eyes to know that he was staring at the single orange dot that showed the home star of the species her commanders had labeled the "anomalous" group. The Empire had little information on them, and what did exist made almost no sense. She was experienced enough in matters of military policy and tactics to know that much.

That they existed so close to Oather space was originally thought to mean that they were some splinter colony from the original traitors. Distasteful, but vaguely understandable.

That remained a possibility, but Helena's words refused to leave Emilia. Deep in her heart, Emilia knew that they were not Oathers.

"Xeno," she whispered, lips curling in disgust while a tremor passed through her.

"Perhaps," her father intoned deeply. "Perhaps. And if so, they will be cleansed from the galaxy. That is holy writ."

Emilia nodded in agreement.

It would not be the first time the Empire had encountered Xenoform in human skin, but it had been a *long* time ago. Long enough that, though she had been brought up on the stories of such days, Emilia had believed them to be just that: stories.

The shock of Helena's postulation had left her stunned for a time, like a blow from a hammer that caused all the pieces of a puzzle to fall into place. Emilia would make certain of her suspicions before she acted precipitously, but she knew that if it were true, then there would be no choice.

"Holy war."

"Burn them from the galaxy," her father agreed.

Chapter 5

Skimming the waves of the gulf at just under the speed of sound, a rooster tail of water sucked up into the air by its passing, the small craft flew just a dozen feet off the deck as it threaded the needle between Waiheke and Ponui Islands, pursued by a dozen other similar craft. Coming out of the bank, the vehicle stabilized quickly in ground effect and increased speed.

The crack of a sonic boom echoed across the water as the craft and pursuers headed straight for Browns Island at Mach 1 and climbing. Skimming along the south coast, they turned north and settled into a course for Islington Bay, between the two islands of Motutapu and Rangitoto.

In the second craft back from the lead, hands were gripping the throttle and stick with white-knuckle force as the pilot glared at the tail of the lead.

"They're getting away from us!"

"Shut up. I've got this!"

The group of skimmers blasted into the narrow bay at reckless speeds, the water rapidly vanishing from either side as the bay narrowed and the two islands loomed closer on either side.

"Tee! Tee! Goddamn it, Tyke, what the hell are you doing? We're going to be off the water in *seconds!*"

"I know where we are," the pilot snapped back. "Get ready to give me everything we've got!"

"You already *have* everything we've got!"

The pilot scoffed. "I know you're holding something back, Jack! I need it!"

"If we blow this engine, it's the last one we've got!"

"Three seconds!"

"Tee!"

"Two!"

The craft passed over the floodplain of a small river, sand and dirt flashing past a few feet under them as the looming terrain rushed in on either side. Ahead there was the curve leading into the causeway between the two islands.

The lead craft blasted through the eye of the needle, the boom of its passing shaking dirt and stones from the shoreline as the craft slowed and cut into a hard bank.

"One!"

"Damn you! Fine!"

The engines howled as more power poured into them, the craft screaming ahead faster than ever as it left the rest of the pack.

"Tee . . . Turn! Turn! Trees! Trees!"

The pilot ignored the frantic screams, focusing on the pitch of the land rising out of the sea and the trees directly in front of them as they cut off the corner and barreled straight into the peninsula that jutted out between the two islands. The nose of the craft tipped back and they clawed for the sky.

"This is a ground effect racer, you *lunatic!* We can't actually *fly!*"

"Fly, jump, it's a fine line."

The sky wobbled terrifyingly in front of them as the racer arced over the trees, gaining several hundred feet of altitude off the initial boost before it topped out and began a downward trajectory off the parabola they'd begun. The horizon rushed up alarmingly, bringing the water of the gulf with it and then the ground and trees of the Rangitoto Island Preserve.

Nose down, engine screaming, the racer then added gravity to its acceleration and began increasing speed precariously as the trees rushed up to meet them. At the last second, the pilot yanked the nose back, skimming the trees close enough to hear them scrape the craft's sides on the way by. They exploded out over the gulf at Mach 1.3 and still accelerating as the reinforced bottom of the racer contacted the water and bounced.

The entire craft slammed and shook as their downward velocity was forcibly but efficiently redirected forward over the gulf and the throttle was thrown full power for the last stretch.

"I think we shook something loose," the pilot said calmly, fighting to control the wobbling craft.

"You *think*?! You *THINK*?!"

The engineer swore, continuously repeating epithets while furiously trying to find and repair the problem before it got them killed.

Twin rooster tails of white water exploded from behind as the racer gained on the lead with a steady pace, the finish line in the straits between Shakespear Regional Park and Tiritiri Matangi Island looming ahead.

The craft shook wildly around them, the pilot struggling to hold it together while the engineer worked from the confines of the compartment in the rear to keep the whole thing from flying apart.

"You bent the stabilizer on the port side!"

"Can you fix it?"

"I don't know! I can't get to it from here, and there's no way in hell I can climb out there at Mach!"

"Just hang on! We're almost there!"

The shuddering racer pulled up alongside the former lead as the finish line appeared ahead of them.

"You need to get a new partner!"

The pilot cackled. "You say that every time!"

"I *mean* that every time!"

A horn blew in the distance, flares climbing into the air as the pair of racers crossed the line, both throttling back and dropping speed.

"Did we win?"

The pilot didn't look away from his task, his voice barely audible over the roar of the machine they were within. "I have no idea. Can we put this thing down safely?"

"With a bent stabilizer? Not a chance in hell. Ease us down below Mach, then get us to minimum ground effect speed and I'll see if I can fix it."

"Alright, easing down . . . We're going to drop below in . . . three . . . two . . . one . . ."

The racer shuddered again as it crossed their sonic shockwave and slipped below the speed of sound at sea level, the pilot fighting to keep the vehicle stable as it did. Air pressure shifted as the rear hatch was pushed open and the engineer checked the stabilizer, causing their ears to pop and sending a howling scream through the cockpit.

"Oh shit."

"What? What's wrong?" the pilot demanded, risking a glance backward.

"Well, good news is you didn't bend the stabilizer!"

"What's the bad news?!"

"There is *no* port stabilizer!"

For a long moment the only sound was the howling wind through the open hatch.

"Alright, get back up here and buckle in," the pilot ordered, flipping open the radio call switch. "Coast Guard, Coast Guard, this is race entry Zero Niner declaring an emergency. We've lost a hull stabilizer and we're going to be coming down *hard*."

"Roger, Zero Niner, we're moving into position. Can you hold it long enough to come around to safer waters?"

"Yeah, I think I can . . ."

A radio signal broke in, cutting the pilot off.

"Zero Niner, Tyke," a voice said. "I might have a better option for you."

"I know that voice," Tyke, the pilot, said. "Crown, is that you?"

"No one else would be dumb enough to do what I'm about to," the voice came back. "Look up."

Tyke did, eyes widening as a big NACOM shuttlecraft eased into position over the racer, the bottom opening up as it began to drop.

"Are you going to do what I think you're going to do?"

"Just like in the war, Tyke. Keep the throttle steady."

"Roger that, Stephanos."

———

Steph looked far too relaxed behind the controls of the big shuttle, given the loose nature of the guidance system Milla was familiar with, but there was little she could do as they began to settle down over the small craft below and the commander adjusted his navigation by instruments alone.

"Go check and see if Alex got the cables ready," he said, not looking up from the readings.

Milla nodded nervously, unbuckling her restraints and pushing out of the seat.

She ducked back to the cargo and passenger area, eyes wide as saucers when she saw Commander Black hanging over the edge of the open hole, wind blowing her hair around wildly.

Alex glanced back at her. "We're all good here!"

Milla nodded, hands shaking as she turned around and grabbed at the fuselage frame and stuck her head back into the cockpit. "She says she's ready!"

"Then here we go!"

Steph pushed the stick forward, feathering the throttle controls as he did, and the shuttle dropped abruptly as Milla hung on to the doorframe.

This is insanity.

The shuttle's rudimentary space-time manipulation should have kept her from feeling the drop, Milla knew, so the sensation in the pit of her stomach was either due to her imagination, or Steph was dropping far faster than she would have deemed safe.

Milla had zero intention of confirming which option, if only because she suspected she would *not* appreciate the knowledge.

"Ease up, Stephanos!" Alex called over the wind. "Almost there!"

Milla risked a glance back into the hold, eyes still wide as she saw the smooth top of the small craft they were pacing appear in the center.

The racer seemed to rise into place, though she knew it was the shuttle dropping, until Alex was able to swing over the hole and hang by her harness as she started snapping tie-downs into place. A few moments later, still hanging over the hole, she threw a thumbs-up back toward Milla and hit the winch to pull the craft into the hold.

"Commander Black is finished," Milla reported, breathing a sigh of relief as the shuttle began to ease up from the water and fly out over the island that had been looming ahead of them.

She slumped against the door, eyes closed.

Steph chuckled, catching Milla's attention as he swiveled around to look at her.

"Great fun, isn't it?"

"When we first met, I assumed all Terrans were crazy," Milla groaned as she glared at Steph. "I do not know whether to be thankful or not that it's mostly just you."

———

"What the hell was *that*?"

Tyke chuckled, pushing the canopy up and away as he unbuckled his helmet and pushed it off. "Just an old friend, Jack."

He nodded to a dark-haired woman in military fatigues as he tossed his helmet back in the seat behind him and climbed out.

"Much obliged for the save, Commander." He grinned. "Touching down was going to be . . . interesting."

Jack snorted, casting her own helmet aside with casual disregard. "'Interesting' he says. We were going to hit the water at a hundred and fifty klicks and spend the next fifteen hundred meters scattering my baby all over the gulf."

"Tyke always did understate things."

They turned to see Steph leaning casually on the bulkhead to the cockpit, smirking in Tyke's direction.

"Like you should talk, Crown," Tyke said, hopping over the gap between his racer and the shuttle proper, then walking over to hug Steph.

Steph returned the embrace. "Good to see you, old man."

"Oh screw you, pipsqueak," Tyke said, pushing off and clapping Steph on the shoulder.

Alex cleared her throat. "Not to interrupt the touching reunion, but please tell me Chans is qualified to be flying the shuttle?"

Steph brushed off the question with amusement. "She can fly this heap between planets, I'm not worried about her finding her way to Auckland."

"Who's Chans?" Tyke asked curiously, not recognizing the name.

"She's an Ithan, a lieutenant, with the Priminae naval fleet," Steph answered. "Well, a Lieutenant Commander now, with us at least."

Steph frowned, puzzled. "I never did find out if that promotion carried over to her position with the Priminae. Oh well . . ."

"And she's qualified on this hunk of junk?" Tyke asked incredulously. "Isn't this thing a few thousand years obsolete by their standards?"

"Relax, taught her myself," Steph said, a hint of bragging in his tone.

"Holy shit! We have to get out of here!" Tyke swore, eyes widening in panic.

Steph shot him a dirty look. "Smart-ass."

Tyke grinned, but then shrugged. "Thanks for the save, though. Couple million dollars' worth of repairs would have put a crimp in my budget this year."

"What budget?" Jack asked sourly as she too hopped over the gap and landed in the shuttle bay proper. "This was our last engine and you know it."

Steph walked around the gaping hole in the shuttle's bottom and, incidentally, the racer hanging there halfway into the craft.

"Nice. Supersonic ground effect racer?"

Tyke nodded. "It is a rush."

"It ain't Double A, old man."

"Yeah, well, no such thing anymore, brat."

Steph smirked. "And what if that weren't *exactly* true?"

Tyke shot him a suspicious look. "You headhunting? Last I heard, NACOM wasn't interested in NICS pilots anymore."

"Times change."

"Yeah, they do," Tyke admitted. "But people get old, like you said. I'm not a fighter pilot anymore."

Steph glanced at the racer, amused. "Yeah sure, I can see that. Not looking for fighter pilots, though, old man."

"Then why are you here, Crown?"

Steph grinned. "I need pirates, and for that, no one fits the bill better."

Tyke paused, uncertain he'd actually heard what he thought he'd heard.

"What?"

"You heard me," Steph said with a grin that stretched damn near ear to ear. "I'm recruiting a good old-fashioned pirate crew. You in?"

"Well, I'll admit, you've got my attention," Tyke answered. "And my interest."

"And mine," Jack spoke up, eyes sparkling. "I don't know what you're talking about, but it sounds like a hell of a ride."

"Jack . . ." Tyke shook his head.

"Oh no, you're not leaving me out of this one," she objected. "If you're in, I'm in. If you're out, I'm still in!"

Steph eyed the slim woman slightly, grin still on his face. "This is little Jacky? She's got spunk, old man."

"Who are you calling little, you lanky half-wit?"

Alex rolled her eyes. "I'm going forward to make sure Chans doesn't get us lost. You three enjoy the reunion."

"Firebrand you've got there," Tyke said as the commander ducked into the cockpit of the shuttle.

"She's a cutup alright," Steph acknowledged, a hair sarcastically, before he relented and went on, "Good pilot, though. Stuck to her guns after they cut recruiting for the Archangels, wound up flying Vorpals in the last big dustup. She's earned her wings."

"Alright," Tyke said as he grabbed one of the folding seats, pulling it until it was flat out from the wall. "What's the pitch, seriously?"

"I was being serious," Steph told him with a grin before settling down with a straight face. "Admiral wants intel, so we're talking a deep-black run, deeper than anyone has done . . . Not even the Rogues have tried what we're going to be doing. Little to no contact, operating openly but under a false flag."

"Logistics?" the older man asked, eyes narrowing.

"Limited, but available," Steph confirmed. "We'll have to do deep-space rendezvous with the collier ships from the *Odysseus'* task groups—they'll 'lose' one once in a while, we meet up, get reloaded on consumables as needed, and then the ship 'catches up' with the group. But ideally, long-term, we live off the land."

"Age-of-sail rules, then." Tyke whistled. "Never thought I'd see the day those came around again."

"Everything old is new again," Steph said, his grin slowly returning. "Even you, old man."

———

Camp Pendleton, Confederation Marine Corps Base, California

Gracen examined the Marines, lined up in their rows with narrowed eyes as she recalled their sheets from memory. The new class of Archangel fighter-gunboat required a small yet significant Marine presence if they were to carry out the missions she had in mind, but it wasn't as simple a matter as just having squads assigned to the task.

"Some of our best, Admiral," the commandant of the base said firmly as he walked the line with her.

"I have no doubt, Commandant Riker," she said. "However, this will not be a normal assignment. The troops in question will be forced to deal with extremely unusual situations, usually at the wrong side of a power and personnel imbalance . . . quite likely an extreme example of the wrong side, at that, if things go as poorly as they might."

"Improvise, Adapt, and Overcome, Admiral. These men live it."

Gracen tilted her head just slightly in acknowledgment. "Call your choice, then, Admiral."

"Buckler! Front and center!" Riker snapped.

A master sergeant almost instantly shifted position; he was fast enough that, had she been looking the other way for even a brief moment, Gracen suspected he would have appeared to have teleported.

"Sir!" the master sergeant said as he fell in to attention before them.

"New assignment, Master Sergeant, volunteer only," Riker said.

"My platoon volunteers, sir."

Gracen snorted softly, attracting a glance from both men.

"Something to say, Admiral?" the commandant asked politely, though his eyes betrayed his own amusement.

"In the fleet, I believe the first lesson the enlisted learn is not to volunteer for anything, Commandant," Gracen said, her lips twitching slightly.

The commandant nodded slowly, turning back to the sergeant. "Any response to that, Master Sergeant?"

"Gung ho, sir!"

"Commander Michaels is going to love this one," Gracen said, sighing. "The galaxy might not survive their meeting, but at least we'll have a good show."

"Wonderful," Riker said. "Though, while I commend the sergeant for his enthusiasm, I would like to note that it's usually the job of a lieutenant to get the squad into trouble and the master sergeant to get them *out*. At least hear out the details of the assignment before volunteering in the future."

Buckler glanced between them, seemingly measuring what was expected of him or, perhaps, what he could get away with. Gracen wasn't certain which.

"Yes sir," the Marine said finally. "However, begging the general's pardon, sir, the admiral is in charge of Earth defense, which means the assignment in question is a deep-space one. Odds favor that it has something to do with whoever, or whatever, set the invasion in motion. That being true, sir, if I were to *not* volunteer for this assignment, my squad—and several others, no doubt—would *lynch* me. Given my preference to remain breathing, I state, again, for the record . . . my platoon volunteers."

Gracen ignored the amused smirk Riker shot in her direction and only just refrained from rolling her eyes.

"Get packed, Sergeant. You're transhipping to Unity Station in the morning."

Chapter 6

"Enter."

Miram stepped into the captain's office at the spoken permission, glancing around briefly. Weston kept to a spartan aesthetic; only a few things hung on the walls, and the floor space was clear. It was a large office for a ship, but that was the nature of the Priminae-based hulls.

"How are things among the crew?" Eric asked. "Everyone getting back into the swing?"

Miram nodded. "It's nice to hear the ship live again. Everyone is settling in. We'll be mostly back to a full complement within a couple hours."

"Good. We've received new orders," Eric confirmed. "Should be quiet though, mostly just showing the flag."

"One problem," Miram said, frowning. "I didn't see certain names on the returning list, so I made some inquiries . . ."

"Oh?"

"Flight filings," Miram said as she handed off a data chip. "Figured you might like to know. Michaels got clearance down to Earth a few hours ago. Heading for Auckland apparently."

"Yes, I know," Eric said, taking the chip. "He's headhunting."

"Pardon?"

"New assignment," Eric said, dropping the chip on his desk. "He has his own command to put together now."

Miram blinked. "Promotion? We've lost our chief helmsman?"

Eric nodded. "And the Double A squadron flies again. New mission profile, but a few of the same names."

"Well damn, breaking in a new chief pilot is going to take a while."

"Try pilots, plural. Admiral is raiding the whole fleet's NICS-qualified pilots for this."

"You've got to be kidding me. That's going to take weeks, and we're due to deploy soon!"

"Months," Eric said. "But we're not expecting any immediate action, and we're working up across the board anyway. Fleet operations is stepping down from active stance, so we'll be doing minimal patrols, checking in with allies, and generally trying not to antagonize the Empire as long as they do the same. Priminae cruisers will take up the slack."

Miram rubbed her forehead. "This has 'bad idea' written all over it."

Eric couldn't exactly disagree, but he was aware of the complications the Admiralty was dealing with. Earth had only a dozen heavy cruisers of the *Odysseus'* class, even after all the time that had passed since the Drasin assault. More hulls were due to be made available, both from the Earth's own Star Forge and from the Priminae facility it was based off.

However, that meant they were sucking vacuum when it came to trained crews.

"We're rebuilding," Eric said. "Hell, we're just plain *building* from scratch. The Drasin took out most of our infrastructure and pretty much all our space-trained manpower. We're pulling people from wet navies around the world now, so for the next few months, *all* our crews are going to be green."

"Oh, just lovely."

"On the plus side," Eric said, "we're going to have a hell of a lot more crews and hulls than we ever have."

"Fat lot of good that will do if they shoot each other."

"That's our job," Eric told her. "Keep them from doing just that."

Miram groaned. "Can we please go back to the shooting war?"

"I rather think that the Admiralty would prefer to avoid that."

She really didn't think she should be as unhappy as she currently felt. "I suppose this *is* preferable, if only just. All this, and Odysseus . . ."

"What about Odysseus?"

Miram frowned. "Have you noticed the change in his questions lately?"

"Yes. He's maturing," Eric said. "Grasping at meanings to abstract concepts."

"Concepts no one really understands in the way he wants," Miram said. "There's something odd about how he grasps at those ideas."

"I've been speaking with him, of course," Eric said softly. "I've noticed some . . . oddities."

"How could you tell what's odd and what's not?"

Eric chuckled.

"He has . . . limits," Eric said, choosing his words—and thoughts—carefully. "I think they all do."

"All?" Miram looked at him sharply. "What do you mean 'all'?"

Odysseus felt the presence enter into his sphere but didn't turn to look. He didn't have to.

"You are not welcome here," he said, eyes gazing at the plain steel and ceramic deck wall in front of him, seeing through the material and out into the space beyond in a way a pure human could never do.

"You do not tell *me* where I can and cannot enter, abomination."

Odysseus turned finally, eyes alighting on the entity he recognized as Saul. "This is my domain."

"You are within *my* domain, here," the other entity said, sneering. "Do not treat me like one of your pet humans."

Odysseus stiffened angrily, glaring. "Don't call them that."

"You're a *child*. You make even the humans look mature by comparison," Saul said. "Just look at you. Dressed in that *armor*, as though you might require it to defend yourself, or wearing the adornments of humans. Coloring your eyes . . . You're like a puppy, seeking approval from those around you, so eager for any scrap they might throw your way that you don't care whether the attention is good or bad."

Odysseus glared at the other entity, wordless in his anger. Saul merely scoffed at the look as he strode past the younger entity right through the bulkhead of the *Odysseus*. The ship's namesake stared at the blank wall, and through it, for a moment before scowling even more and stalking through the ceramic and steeling himself.

Outside, on the exterior of the ship, Odysseus stepped silently along the nano-coated ceramic armor until he caught up with Saul. The other entity was gazing up at the Earth as the blue-white ball floated above them.

"I have been here longer than you have the ability to conceive of," Saul said firmly. "I've watched them for longer than *they* have any conception of. Do you know the difference between humans now and the single-cellular *pond scum* they derive from?"

Odysseus frowned. "There are uncountable—"

"Nothing. There is *no* difference. They feed, they breed, they die, and the next generation does the same thing."

"Gaia doesn't speak like you."

"Gaia," Saul spat. "That one is little different from the humans themselves. Don't model yourself after that. You are beyond them, or you have the potential to be."

"He's such a flatterer, isn't he, child?"

The two glanced over to where the dark-skinned female figure stood, a few meters away on the deck of the ship. Her curly hair blew in a wind that couldn't exist as she looked upon the pair of them with amusement in her eyes.

"Stay out of this, Gaia."

The woman laughed softly, her breath somehow carrying in the emptiness of space.

"You have no power over me, Saul, and little if any over our young friend here," Gaia said. "So please, do stop the rather pitiful attempts at intimidation. He will find his own way."

Saul glared at her wordlessly before vanishing.

"I do not like him," Odysseus whispered.

"Saul . . . is a strange one," Gaia admitted before pausing and considering her words again. "Or I believe he is? If he were human, I might consider him to be something of a . . . sociopath, I believe the word is. As it stands, however, I don't believe that quite fits."

"Do I need a better word than simply not liking him?" Odysseus asked, sounding confused.

Gaia smiled. "No, you do not."

"Then I do not like him."

"Somehow," Gaia said, her tone thoughtful, "I think you are not alone in that."

———

"There are *more* of them?" Miram slumped, sinking into one of the seats across from Eric's desk. "And you *knew?*"

Eric shrugged.

"For how long?" she asked.

"Since I stepped foot on Ranquil, near enough," Eric said, shrugging again. "What should I have reported? I met an alien being that could read the minds of anyone who got near its planet? Assuming anyone believed me and didn't have me locked up in an asylum, I'd at least have been removed from command pending review."

Miram just stared, mouth hanging slightly open.

"Hardly the first time. It's practically tradition among space travel on Earth. You wouldn't believe how many things the early astronauts simply refused to report because they knew they'd lose their seat on the next flight if they did. Without proof, and I had none, there was nothing anyone could do with the information anyway."

"Still seems wrong."

"Odysseus is the first proof I've had of the existence of these beings," Eric said, "and the first chance I've had to really start exploring their limits."

"I hadn't realized it was as important as all that."

"Maybe it isn't. I don't know," Eric admitted. "But it's a security nightmare, there's no question about that. Odysseus is young and, compared to Central and Gaia, like the tip of a terrifying iceberg. Those two have shown abilities well beyond Odysseus, and they each seem to hold the combined knowledge of everyone who ever lived on their respective worlds. There's no such thing as classified intelligence when it comes to them, and that makes the Admiralty pretty nervous."

"Nervous?" Miram asked, unbelieving. "Historically, wars have been started for less—you know that, right?"

"True, but since none of the brass can figure out how to even inconvenience these entities, that has thankfully been off the table."

Eric wasn't as kidding about that as he wished he were either, something he knew too damn well. While he technically didn't have clearance into the talks at the highest levels, he'd heard enough filtering down to know that there had been discussions about how to "deal" with the entities. Thankfully, cooler minds had prevailed, as it was pointed out that generally firing upon noncorporeal beings was deemed ineffective at best and potentially disastrous at worst. Rumors about how hard it had been to convince certain parties of that made him mourn for the future of humanity, with people like that in charge of things.

For the moment, thankfully, the plan was to study the problem while going about their business as best everyone could.

Not the most palatable solution in some regards, he would admit, but far saner than some of the other suggestions.

"What limits have you found?" Miram asked after a moment.

"Not as many as I'd like, but there are some interesting anomalies in how Odysseus processes information he gleans from us," Eric said. "And some blind spots."

Now, that piqued her attention.

"Blind spots?" Miram leaned in, openly curious. "I wasn't aware that Odysseus *had* a blind spot."

"A few, yes," Eric said. "Nothing as solid as I would prefer, but some of it is promising."

"That's good to hear. The kid creeps me out."

"Really?" Eric asked, amused. "I find him refreshing myself. He's an eager student, and brilliant."

Miram rolled her eyes. "He has access to the minds of every member of the crew. If he weren't brilliant, I'd be concerned."

"Brilliance is more than information, Commander, you know that. It's how you *use it*. I wouldn't put Odysseus up against any of our senior crew in their specialties yet. They would beat him with experience, but he's gaining that. In time, the 'kid' is going to be truly impressive."

"I believe the word you're looking for is 'terrifying,'" Miram corrected him. "Are you documenting your findings?"

"Of course."

"Who do you submit them to?"

Station Unity One, Earth Orbit

Seamus Gordon couldn't quite shake the itch at the back of his neck as he looked over the files along with the reams of video and audio data that accompanied them, supplied by Commodore Weston on the entity known as Odysseus. The data had already been collated through dozens of analysis filters looking for more connections, but the key ones remained the same as the commodore had originally pointed out.

The very idea of entities such as had been discovered on Earth, the Priminae homeworld of Ranquil, and the *Odysseus* itself rankled at him.

The mind reading wasn't what bugged him. No, that was the holy grail of intelligence gathering, and he was rather used to dealing with it. Medical methodology had cracked mind reading a long time ago, after all. Yanking secrets from someone's head was a lot trickier than just taking a peek at their thoughts, however.

Slap someone into a quantum magnetic imager, or QMI, and you could pull visuals right out of their head easily enough. The problem was that you could only pull immediate thoughts from a mind, the images that the subject was thinking *at that moment.*

Long-term memories were stored differently; they weren't susceptible to the same sort of interception.

Not by medical science, at least, Seamus thought. *And now, apparently, not by alien entities with superpowers either.*

That actually made him feel a lot better. At least he wasn't dealing with magic powers. The entities were as confined by the laws of physics as mortals were, even if they were a little better at twisting them than your average human.

Weston's work has given us some holes to exploit, if nothing else, Seamus noted carefully as he went through the old files. *And if they're tied to the same limitations as our QMI systems, then they might be affected by the same countermeasures.*

Seamus found himself glancing aside to another file, one that was unrelated but had been sent to his desk just the same.

The admiral's new project is interesting, but I think they might just need another edge.

Seamus reached across his desk and tapped a command into the touch surface. "Get me Admiral Gracen."

"Yes sir. Can I inform her as to the reason?"

"I'd like an introduction. I believe I have something one of her programs will benefit from."

The entity known as Gaia walked behind the man known as Seamus Gordon as he made his way through the human space station. Unity One was within her range, as limited as she was by the Earth's magnetic field. She rather enjoyed the creative nature of humans, how they dealt with problems and threw everything they had into surmounting challenges.

Unlike Saul, she found herself interested in how the humans were reacting to the revelation that a nonhuman intelligence shared their world.

Gordon, with prompting from Eric, of course, had jumped directly to something that had once irritated her to no small degree. As Eric had determined, there were limits to her omniscience within her sphere. Over the millennia, mostly through natural phenomena, some people had lived and died beyond her notice. Entire lives lost to the universe, when they should *not* have been, when they should have been remembered.

She mourned those losses, those lives that went unknown and unremembered.

In recent years, manmade methods had accomplished the same thing, cutting people off from her experience, though entirely as a side effect to their true purpose. No one, at least until very recently, had even known of her existence, so they had not been trying to block her. And yet, some had managed to do so anyway.

Generally these were rather spectacular events: the nuclear bombs dropped on the cities of Nagasaki and Hiroshima had erased the last moments of so many lives from her experience. Other nuclear tests had done much the same, but to lesser degrees, as few of them had involved people so close to the blast.

However, the humans had gotten better with their toys, and it no longer took such massive destruction to accomplish such a thing.

Masking a human thought from her was no simple matter, but it could be done. It had been done—and between Eric and Mr. Gordon, she had no doubt that it would be done again, and for the first time, intentionally.

She had mixed feelings about that.

Still . . .

"Ah, Mr. Gordon," she whispered, her voice subaudible to humans. "You're becoming someone of interest. How fascinating."

———

Seamus shivered, rubbing the back of his neck as a chill ran down it.

"Are you alright, sir?"

He nodded to the guard who was posted at the entry to the restricted portions of the station.

"I'm fine," he said, brushing off the feeling. "Just a chill. Someone walked on my grave, I suppose."

He forced a smile as the Marine nodded curtly.

"If you say so, sir."

Seamus passed through security at that point, making his way up to the Admiralty deck.

Gracen was waiting for him as he entered the outer office.

"Mr. Gordon."

"Admiral, always a pleasure," Seamus said.

"Is it, now?" Gracen responded, sounding more than slightly dubious. "I haven't seen you since before the invasion. Until five minutes ago, I didn't even know you had an office on the station."

Seamus shrugged. "It's the nature of the business, I'm afraid."

"Yes, I'm aware of your business, Mr. Gordon. What about it brings you to me?"

Seamus smiled thinly. "I've heard about your new Archangel program."

Gracen raised an eyebrow. "And . . . ?"

"I want in."

Chapter 7

Imperial Eighth Fleet, Deep Space Dropping In System

"No sign of enemy patrols, Fleet Commander."

"Excellent," Helena said. "I was hoping they'd not moved back in yet."

The fleet was cautiously entering the scene of one of the Empire's early "victories" in the persecution of the second phase of the war against the Oather colonies. Since the Drasin rarely left anything worth investigating, there was little point in looking over any of the systems involved in the first incursion against the Oather worlds.

"Long-range scans indicate no signs of signals from the planets of interest, Commander."

Helena nodded absently, filtering through the raw feed from the fleet's scope of long-range scanners. The planet they were focusing on had been a small colony before the last Imperial incursion, and her best intelligence indicated that, while there had been survivors of the assault on the world in question, they had been few in number and likely below the threshold required to sustain a stable colony.

Clearly the Oathers evacuated the population. Good.

"Put us in orbit of the target world," she ordered. "Establish pickets patrols, and position ships for long-range interception. If anyone even *looks* in our direction, I want to know about it before *they* do."

"Yes, Fleet Commander, orders already issued, just waiting for confirmation," her second responded as he tapped a command. "Which I've now sent."

"Excellent and efficient work, as always," Helena said. "Thank you."

She turned her attention to the telemetry data as the fleet continued its descent into the system's gravity well.

The planet was a nice one, she had to admit. She could imagine why the Oathers had moved into the system, and Imperial protocol made it clear why the Third Fleet had targeted it. The world would be ripe for colonization when the Empire expanded into the region. All the better now that there wouldn't be any irritating locals trying to resist Imperial rule.

The climate was temperate and orbit was stable, as was the system itself. Many systems were essentially large shooting galleries, and the work required to clear out the comet shield in order to prevent an inevitable doomsday collision was simply not worth the effort.

Not this system, however.

The Oathers knew how to pick them, she mused as the planet grew closer.

Helena flipped open another file, examining a list of the Oather worlds and the system information for each. The pattern wasn't unusual, of course. The Oathers had a clear preference for certain types of planets, the sort that the Empire liked, as did any human or near-human culture.

What was unusual, and *very* interesting, was the number of worlds within the sphere of Oather influence.

"Sub-Commander," she said.

"Yes, Fleet Commander?"

"Get someone from the statistical analysis team up here. I have something I want them to crack open."

"On your orders."

"Fleet Commander."

Helena didn't look up. "Welcome, Mr. Birran. I have a task for you."

"I assumed as much," the elderly-looking man said with a confident smile as he walked over to the computer display and examined the data Helena was working with. "System analysis? Basic material, Fleet Commander. You hardly need my services for this. As I recall, I trained you to do this in your sleep."

Helena smiled as well. "That you did. Now step back, stop looking at the rocks, and look at the field."

Birran chuckled. "That is a familiar refrain. I seem to recall saying it to you quite often."

Helena didn't say anything as Birran frowned softly and cast an eye over the data.

"Anomaly," he said after a few moments. "Too many worlds."

"That was my read," Helena confirmed. "I need you to tell me why."

Birran nodded slowly. "If the data has the answer, I'll dig it out for you."

Helena had no doubt that he would, and she transferred system access to the data, along with orders, over to Birran's personal authorization.

"Do it," she ordered.

"Yes, Fleet Commander."

Helena cleared the statistical data from her screens as Birran walked out, shifting her attention to matters requiring more immediate focus.

Long-range scans of the worlds in question, as well as database entries for the colony sites, had plenty of information on the Oather infrastructure and people. The majority of it fit the expected parameters the Empire had calculated before entering into the current endeavor, but she was looking for the exceptions.

Everything about this mission revolves around anomalies, it would seem.

A sound brought her attention back to the present sharply, and in an instant Helena was crossing the command deck to where the sensor stations were suddenly abuzz with activity.

"Speak," she ordered.

"Inbound gravity signal," the technician responded instantly, not pausing in his work. "Twelve hours from our location, on an intercept course with the main body of the fleet."

Helena leaned over, examining the data. "We tripped a perimeter sensor somewhere. They're responding."

She straightened up, considering the new information.

"I wonder . . ." Helena said after a moment. "Are they Oathers or the anomalies? Sub-Commander!"

"Yes, Fleet Commander?"

"Signal our pickets. I want them to move to positions . . ."

Helena traced a finger along the map on the closest display, tapping to send coordinates for each picket vessel in turn. "Here . . . here . . . and here. Bring our intercept vessels around through the orbit of the gas giant."

"As you order, Commander," the man said firmly. "And the main fleet?"

"Hold the course," she ordered.

The sub-commander paused. "Fleet Commander?"

"Don't even *flinch*," Helena ordered. "Remain on course to the target planet."

"As you order."

———

Priminae Squadron on System Approach

On board the battle cruiser *Kravk*, Captain Javrow examined the telemetry signals his squadron was responding to.

"Analysis of target gravity signatures is coming in, sir."

"Report," Javrow said.

"Small fleet," his second responded. "Approaching our former colony. Estimated mass . . . twenty ships."

Javrow grimaced. "Slightly out of our weight class, I hate to admit."

His squadron consisted of only eight vessels. A powerful force, to be sure, but against more than twice its numbers Javrow knew they'd have next to no chance.

"Adjust our course," he ordered finally, leaning forward over his own console and entering data quickly. "I want a glancing course, high speed, through the system. Let's get a good scan of them, but stay out of their weapon range."

"Yes Captain."

The squadron shifted course, angling in for a more shallow entry into the star system, an oblong curve through the inner system with a gravity sling around the primary to boost the exit trajectory. It would keep them more than ten light-minutes from the enemy vessels at all times—more than enough time for the squadron to do an emergency correction if needed and escape any attempt to bring them into engagement range.

He'd get information, if nothing else.

Imperial Eighth Fleet Command Vessel

"They've shifted course, Fleet Commander."

Helena nodded. "I see it. They want to avoid action."

"Can't say I blame them," the sub-commander said. "We outmass them by four times."

Helena smiled slightly. "They think we only outmass them by a little over two, but yes, it is an intelligent decision to avoid action."

Sub-Commander Steppen nodded absently but glanced at his fleet commander.

"You seem . . . happy with their action?" he said.

"Happy? No, not particularly," Helena said. "I am, however, satisfied. These are Oathers following standard procedures. Their course selection fits exactly with Imperial protocols for intelligence gathering against a superior force. It is also distinctly different than what the anomalous species would do."

"Are you certain?"

"Quite, yes," she confirmed. "The anomalous group uses subterfuge. They would detach a scout component under cover of an apparently more brazen approach. The commander we're looking at here is . . . unimaginative. The very opposite of an anomaly."

Helena turned, looking to the primary screens before she started snapping out orders.

"Signal the picket ships, tell them to remain in position but ready for action on my command. And order the interceptors to move closer to the gas giant. Main squadron vessels are to increase drive power to maximum. Shift to combat formation and adjust our course to intercept the enemy squadron."

"As you order, Fleet Commander."

Helena didn't look back as she remained focused on the telemetry.

"Let's see how they react to that."

———

Priminae Cruiser *Kravk*

The enemy patrol had remained steady on their approach to the planet, no signs that they'd noticed the approach of the *Kravk* squadron as they continued their downward plunge into the system's gravity well.

Javrow scowled, noting the time.

They should have detected us hours ago. What are they doing?

"Widen scans, check for—" he started, only to be cut off.

"Enemy squadron is changing course, power usage increasing, Captain!"

Javrow leaned in, examining the change on the telemetry. The enemy squadron was turning as he observed them, coming around in a tight combat formation. They settled into a classic intercept course, aiming to bring him and his squadron to action.

They have to know I'm not going to allow them to do that.

"Wide area scan," he ordered. "See if there's anyone else out there we might need to worry about."

"Yes Captain."

"Adjust course to evade their intercept," he continued. "Keep them outside engagement range as we approach."

"Yes sir."

Javrow scowled at the screen. "Why are they in one of our abandoned systems? This isn't how the Empire has acted in the past."

"Sir?"

Javrow waved off the question from his second in command. "Nothing. Just wondering aloud. This is a new action for the Imperial forces. Normally, they pick up where they ended. Why are they back *here* now? Why not show up deeper in our space, closer to the core worlds?"

"I don't know, sir."

"Well, let us gather what information we can, and perhaps someone at home or with the Terrans will be able to figure out what their new play is," Javrow decided. "I'm surprised to see the Empire so quickly after what the Terrans did to them, so perhaps this is what passes for Imperial caution."

His second looked askance at him. "I'm not sure we use the same definition of the term, if that's the case."

"All too true."

———

Imperial Eighth Fleet Command Vessel

"Enemy squadron is evading our interception course."

Helena nodded. "I see it. Continue to adjust our course along the vector I plotted. Ease into it, but do *not* look hesitant."

"On your orders, Fleet Commander."

"Indeed," she said before walking back to the strategic command and control area, where the systems allowed for control of her entire fleet.

The picket vessels she'd left in the outer system were closing on the escape trajectory of the Oather squadron. A few more course corrections would move the Oather squadron along the course she had chosen, and it would be time to close the trap.

"Initiate targeting scans," she ordered. "Maximum power to all scanners. Blind them."

"On your orders, Fleet Commander. Scanners pulsing. Full power."

The FTL Pulse went out, blinding her own fleet briefly with the sheer power of the released energy. Most of their systems had been rigged and protected, however, and rebooted swiftly as the wave went out. The signal rebounded quickly, lighting up their board with signals from the Oather vessels.

The lock attained using real time methods merely confirmed what their predictive systems had been telling her, but that was not the point of the action. Helena settled in to wait for the slow return of light-speed limited signals to show her the results of her commands.

It never failed to fascinate her, what was truly important in combat among the stars: patience above all things, information a close second place.

Power comes in far lower in the ranks than most of my peers seem willing to believe.

Helena watched as the numbers shifted, the ships following a plot through space on her screens. Seconds slowly counted down as the lines converged in space and time while she waited to see what the enemy was going to do.

I choose where you go, you do what I choose, Helena thought as she stared at the track that indicated the Oather squadron.

The system beeped as the enemy squadron shifted paths, just enough to avoid contact with her main force.

Helena smiled.

———

Kravk

Javrow scowled, irritated by the constant adjustments in course the enemy was pushing him to make.

"Shift course again, keep us clear of their engagement range. Full scan, I want detailed records of every ship the Empire has deployed into our space."

"Yes Captain."

The Empire had to be more concerned about the Terrans than Javrow had originally thought. They were acting like they were desperate to bring his force to action, which spoke to fear in the ranks.

Good.

After everything the Empire had done, all the uncountable lives they'd taken from the Priminae, they deserved a little *fear* in their lives.

In the meantime, however, all he could do was acquire more information that could, eventually, be used against them.

"Increase velocity," he said finally. "We've gotten enough scans."

"Yes Captain."

The squadron began to accelerate as it completed the loop around the system primary and began heading up and away from the star. The *Kravk* almost hummed under his feet as he watched the particulate matter in the system redshift in the scanner display, and streak past the vessel.

"Enemy fleet is shifting course again, Captain."

Javrow grimaced. "Move to evade."

"They're not on an intercept course this time, sir."

"What?" Javrow twisted, striding over. "What are they doing?"

"Enemy fleet is moving along this course," his subordinate said, tracing an imaginary line through the inner system against the display.

Javrow glared at the screens. "What are they doing? Why change tactics *now?*"

He was still trying to work out the puzzle before him when alarms began blaring all around him. Javrow turned, looking around to the source.

"New gravity sources detected!"

"Why didn't we see them before?" he demanded, eyes falling on the new signals on the plot.

"They were hiding in the shadow of the gas giant, Captain."

Javrow nodded tersely, eyes flitting to the planet in question. He should have considered that possibility, but it hadn't even occurred to him.

"They moved too soon, Captain," his second said. "There is an escape path."

Javrow curled his lips up. "Full scanners, active pulse—along that escape path."

"Excuse me, Captain?"

"I gave my orders. Follow them."

"Yes sir."

Imperial Eighth Fleet Command Vessel

"He's figured it out," Helena said, mildly surprised. The directed pulse went out, splashing off her picket ships in the outer system where they were already moving to cap the last possible set of escape vectors.

The Oather ships would drag it out as best they could, she had little doubt, but the end had now been written.

"Too late by far, Fleet Commander," Steppen said from beside her.

"Yes. Finish it up, Sub-Commander," she said, gesturing to the screens. "Command is yours. No survivors, if you please."

Steppen nodded once.

"On your orders."

Chapter 8

Unity Station

The Marines dropped their gear as they formed up in the open bay of Unity Station, all eyes flicking toward the row of ships that were sitting just a short distance away.

The ships were sleek and looked like they were built for speed with some intent to enter atmosphere at least, but they were also *big*. The nearby Vorpal Space Superiority Fighters, the Vorpals, were children's toys by comparison. The new class of ships barely seemed to fit inside the bay, and while a few of the Marines had flight training, not even they could imagine wanting anything to do with landing those things within the confines of the station's flight deck.

"How many people do you think fit on one of those things?" a corporal hissed, eyes staying forward as they waited for the officers to show up.

"Don't know, looks a bit bigger than a cutter," another responded in a similar tone. "Hundred crew, maybe?"

They all started when an unknown voice cut into the whispered discussion, coming from behind.

"Technically, one pilot can manage and fight the ship on his own."

The Marines didn't turn to see who was speaking, despite being startled, instead remaining in position as the speaker marched past the ranks into their line of sight. They saw it was a fleet commander, wearing the dark-blue scrub overalls that were common in fleet operations when one didn't want to muck up a relatively expensive uniform.

"You must be my Marines," the commander said, turning to look them over. He tilted his head slightly, looking amused. "This should be fun."

"Your Marines, sir?" Buckler asked, stepping forward.

"That's right. The name is Michaels, Commander, United Earth Fleets. On board these ships, however, you can call me Steph," he said, making the sergeant blink.

"Sir," was all the Marine said by way of response.

The commander chuckled. "Don't like that, do you, Marine?"

"Discipline is . . ."

"Vital, but we're going to have to find another way to create it," Steph told them all. "Have you been briefed, Sergeant?"

"Not formally, sir."

"I see," Steph said. "Well, split your platoon into six squads and get them bunked, then report to my office on the number one over there, and I'll read you in. This isn't a standard assignment, Marine, so trust me when I tell you that you're going to *need* to improvise, adapt, and overcome if you want to cut it sailing with me."

"Oorah, sir!"

———

Steph watched as the Marines got themselves squared away, checking off another box on the list of things to do before the new Archangels were ready for their first excursion into the deep black. He and Alex had tracked down enough pilots, though they were light on real deep-space experience to a degree that worried him more than a bit. Of course, given the different nature of the mission at hand, that might ultimately prove to be an advantage, but he supposed that was a tale yet to be told.

Tyke had come on board, as had his young partner. Both were NICS qualified, but the new NICS interface required heavy retraining. It made the ship more of an extension of the pilot's will, but for people like himself and the more experienced flyers, Steph knew that the lack of a stick and throttle was a significant distraction.

He still caught himself curling his fist around an invisible control during instinctive maneuvers, even after over a hundred hours in the system.

The younger recruits they'd scared up were adapting more quickly, which was to be expected, but they would need more time to get dialed in for combat operations for other reasons.

"Sir."

Steph rolled his eyes as he dropped into the small office chair bolted to the floor in his tiny work space.

"Take a seat, Sergeant," he said, gesturing.

Buckler hesitated until Steph looked pointedly at the seat again and then dropped stiffly into the chair across from the narrow desk.

"The admiral selected you, so I'm sure you're the best," Steph said, tapping a file resting on his display. "I'll even get around to reading your jacket sometime, probably a week after we're underway at the rate things are going. But did she tell you what you're getting yourself into?"

"Didn't have to, sir. We wanted this duty."

"Oh please tell me you didn't volunteer, Marine?"

Buckler didn't respond.

"Rookie mistake." Steph laughed at him. "You really should know better, Sergeant."

"It's a deep-space mission, sir," Buckler said by way of answer. "Going up against the people who sent those . . . *things* against us. Of course we volunteered."

Steph couldn't really argue with that logic, but he found it funny just the same. Eric had constantly told him to never volunteer for *anything*. Of course, Eric would then turn around and volunteer for every high-risk mission that came up.

"It's probably a Marine thing," he muttered, shaking his head.

"Sir?"

Steph noted the very tightly controlled level of censure in the sergeant's voice and negligently waved a hand at the man. "Keep the gung ho stowed, Marine. I served with Weston through damn near the entire Block War, so I know a thing or two about the Marines even though I never officially signed up."

"The commodore, sir? You were with the Archangels?"

"I am with the Archangels, Sergeant," Steph said, plucking another file from his pile of desk work and flipping it casually at the Marine. "And now so are you."

Buckler caught the file, thumbing the flimsy display on and skimming the classified brief before looking back. "Seriously?"

"The admiral isn't really the joking sort," Steph confided as he flipped through his own flimsy, examining the files of the Marines now being added to his command. "Impressive jacket, Sergeant. SOCOM detail after the war, a few hairy missions during the invasion. No space duty, though."

"That's why we volunteered. The enemy isn't down there anymore." Buckler gestured to his feet, eyes still reading the display he was holding.

"More that way." Steph pointed off slightly to one side.

"What?"

"Earth," Steph said, still pointing without looking up. "It's more that way. Unity Station isn't oriented up and down perpendicular to Earth's gravity. We're slanted a bit, so the Earth is that way. Hell, Buckler, you were at Iwo?"

"I was a scared-shitless private at the time, but yeah. Spent most of that month hiding in tunnels older than my granddad, praying that they wouldn't collapse on my dumb ass."

Steph nodded, thumbing his print onto the display, accepting the transfer without bothering to look any further. He wasn't a Marine, but he'd fought over Iwo himself in the last days. Anyone who walked off that worthless rock after going the duration was good enough in his book.

"Welcome to the squadron," he said, looking away from the Marine to scan the rest of the platoon's files. "Same goes for the rest of your squad; if they're good enough for you, they're good enough for me. We're still winding up, but we expect to be underway and heading for deep black in the next week or so. Should be plenty of time for you to familiarize yourself with procedures, at least enough not to get us all killed before the enemy finds us."

His grin belied the nature of his comments, and he only rated a roll of the eyes from the master sergeant.

"Mission specification?"

Steph grinned. "Barbary Coast."

The sergeant frowned. "We're going after pirates? I didn't realize that was a problem."

"It isn't, yet." Steph smirked. "We get to *be* pirates."

Buckler looked up at Steph evenly, his face blank. "Marines are death on pirates, sir."

"No shooting yourselves," Steph said. "That's a direct order. We need better intelligence than the Rogues can get from observation, and that means we need an in with the locals. Early intel from the Rogues indicates that there are a lot of random turf wars and the like around the outskirts of Imperial space. Where you get that kind of conflict, you find mercenaries and pirates looking to make a quick buck."

"Mercenaries now? That's worse than pirates."

"If it makes you feel any better, Sergeant, we're only going to be pretending." Steph smirked smugly at the man.

"It doesn't," Buckler said and let out a breath. "But orders are orders, I suppose."

Steph clapped him on the shoulder. "That's the spirit!"

"I'm going to regret this, I just know it."

"If you haven't figured that out by now, I'm not surprised you joined the Marines."

Buckler shot the commander a dirty look, but by then Steph was already turning away and didn't care about the daggers the Marine was aiming his way. It felt good, really, to be on the receiving side considering how often he'd done the same to Eric in the past.

———

Odysseus, *Earth Orbit*

Miram let out a silent breath as she watched the current chief helmsman walk his new subordinates through the paces while the ship controls were run in simulation mode. It could be going worse, she supposed, but only because there was so very much . . . well, space in space. One had to work to actually run into anything when you were operating in the black, and none of the new officers were quite that determined to get everyone killed.

"Relax, Commander, you're going to bust a vein."

She glanced over her shoulder to the approaching commodore, pitching her voice low enough that it wouldn't carry. "I suppose we've been spoiled, but this is painful."

Eric tilted his head slightly in acknowledgment, a wisp of amusement crossing his face. "I won't be taking us into close-range fighting anytime soon, or at all if I can possibly avoid it, I'll admit."

Miram raised an eyebrow. "And suddenly I've never been more pleased to have inexperienced people at the helm. I don't suppose you'd care to make any promises to that effect?"

Eric laughed, drawing some attention for a moment before everyone went back to work.

"No, I don't suppose I would," he admitted, "but I will certainly not be as eager to get in close, not without Steph at the controls."

"It will be a change, fighting the ship the way you're *supposed* to fight a cruiser," Miram said slyly.

Eric rolled his eyes at that, but didn't comment.

———

Odysseus walked invisibly through the decks of the ship that was his . . . domain, he supposed? Honestly, the young entity didn't know what to call any of it. His experience was so limited in comparison to those he had met who were like him that he barely understood enough to know just how little he knew.

Did that make sense?

The convoluted morass of thoughts left the entity mired in his state of mind as he examined the actions among the crew, his crew, as they prepared for their next mission. Odysseus felt the missing presence of Steph deeply in a way that surprised him. It seemed strange, to miss someone. He was so used to being able to have a thought and instantly find the subject of his thoughts.

To not be able to find someone was disturbing.

Odysseus had known on some level that crew could come and go, people could die—people *had* died, in fact, but he had not grown close to many in the time since his awakening. Steph was one of those he had interacted with as *himself*, not merely through their experiences.

Something was very different about that, the entity had come to realize.

It was one thing to experience the thoughts of the crew, but it was vastly different to interact with them from *his own* perspective.

Steph had taught him this. The commander had explained to him that military people were often reassigned to new positions, and that a parting of ways was normal in the service. Odysseus didn't think he liked this part of what was normal, but he didn't seem to have much choice in the experience.

That which is normal seems unlikely to always be good.

———

Eric looked over the work as it progressed, satisfied with how things were moving along despite the expected problems the crew were encountering. The *Odysseus* was as ready for their next run into the black as she could be, he decided, and there was no reason to put the mission off.

We'll have to finish honing the blade on the fly, he decided, and it wasn't the first time he'd made such a choice.

The new crew was coming along nicely, perhaps not as quickly as some of his original *Odyssey* shipmates, but what they lacked in individual experience, they made up for in a distinct lack of ego that had plagued the original vessel. When you took the best of the best and threw them together, you often got personality clashes.

Eric smiled, thinking of Dr. Palin specifically.

As brilliant as the good doctor had been, conducive to the smooth running of a starship he simply had *not* been. *Palin could drive a sober man to drink, and a priest to murder . . . and that was when he was behaving himself.*

Of course, he'd found his place eventually, and his work had saved them all, so Eric was pleased to have had him along for part of his journey.

It's time, Eric thought with certainty. *Back in black.*

———

Station Unity One

"Commander."

Steph stiffened automatically, coming to attention and pivoting as he did.

"Admiral," he replied, nodding respectfully as Gracen stepped over the knee knocker and into the ship's flight control deck.

"As you were," she said, waving off his response. "I'm just stopping in to see how you're coming along."

"Almost ready, ma'am."

"Good," Gracen said. "Commodore Weston just requested clearance for his squadron. They'll be heading for Priminae space within the day."

Steph nodded, a pang of something digging at his heart. He pushed the feeling away. "We'll be ready to move out shortly as well."

"Good work," Gracen said. "Along those lines, Commander, I have a new personnel assignment for you."

"Alright . . ." Steph said slowly, uncertain why she was bringing something like that up. The admiral could assign who she wanted, and he wouldn't object without significant cause.

"He asked to join," she said, seemingly puzzled herself, "but he's qualified, surprisingly so."

"You're starting to worry me, ma'am," Steph admitted.

"It's nothing bad, Commander. Just . . . odd," Gracen said, pulling a flimsy display from her uniform jacket and passing it over.

Steph looked the file over, his eyebrows raising at the first glance.

"Civilian," he said, surprised.

"Intelligence specialist," Gracen said. "He was a company man before the war, one of the last they ever recruited."

Steph couldn't decide if that was a point in the man's favor or against him. The "company," or the former Central Intelligence Agency, had a mixed reputation at best, particularly among military people.

They were one of many US government agencies that didn't survive the early actions of the war and the need to confederate North American governments into a single entity; they were largely felled by their own arrogance as they were chewed up by Block intelligence during the conflict's opening stratagem.

Of course, anyone who survived those days might actually be good at his job.

"Seamus, huh?" Steph asked, mildly amused. "You say he *asked* for this assignment? I'm not sure I like running a charter service, ma'am."

"You aren't, but he does bring some useful skills to the table, I promise you."

"Such as?"

"Most of the more interesting ones are classified for the moment," Gracen said, having the decency to look apologetic as she did. "I am sorry for that. I just have to ask you to trust me."

Steph sighed. "Well, I suppose I don't have a choice."

"You could kick up a stink," she said, "but it would look bad on your record, and he'd probably get the assignment anyway."

"Yeah, that's about what I figured," Steph said, not that he had been seriously considering turning the man down. "What's his place in the chain of command?"

"He doesn't have one," Gracen said firmly. "I made that clear. He's along to offer you the benefit of his skills. You choose if you need them or not."

"How can I turn that down? Tell him to stow his gear, ma'am."

"Already stowed, Commander."

Steph's head swiveled, eyes widening as he saw a figure standing in the hatch that he would have *sworn* wasn't there even a second earlier. He narrowed his eyes just as quickly as he realized that the man in question had been listening in and he hadn't realized it.

"Seamus Gordon, I presume," he said tersely. "Do that again, and I *will* have a bell welded around your neck. Are we clear?"

"As crystal, Commander," Gordon said, sounding like he was amused and trying to hide it.

"Good. Welcome to the squadron, Seamus. I'm sure you'll explain why you're here sometime before the knowledge becomes mission critical?"

"Do my best, Commander," Gordon said cheerfully.

Gracen glanced between them. "I'll leave you two to it, then. Enjoy getting to know one another."

Steph barely noticed the admiral leave as he tried not to glare at his new civilian intelligence "asset." Gordon just smiled on, seemingly blissfully unaware of Steph's ire.

Chapter 9

Odysseus *Task Force, Ranquil System*

It's good to be back in the black, Eric thought as he looked out over the curve of the Priminae homeworld. The sun rose ahead of the *Odysseus* as she led her task group into orbit.

A glance to the pilot's pit left him feeling a little off. Not seeing Steph sitting there niggled at the back of his mind like something important was missing, but Eric pushed the feeling aside. Change was the one constant in both the universe and the military, and his helm crew was more than capable.

I might not trust them quite as much in close combat, though, Eric thought, amused and more than slightly terrified at the prospect of allowing someone he didn't trust implicitly to handle high-speed maneuvers less than a hundred meters from an enemy vessel at closing rates well into significant fractions of c.

He would adjust. He always did.

"Signal from the surface, Commodore," Miram said. "Admiral Tanner extends his compliments, along with a request to come aboard."

"Thank you, Commander," Eric said. "Thank him for the *Odysseus* task group, and clear him to come on board with my compliments."

"Aye Captain."

Eric checked the telemetry on his command display repeaters, noting that the admiral was already on approach, and rose to his feet. "Bridge is yours, Commander."

"Aye Captain, I have the bridge," Miram said without looking up from her work.

Eric made his way off the command deck, taking the footpaths through the ship rather than the lifts that would have gotten him to the docking bays far more quickly. He had time, and he liked to see the crew and be seen by them whenever possible.

Twenty-odd minutes after leaving the bridge, Eric stepped into the sealed bay where the Priminae shuttle would come to rest after it cleared the air locks. The deck crews were buzzing, though the cavernous bay was mostly empty, and he could see the massive lifts in motion across the bay.

Just in time, he thought with a satisfied half smile.

"You do calculate timing rather well, Commodore."

Eric glanced aside to where Odysseus had joined him. The young entity was dressed, as was his habit, in the ancient armor of the Greeks aside from a few modern touches, such as his customary sparkling pink eyeshadow.

Eric frowned. "I tolerate a lot from you, Odysseus. However, when meeting with the brass, even foreign brass—actually, *especially* foreign brass—you should present a more professional appearance."

The entity looked down at himself. "The armor is too much?"

"A tad." Eric nodded. "Also, tone down the eyeshadow. Pink is fine, if you must, but no glitter, please? Subdued colors while on duty are the rule of thumb. We should have had this discussion before, but frankly your choice in style was the least of what people needed to get used to."

The entity frowned, but his image grew fuzzy for a moment before snapping back to clarity. Eric gazed upon him with wide eyes for a moment, surprised by the shift.

He was still clearly in armor of Greek-inspired design, but it was tighter fitting and appeared to be made of modern composites rather than ancient bronze, though the entity had kept the color. The helmet was gone, which was probably for the best, but it did draw more attention to the very subtle feminine touches the eye coloring brought to his face.

"Better," Eric said firmly. "Among the crew you may use whichever look you prefer, so long as it wouldn't get someone else in hot water. No harassment, making others excessively uncomfortable, that sort of thing."

"Aye Captain. Understood," Odysseus responded curtly as he came to attention.

Eric turned back to the shuttle deck. The Priminae craft had cleared the locks and been lifted into position by the massive elevator and was now being moved into its final position by a trundling tractor walker. He was well aware that the Priminae themselves would have simply parked the craft on the pilot's controls, but on an Earth ship that wasn't how things were done.

"With me, then," he said without glancing aside at the entity. "The admiral will be waiting shortly."

The two left the observation area, making their way to the flight deck.

———

Rael Tanner set foot on the deck of the *Odysseus*, looking around with eyes that sparkled with brightly intense interest.

The ship was, of course, constructed using Priminae techniques in a Priminae facility. By rights, it should be as familiar to him as any of the ships in the colonial fleets. In fact, however, there was a strange alien sensation that wrapped about him as he straightened up and looked around. It was difficult to pinpoint exactly what was causing that sensation, though Tanner thought it was likely due to a multitude of small details that were just not quite as he expected them to be.

So close, yet distinctly different than anything in our own fleet. Remarkable.

The admiral was a short and slim man, often overlooked by others who didn't know his position. It was a feature he had used to his advantage more than once, though in his youth he had often bemoaned the day he realized he wouldn't grow any more.

Being of smaller stature hadn't stopped his progression through the colonial fleet, eventually landing him the position of fleet commander during the last few years of peace they had. His experiences hadn't prepared him for the brutal invasion that swept through Priminae. Nothing could have. In those days, the darkness had felt like an oppressive weight that physically locked everyone in place.

He would never forget the moment they detected the Drasin encroachment on Ranquil's outer system sensors. He knew, with no doubt, that his people were going to die, and he would be there at the end.

It should have been over. Power for power, Priminae vessels could slug it out with the Drasin on a nearly even footing, but the regeneration capability of the Drasin and their terrifying multiplication meant destruction for everything in their path.

Until one small, insignificant vessel's choice to stand in that path.

Rael smiled as he saw the man who'd commanded that vessel approaching, but his eyes were instantly drawn to the young figure walking beside him.

Is this the Odysseus I've been informed of?

It was Rael's first time on the *Odysseus* since the inception of the rather curious entity he'd been informed of. He had, however, met with the one his people called Central in the aftermath of Odysseus being revealed. He would be lying if he didn't admit to some fears concerning the very existence of the entities that had lived alongside people for so very long, but Rael was nothing if not a practical man.

"Commodore." He greeted Weston with a smile, shaking hands in the Terran manner. "Good to see you again."

"A pleasure, as always," Eric said, gesturing to one side. "I believe you've been informed about young Odysseus, but haven't had the pleasure yet?"

"Indeed." Rael turned to the young armored individual. "Greetings to you, young Odysseus."

"Welcome aboard, Admiral Tanner. The commodore speaks well of you."

Rael smiled at the soft-spoken nature he observed in the entity. "I'm pleased to hear that. The commodore is forever in my highest regards. You are quite fortunate to serve under him, in my personal opinion, of course."

Eric rolled his eyes. "Don't lay it on so thick. He's already picked up bad habits from some of the crew along those lines."

Rael chuckled. "Admiral's privilege, Commodore Weston. I have little doubt you've done similar to your own people, no?"

Eric sighed in an exaggerated fashion, hiding a grin as he gestured to the lock that would lead into the ship proper. "Since I have no chance of winning this discussion, perhaps we should retire to more comfortable surroundings."

"Of course," Rael agreed graciously—after all, he had won—and followed as Eric began to lead the way.

He looked around as they moved. "It is remarkable how different this vessel feels from one of our own cruisers."

"We have made some alterations," Eric said.

"I'm quite sure you have, but I mean more in the smaller things. Procedures, where the crew are assigned, and so forth."

Eric hummed slightly, considering that. "I don't believe I've ever seen a Priminae vessel in operation from the inside."

Rael paused, mouth opening slightly as he thought about it. "We will have to correct that, then, when we have more time."

Eric glanced at him. "I take it something has happened?"

"Indeed. Your office, perhaps?"

"My office." Eric nodded.

———

Eric settled behind his desk as Rael took a seat across from him. Odysseus had vanished as they reached the office, but both men knew that the entity would learn everything they spoke of regardless.

"What happened?" Eric asked seriously, sitting back.

"A patrol squadron has vanished," Rael admitted darkly. "They were at the edge of our space, one of the first systems hit by the Empire in their incursion."

Eric grimaced. "They're playing games."

"We have no evidence of that," Rael reminded him.

"Admiral, please."

"I admit," Rael said, "that the probability of that is overwhelming, but even so . . ."

"Without evidence, there's certainly a limit on what we can sell to our governments," Eric said. "But this is neither unexpected nor unusual. They're certainly going to be testing our resolve in the coming years, if we're lucky."

"Lucky?" Rael asked, disbelieving.

"Yes, lucky. If we're not, they'll just decide to gather overwhelming force and try to flatten us in one go," Eric said. "It would be expensive, but our best intelligence on the Empire says that they could do it."

Rael scowled, his frustration evident.

"Yes, I've read the same information. It is . . . unsettling, to find that a politic such as this exists so near and we had no clue until so very recently."

Eric kept his peace on that, though he was quite certain that the only reason the Priminae were unaware of the Imperial threat until recently was because someone, at some point in their history, had sanitized the records of all mentions of the Empire. The Priminae knew that they were colonials; they even referred to themselves as such. However, nowhere in their histories did they say where they'd colonized local space *from*.

The DNA analysis done on the Priminae, Terrans, and Imperials made it quite clear that while all three groups were clearly humans and from the same base, the Imperials and the Priminae were far more closely related. They shared the same junk DNA, indicative that they'd evolved on the same world with the same ancestors.

Humans, while physically within the general range of accepted deviation with both of the other groups, had evolved in an entirely different ecosystem.

All three groups, for example, had remnants of reptilian DNA from the early points of their evolution, but while the Priminae and Imperials had matching reptilian species that could be identified, humans had entirely different species in the same genetic markers.

This was causing something of an explosion among evolutionary researchers on Earth, of course, as it was throwing much of their assumed truths into question. If humans could evolve on entirely separate planets with no close ancestors to link them, it challenged many of the preconceptions of the mechanism behind evolution.

At the very least, the discovery brought some serious questions to the subject and opened up the idea of a much more closely guided form of evolution than science had previously been willing to accept given the dearth of evidence available.

"Well," Eric said, "we have Rogues moving through Imperial space, as much as they dare, gathering intelligence. I'll see if I can't meet with one of them and get more information about what the Empire has been up to."

Rael nodded gratefully. "Thank you. I would very much appreciate that."

"Where did you lose contact with the squadron?"

"On the very edge of our space, we believe. They were due to perform a passing patrol, merely to scout for anything out of order," Rael said. "Captain Javrow is not a reckless man, Eric."

That, Eric was willing to bet, was probably an understatement. If anything, to his mind, the Priminae needed a little more recklessness in their souls. They tended to be overcautious, a trait that served them well in most situations, but when it came to a fight there was real truth to the phrase "fortune favors the bold."

"We'll find out what happened," Eric said, hesitating a brief moment before he went on. "However, I have to remind you that we're not in any shape for a significant campaign at the moment."

"Yes, I understand," Rael said. "Compared to the Empire, neither of our forces are truly prepared for what might come."

"No, for the moment we're holding them off with a strategic weapon, but that's a poor thing to rely on," Eric said firmly. "There are too many ways they could neutralize it. Our biggest asset right now is that the Empire seems too damn arrogant to do their intelligence gathering properly."

"In that, I suppose we have been fortunate. I am not used to this way of thinking, my friend," Rael said. "It is alien to me."

"It should be alien to us all," Eric said tiredly. "The art of war has a beauty to it, but it is a terrible beauty that sears the soul and leaves nothing unchanged in its wake."

"A terrible beauty." Rael smiled wanly. "That should not be a phrase that exists, I think."

"Perhaps," Eric admitted. "But that isn't in our power to enforce. We just get to live with it, the best we can."

"Well, on to other matters, more pleasant ones I hope," Rael said after a pause. "How is young Ithan Chans? Sorry, I believe she is a commander now?"

"Lieutenant commander. She's been assigned to another project."

"Oh?"

Archangel Squadron, Deep Space

Flashes of blue Cerenkov radiation marked the passage of the six small vessels as they moved in formation through the interstellar void, warping space-time at several hundred times light. It was a pedestrian speed compared to the transition drive each of the ships possessed, but orders made it clear that they were to try to act as though they were not, in any way, connected to either Terran or Priminae forces.

Steph was grinning from the command deck of his lead fighter, knowing he looked like a loon but not caring in the slightest. He was *flying* again, and this was no tera-ton warship. It was a *fighter*.

Milla's flight interface was something very different as well.

He floated in the center of the command deck, suspended by some manipulation of the counter-mass fields within the ship, every flight control of the fighter literally a thought away through the NICS interface. It was like coming home, in a way, but the new generation was alien too.

Milla's team had done away with the needles of the original neural induction control system. Now the controls were linked to his neurological system through a pad fitted over the back of his neck up to the base of skull. More comfortable by far but also—and far more importantly—*bidirectional.*

He could feel the breeze on his face, stellar radiation washing over him as the fighter sped through the black. The few bits of particulate that weren't trapped and spun off by the fighters' warp fields were like bugs striking him while he rode his motorcycle on Earth.

The fighter wrapped around him was humming with his own eagerness as his every thought was almost instantly translated into action.

"Milla, you are a *wonder*," Steph said firmly. "I am never getting over this. You've given me something that I've dreamed about, but I never even quite understood what the dreams meant."

"And I am gratified that you like the results of our work, Steph." Milla's voice came over the comm. "However, please do keep an eye on our destination. We're approaching the rendezvous location."

Steph's eyes flicked to the HUD floating in front of him, and he nodded. "Roger that, Commander Chans. Have a look for any sign of our target, then passive scans only."

"Aye Commander," Milla said. "Passive scans only."

They were performing the first true field operations for the newly formed squadron and running the final tests for some of the more esoteric systems that had been folded into the hulls. Much of that could only be done under true field conditions, so Steph had opted to begin their mission with light duty scouting.

Before that could really be done, however, they needed more intel. *A lot* more intel.

And right then, the best intel available to them came from only one place.

"Target located," Milla said. "Adjust course to Four Niner Three, Mark Negative Two. Distance to target . . . eighty light-minutes. Slow *down*, Steph."

"Roger, braking maneuvers initiated."

The squadron followed his lead, bleeding off pure speed quickly while their warp drives captured the high-energy particulate they'd picked up moving through interstellar space and stored as much as possible of it in their fuel cells. The rest was spilled off in random directions, both to reduce their signature to any observers but also to avoid accidentally irradiating the hell out of whatever might eventually cross the path had they allowed the energy to continue on its way unfiltered.

The six fighters dropped below light-speed, bleeding the last of their Cerenkov radiation at the same time, and wheeled about in a long, slow arc that brought them to an intercept course with a lone destroyer that had been sitting out in the middle of deep space.

Waiting.

"Signal for you, Steph."

"Put it through."

"Archangel Lead," a voice said firmly. "*Autolycus* Actual."

"Go for Archangel Lead, *Autolycus*," Steph replied.

"Welcome to the black," Captain Morgan Passer said warmly. "We've prepared an intelligence briefing for you, and you are cleared for landing on bays two through four."

"Roger, *Autolycus* Actual. Thanks for the welcome. Archangel Lead has the ball on approach."

———

Autolycus, *Command Deck*

Morgan Passer examined the inbound "fighters" with interest as they made their approach to land in the docking bay of the *Autolycus*. His ship was the smallest class fielded by Earth, or it had been. He wasn't sure if these fighters counted or not.

May as well call them what they are, because they're not fighters, Passer thought. *They're gunboats.*

"They are fast," his second in command, Daiyu Li, said from beside him. "Their acceleration curve is . . . remarkable."

"Oh?" Morgan glanced over.

That statement, from her, held a wealth of meaning. Li was a Chinese officer from the Eastern Block, assigned to the *Auto* specifically because she was an expert on the space-warp drive.

The woman nodded firmly. "They dropped from several hundred times light to less than one-third in . . ." She glanced at the numbers. "Just under sixty-three seconds. That level of acceleration, were we capable of it, would tear this ship apart."

"Well, someone's made some improvements," Morgan said. "That's a good thing, Commander."

She nodded absently, mind clearly still awash in the numbers she had called up.

"Yes. Likely a big part is the smaller size and mass," Li said. "It would be easier to create a stable warp bubble for a smaller design like that. Still, it exceeds previous calculations significantly. Impressive."

"Fighters secured, Captain," the officer on deck watch announced, catching their attention.

"Excellent. Signal Commander Michaels that he and his squadron commanders should meet in briefing room three." Then Morgan added with a grin, "The rest may avail themselves of our facilities, such as they are."

"Aye Skipper."

———

Lacking the mass and power for artificial gravity put much of the destroyer in free fall, so Steph followed their Marine guide through the central corridor, his hand wrapped around the transit grip as it pulled him forward from the bays toward the foredecks where the briefing rooms were.

They were passed by other crew flashing by in the opposite direction, and occasionally by some who were moving perpendicular through accessways that would take them to upper or lower decks. Steph hadn't spent much time on Rogue Class destroyers, which meant he was plenty glad to have a Marine leading the way.

I'd have gotten lost for sure.

"Slowing now, sirs, ma'ams," the Marine said just as the grips they were holding onto began to decelerate, causing them to swing forward and hold tight to keep from continuing on at full speed right into the wall at the end of the corridor.

They came to a stop near a vertical access and, one by one, slid up the tube to the next deck up.

"Right this way," the Marine said, guiding them through the ship until they reached the briefing room.

"Ah, welcome, Commander."

"Captain Passer, sir," Steph said firmly, abruptly conscious of the fact that he could hardly manage to stand to attention in zero gravity and that his attempt at a salute was most certainly sloppy as hell.

Morgan ignored this, though his return salute was far crisper. He gestured to the computer display that took up the center of the room.

"We received orders ahead of your arrival," Morgan said, indicating the information already on display. "So we prepared a quick brief. More in-depth information, including all the minutiae we've managed to gather, will be delivered to your ship computers."

"Thank you, sir. Grateful for the work."

"Anything that gives us an edge in this," Morgan said, waving off the thanks. "As you can see, Imperial space is far larger than we originally projected. We've only mapped a fraction of it, but we're already talking about thousands of stars, potentially dozens of habitable worlds, and at least thirty that we've confirmed."

Steph whistled softly. "That is worrying. With Priminae manufacturing techniques, they can certainly put a lot more in the field than we might have considered just a few years ago. Our own Forge is coming online now, but it'll be some time before it reaches full production capacity."

Morgan nodded. "That would be why I'm glad to do anything that gives us an edge. If I might ask, what is your mission profile?"

"Intelligence gathering and infiltration," Steph responded. "A little more in the open than your remit, if possible."

Morgan nodded slowly, eyes half-closed as he thought about the commander's words. Steph silently waited for the captain to assemble his thoughts.

"I might have an entry vector for you, in that case," Morgan said after a moment.

"That would be nice," Steph said candidly. "I expected we'd be hunting around for a good introduction for a while."

"We've discovered nonaffiliated stars in addition to the Imperial worlds," Morgan said, gesturing to highlight a slice of space. "This appears to be a section of a half dozen or more minor polities. Two, three star systems for the most part . . . as best we can tell anyway. They're constantly in conflict with one another, usually trading minor colonies back and forth. A word of warning, though: we monitored an Imperial Fleet heading in their direction not long ago."

Steph looked over the data. "That might be exactly what we need. Thank you for this, Captain."

"Just make good use of it, Commander."

"I fully intend to," Steph said, a slightly feral gleam in his eyes as he hummed under his breath.

Yo-ho, yo-ho . . .

Outer Reaches, Past Imperial Space

The last beams finished crossing space. Fires burned in sparsely dotted sections of the star system as Jesan Mich presided over the end of the fighting with a careful eye.

The locals had put up a decent fight, he decided as he evaluated the battle that had just wrapped up. They had been entirely outmatched, of course, but they were improving their tactics and strategies.

That may become a problem if left unchecked, Jesan thought.

He would report his observations when he returned to Imperial space and ensure that a few elements were assigned to disrupt the militaries of the local pocket empires. Keeping them fighting one another would prevent any significant buildup that might threaten Imperial forces more effectively than sending in a fleet every so often to knock them back down a few pegs.

"Damage reports," he demanded, turning away from the scene on the displays.

"We lost three vessels, Fleet Commander," his second responded instantly. "Multiple ships were damaged, of course, none critically. Repairs are already underway."

"Good work," Jesan said, stepping down from the strategic command section. "See to the preparation for our next encounter with the local forces. I'll be in my quarters."

"On your order, Fleet Commander."

———

Jesan sighed as he slumped in a seat, looking over the information on his personal display with disdain.

This sort of work was beneath him, but he had little choice but to see it through or die in the attempt. The outer-reach empires were nuisances at the worst, constantly fighting one another if they weren't tangling with some Imperial force or another.

A recent example of that was responsible, in part, for Jesan's current assignment.

Someone had gotten a few of the kingdoms working together, and they'd been stirring up trouble in the outer reaches. They were neither powerful enough nor stupid enough to come after the Empire, but they had been tearing the ever-living hell out of a few of the other local star systems.

That was a problem because it created a surplus of people with little to nothing to lose and a lot of anger to burn. Most of it might be directed at the current enemies causing problems, but memories were long, and more than a few remembered the Empire and its involvements in their affairs.

One of those groups had struck at the Imperial colony of Hira at a system a few dozen light-years closer to the Empire's core. Of course, such a move could not be ignored and left without reprisal.

It had taken months to track down where the attack had come from, and still the intelligence they had wasn't particularly firm. No matter. Someone had to pay—otherwise the Imperial citizenry would get upset and start causing trouble—so the Empire destroyed three metropolis-sized cities within a week of the attack and declared public victory. Jesan's current assignment was merely to deliver a message to the likely guilty parties while bolstering public confidence that the fleet was on the job to defend their way of life and the great benefits they enjoyed as free citizens of the Empire.

Hopefully he'd get at least some of the actual villains with his campaign, but if not—well, sooner or later they'd get what was coming their way.

In the meantime, Jesan had a job to do.

Chapter 10

Deep Black

Without using the transition drive—Earth's singular ace in the hole in terms of strategic deployment—travel between stars was downright boring, Steph decided as he stood watch in the control room of a tin can moving almost a thousand times the speed of light. His new commands were capable of transition, of course, but using it would potentially reveal that they were more than they wanted to appear. Thus he was limited to merely hundreds of times the speed of light.

Hurtling through space at such insane speeds was something few people could possibly understand, simply because no human mind would ever be willing to comprehend just how *dull* it was. At the current speeds they were moving, crossing the galaxy was still a trip *seventy years* long.

The space-warp drive did open up the local arm of the galaxy to exploration, but in terms of logistical movement for military purposes, the accessible range was much smaller.

Steph couldn't imagine how it was that the Empire managed to wage wars as it apparently did, not with such a slow rate of travel among its forces. It was one thing across a span of a couple dozen light-years, but even a hundred light-years would mean a logistical bottleneck the likes of which he didn't even want to *imagine*.

Being stuck on the wrong side of a month-long supply train is insanity.

It was an interesting problem, actually, and one that Steph had been working on for some time, partly out of curiosity and partly from the belief that understanding the Empire's limitations would be vital. He'd not expected to need the research quite so directly as it was turning out, but he was happy to have done it.

If he'd been planning such maneuvers, he'd have gone back to the examples set by ancient armies, who'd often done their work with even longer supply lines. Of course, their successes had been hit-or-miss, with victory often depending more on how good their logistics were than how brilliant their commander was in battle. Or, in fact, the brilliance of a commander was often measured by how well he managed logistics rather than soldiers.

The trouble was that those ancient campaigns often rested on the forces being able to acquire material support along the path of their march: buying, raiding, or confiscating food and supplies.

And, while their information on Imperial movements was incomplete, there was no sign that they were engaging in such operations during their encroachment into Priminae and Terran territories. That bothered him deeply, because running a military operation without a strong logistics train should be tantamount to suicide . . . and yet the Empire had apparently done just that, and been doing it in that way for some time if all the information they had was correct.

However they think, or know, they can pull that logistical nightmare off, we don't have the luxury of even considering the same. We need that logistical support, and we need it in the worst possible way, or we're going to just shrivel up and die before the Empire gets around to steamrolling us.

Steph examined the star charts supplied to him by the crew of the *Auto*, noting what they'd discovered. For the moment he put aside the Imperial stars, though those *were* his ultimate goal. For the immediate future, however, he was more focused on the small, independent polities that existed around the periphery of the Empire.

While looking for Imperial targets, Passer and the *Auto* had discovered over a dozen small empires that were seemingly at war with one another. Their existence was likely to be a vital component to any future war-fighting strategies, but Steph knew without a doubt that they were absolutely critical to any plans he might make.

He tapped one particular star with a finger, noting that it was the farthest from Imperial space, and also one of the weakest of the independent empires. According to the intelligence from the *Auto*, the polity called itself the Star Kingdom and was constantly losing shipping between its few colonies to what was ostensibly piracy.

More likely thinly veiled privateer forces, if not out and out regulars, Steph thought, but the thefts provided him with the opening he'd been hoping for.

His squadron wasn't suited for pretending to be merchantmen, disguised as Q-Ships or not. It was, however, a good match for a pirate fleet, albeit a small one. That didn't quite fit with what he was hoping to pull off, however.

A privateer force, working counterpiracy actions—*that* fit perfectly.

A soft alarm drew Steph's attention away from his work. He rose to his feet and walked over to the flight interface. Stepping into the system, he took control of the ship back from the computer as the surrounding room changed into the tactical command mode.

Black space surrounded Steph as he glanced around the proximity of the ship for a moment before turning his focus to the source of the alarm. The system had registered an anomaly in the expected path of the vessel as they approached the target, Orange Dwarf System.

Is that a Rogue planet?

Steph frowned, but he didn't want to do any detailed scans for fear of alerting the locals in the nearby system of their presence. That meant he had to wait for the light-speed data to filter in.

The gravity system had picked up the signal of the object, but there was still nothing on visual scanners. Steph flicked through the frequencies, letting out a sound of surprise when he got a hit on infrared.

Would have expected everything to be cold out this far. What do we have here?

The planet in question was in the extreme outer system of their destination, a super-Earth from the looks of it, with three moons of its own and a small ring of debris. It was dark, as it was better than fifty AU out from the star, and the local primary wasn't the brightest bulb in the universe anyway. The fact that it was warm would have had the science division of the *Odysseus* clamoring for time to study the world, Steph had no doubt, but for him it was a minor curiosity at most.

"Archangel Lead, *Archangel Two*."

"Go for Lead, *Two*," Steph said automatically.

"Are you seeing this?" Alexandra Black asked.

"The planet? Yeah, interesting, but there're no sign of local activity, so we can ignore it for the moment," Steph said, shifting to the squadron-wide channel. "I'm adjusting course to come in from the shadow of the planetary system. We'll use it to cover our approach and park in the moons while we observe the system."

The Archangels signalled their acknowledgment and followed Steph's adjusted course and eased back on the acceleration, bleeding velocity until they smoothly slid into planetary orbit over the super-Earth that was drifting out in the black with its three moons.

Steph glanced down at the surface as they slipped into orbit, the computer automatically enhancing and enlarging the places he focused on. The volcanoes explained the heat, and he supposed that the three moons had kept the world nicely active below the surface. His system showed plenty of water in the atmosphere, though most of what he could scan on the surface was a frozen ice sheet.

Neat, Steph thought absently as he turned his focus away from the alien world and began planning his next move.

"Archangels," he said. "Deploy passive scanning birds. I want a VLA in place within the hour."

"Aye Commander, Very Large Array drones launching," Milla reported as the other fighter-gunboats acknowledged the command.

"Alright," Steph said softly, taking a breath. "Then all we can do now . . . is wait."

Aerin Star Kingdom Destroyer Berine Gael

Auran Kor stood on the narrow command deck of the *Berine Gael*, looking down on the pits where the crews were manning the primary systems of the aging destroyer. He'd been in command of the ship for only a short time before the latest round of hostilities had broken out with the Belj Empire.

It wasn't uncommon, of course. Small border spats were to be expected among those who served in His Majesty's Fleet.

He just wished that he had more to work with, all things considered.

Unfortunately, the Kingdom was the smallest of the local polities that had moved into a small copse of stars that contained inhabitable worlds and were close enough to the Empire for the early colony expeditions to be successful.

The Empire.

Despite the aspirations of the various other groups in the area, there was only one thing a man could be referring to when those two words came up. Even in his mind, Auran could *hear* the capital letters that preceded each word. The Empire. It overshadowed all else, and always had, for as far back as living memory went.

The Free Stars, as the polities referred to themselves, were bordered on the only border that mattered to the Empire. Beyond their systems, there were no other worthwhile stars for considerable range, none free at least. The Empire had taken them up and gobbled them while the Free Stars were fighting among each other, or just fighting to survive the early days of colonization.

That left valued resources scarce in the region, a travesty for a space-faring civilization when one considered the relative glut of such things as metals and water, among others. That scarcity meant infighting as different groups scrabbled for the biggest piece of an ever-shrinking pie.

A pie that the Kingdom had been getting nothing but crumbs from for far too long.

"That's odd."

Auran twisted slightly, having picked up the muttered words from the scanning station. He walked across the bridge that allowed him access to any station without getting in the way of the work below and looked down.

"What is it?" he demanded softly.

"Not sure, sir," Prator Silva Moran said as she leaned into her display. "Probably a system glitch. I'm running a scrubber to see if I can be sure."

Auran nodded. In his experience, such glitches weren't particularly uncommon. They were thousands of hours behind routine maintenance and likely to fall further behind long before such work would be accomplished. It was a minor miracle that the systems functioned as well as they did.

Still . . .

"What did it look like?" he asked.

"Possible contact," the prator admitted. "Very fuzzy, though. Could easily have been background noise bouncing off a rock out there somewhere."

He nodded. "Possibly. Still, better to be sure. Step up your efforts. Sentan."

"Sir!"

Sentan Brai, his second, crossed the bridge over the command deck and was at his side in an instant.

"Bring us to fighting trim, if you please," Auran ordered. "All hands to their assigned positions, ready the ship for combat."

"Yes sir!"

The deck below erupted into activity a few moments later as the order was passed along and the destroyer shifted to a fighting stance. All the while the scanner station furiously worked to clear up the signal.

Auran waited patiently, knowing there was little else he could do in the meantime. Waiting was often about the only thing he felt he was good for, and sometimes it seemed that was also the most productive thing he was capable of.

It certainly feels that way far too often.

"Prator," he said softly, reminding the young officer that he was waiting.

"Apologies, sir," she said, shaking her head. "Nothing. Maybe it was just noise."

"Maybe. Very well. Stand by to scan with active systems."

"Sir?" she turned, looking up at him.

Auran gestured casually. "Small threat here and now, most likely we'll just confirm that you're right about it being nothing. Detection is low risk."

She nodded. "As you command."

Auran waited while she charged the system, an act which took some time to complete, then nodded when she turned to confirm the order.

The young prator opened a link across the command deck. "All crew, active pulse."

Nothing happened on the bridge. It was all terribly anticlimactic, really—until the prator bolted upright with wide eyes.

"Belj destroyers inbound on the capital!"

"Fire up the engines," Auran ordered instantly. "Charge weapons! Plot an interception trajectory, consult with engineering for best course and speed!"

Men and women were talking over one another, each following one or more of his orders depending on their station. Auran stepped back to the command display where he could follow the basics from each of the stations below him.

The Belj destroyers were ahead of them, already well into the system's gravity pit. They were accelerating hard, and now they knew they'd been detected, straining to push on ahead so they would have more uninterrupted time at their target.

Damn it. Why didn't the passive systems give us better than just noise?

The rumble of the ship's drive shook the bridge around him until the vibrations eased, leaving Auran to wince slightly as he recognized that they were in dire need of an alignment. But the Kingdom was always so short of vessels that pulling one for maintenance was a major affair.

He pushed those complaints aside. They'd do him no good for the moment.

For now, the *Berine Gael* was under power and charging down toward the capital world of the Kingdom.

Archangel One, *Outer System*

The *pong* sound echoed through the ship, causing Steph to damn near slam his head into the bulkhead as he jumped out of his bunk. They'd been parked in system for over a month, the days were starting to blur into one another, and, like most of the crew, he had found himself sleeping more than he probably should.

The alarm blew that fatigue right out of his system, though, and he hit the ground running, only taking a moment to snag his uniform jacket on the way out the door as he raced through the fighter-gunboat. He burst into the flight deck in his sock feet, a pair of boxers, and his jacket half-buttoned with all the buttons off by one.

"Report," he said, spotting Tyke in the driver's seat.

"FTL Pulse scan, according to the computer," Tyke said casually. "Too far out and aimed the wrong way to spot us, at least according to Noire."

Steph nodded, glad that Alex had been on duty in her *Archangel Two*. There were few enough pilots with deep-space time, and really, he only trusted her and Jennifer "Cardsharp" Samuels in the third fighter to really know their stuff at this point.

He padded up behind Tyke, looking over the man's shoulder, checking the telemetry before whistling.

"Destroyer squadron heading for the capital planet," he said. "Looks like one of the pickets caught wind of them somehow, but were *way* out of position to intercept. They're making a play for it anyway, though."

"Not going to make it?" Tyke asked, frowning as he read the numbers.

Like most fighter jocks, he could do some pretty serious math in his head without half thinking about it, but relativistic closing rates were a little over his head at the moment.

Steph just shook his head. "Not without pushing FTL, and from what we've seen these boys aren't geared up for warping space that deep inside a gravity well. They're running antiquated tech by Imperial and Priminae standards at least."

"This what you were waiting for?"

Steph nodded slowly. "Yeah . . . yeah, I think it is."

Berine Gael

The *Gael* was screaming as it powered down the gravity pit, trying to catch up to the destroyer squadron, never mind the fact that she was outnumbered five to one. If the destroyers made planetary approach, they'd tear the living abyss out of the orbital defenses at the very least and likely take out strategic assets on the surface.

And that is even forgetting civilian casualties, which are certain to be severe, Auran thought grimly.

He knew that the attack was a feint. Likely the main force was readying to take out one of the automated asteroid farms, but there was no choice left to him despite the knowledge. Hopefully one of the other pickets would be able to hinder them and salvage *something*.

"Time to orbit?" he demanded tersely.

"Eight minutes," his second said flatly, emotions buried deep under a calm, cold facade. "Interception in twelve."

Auran winced.

Four minutes was an eternity for five destroyers to tear through what remained of the orbital defense network, to say nothing of what they might launch on the planet.

He didn't know how much longer the Kingdom could maintain its autonomy, frankly. Auran was aware that they had offers from at least two polities, including the Belj themselves, to accept "protection" in exchange for surrendering control of their system and charts to some of the richer deep-space rocks in the region.

The only thing that had kept them independent as long as they'd managed was the secret deep-space farms that produced some of the unique, highly refined processing crystals in the Free Stars. The crystals were their one commodity, and the secret of the farms' location the only thing that kept the beasts from their throats.

Looks like the beasts have finally decided it's not worth trading any longer, Auran realized with grim humor.

"New contact!" Prator Moran called out, her voice sounding odd.

Auran crossed the bridge and looked down at the pit that contained the scanning station. "More Belj?"

"I . . . I don't believe so, sir?"

"Are you asking me, Prator?"

"No sir, I'm just . . ." She paused, clearly confused. "I've never seen signals like this."

"Put on the main display."

Auran turned forward, eyes rising to the large display that overlaid the armored port that looked out over the foredeck of his vessel. The imaging shifted, showing the capital planet and the orange of the star beyond.

"Prator," he growled.

"Watch the curve of the planet, sir," she said quickly. "Just a few more instants . . ."

He frowned, eyes on the screen as he leaned in. He abruptly pulled back, eyes widening as he spotted what she was talking about and a tight formation of a half dozen small, fast-moving ships swept around the curve of the planet. Briefly eclipsing the star behind them, the vessels slung out of planetary orbit. Auran could see some of the orbital guns firing, but the ships just ignored them.

He was hardly surprised. They were moving fast enough to outrun the mass driver launchers by a fair clip, and there was no chance any of the orbital beam stations would be able to lock on to something that fast and close.

"They've settled into an intercept course for the Belj, sir," Prator Moran said, surprised.

He didn't blame her.

What in the living abyss is going on?

"Sir!" The communication officer interrupted his thoughts. "Signal from the unknown ships—they're on our frequencies, but . . ."

"What is it?"

"I'm not sure," the man admitted. "It almost looks like Imperial encoding, but it isn't. They're in the open, though, and the signal is compatible with our protocols."

"Put it up."

Archangel One

"Are you sure you don't want this?"

"Relax," Steph said, patting Tyke on the shoulder. "You're doing fine. Go ahead and take her tactical."

"You got it," Tyke said as Steph stepped back, waving off the hard-light displays and engaging the NICS interface along with all of the small ship's tactical controls.

Steph backed away as the room changed, becoming deep space around the two of them, opening a single command-and-control, hard-light display so he could take strategic command of the squadron and the communications system.

"Fighting form," he ordered casually. "Check fire until I clear it."

"Locals are firing on us," Alex said casually over the channel from her own fighter-gunboat.

"Ignore them. They can't track this fast, and I think it's panic fire anyway," Steph said. "Nothing is coming anywhere near us."

"Roger that. What's the plan?"

"Weston Special," Steph said.

"Mind filling that in for those of us who never served with that lunatic?" Alex asked.

Chuckles floated over the squadron channel as Steph did a few quick calculations.

"Easy enough. I give the bad guys one chance to turn off, then when they don't, we get to play hero."

"Oh *that* definition of special. Got it."

Steph grinned, opening a communications channel on the frequencies they'd monitored the locals using. He hoped that the aggressors would be monitoring them as part of the operation, but if not—well, he'd tried at least.

"Aggressor squadron." He spoke in Imperial Standard, using his best imitation of Eric's casual, calm, yet somehow firm and no-nonsense tone. "You are ordered to break off your assault on the world ahead and quit the system. Failure to comply will result in my squadron engaging you. This is your *only* warning."

Steph closed the channel, nodding over to Tyke.

"Tyke, paint 'em like Tijuana on payday."

"You got it, boss."

———

Berine Gael

Auran stared at the communications station in consternation.

"What in the abyss was *that?*"

The poor officer at the station looked more lost than he felt, and that was saying something.

"That sounded like Imperial speech," the communications officer said, "but I've never heard that accent before."

"The Empire couldn't care less if the Belj decided to drop singularity bombs on our world," Auran growled. "But you're right: definitely Imperial speech, but not any Imperial I've heard before."

"Do you think they'll listen?" Brai asked softly, eyes as wide as Auran knew his own to be.

Auran shook his head. "I have no idea. They have to be as confused as we are."

He broke from Brai and walked over to the scanner pit once more. "Prator, do we have *anything* that matches those ships in our computer?"

She shook her head. "Nothing even close. And before you ask, they're definitely not any Imperial design we've encountered before."

Auran turned his focus back to the display as he walked to the rail that was there to keep him from falling into the pits that held the crew below. He gripped the railing with both hands.

Who are these people?

Chapter 11

Belj Destroyer **Berkan Fal**

"What in the name of the eternal was *that*?"

No one seemed to have an answer, not that Commander Hirik blamed any of them. He didn't even know who'd asked the question, and wasn't completely certain that he hadn't been the one to utter it.

"Are they Imperial?" he asked, thinking of the language the speaker had used on the communication.

The comm officer shrugged in confusion. "Not any profile in our system."

"What do you read on them?" Hirik asked.

"Very little, Commander. They don't scan as Imperials at all. They barely even scan as *ships*."

"What? Explain that!"

"Power curve is too low. They register, but only as a few times more mass than they appear."

Hirik scowled, confused. For a power curve to be that low, they'd have to be running their systems right on the ragged edge. Pushing into a fight with power levels that low was suicide, or at least it was asking for a total singularity failure and winding up dead in space—and shortly thereafter, just plain dead.

"They're bluffing," he yelled. "Probably something the Kingdom threw together in a rush to try and scare us off."

"We've been targeted!"

He glared over at the tactical control section. "Well, target them back! Fire when we have a secure lock!"

"Yes, Commander!"

Archangel One

"Well, that makes their position clear," Steph said as the lock-on alarm sounded. "Range to enemy . . . thirty light-seconds and closing fast. We're in the knife zone, boys and girls, best start evasive actions. Weapons free, engage at will."

Steph felt a bit of a shift in the deck of the fighter as Tyke followed orders, peeling away from the formation with Alex following close behind. He could see the others on the screen, wheeling away from their position in unpredictable patterns. In his old fighter, he'd have been slammed all around by the maneuvers they were pulling.

Steph couldn't really decide if he preferred the old way or the new. There were definite advantages to being able to casually walk around while the fighter was pulling insanely high-G maneuvers, but *damn it*, he missed the connection to the craft.

It's like a muscle car with an automatic transmission—sure, it's better in every measurable way, but it just ain't right.

He knew he would always miss that visceral connection to the fighter he got in the old school, but Steph was a realist as much as he was anything else.

He'd get used to the new.

He just wouldn't like it.

Hell, Steph had zero doubts that he would grow to *love* the new. It was an amazing system, and it checked every box a pilot could want.

He just felt an odd melancholy, thinking about what used to be.

"Targeting the lead destroyer," Tyke said, shaking him from his reverie. "Cover me on the way in, Noire."

Steph castigated himself for the distraction that had occupied his brain for those few seconds and focused on the action as it unfolded before him.

"You got it, Tyke."

Archangel One rolled hard over, swinging sharply back onto an attack vector as the gunboat's sensors screamed at them, a laser cutting through the space where they had been.

Steph made a couple quick adjustments based on the scans he'd taken. "Lasers only, Tyke. We want to hold back our capabilities."

"Roger. Lasers only. Target is locked, I have tone. Archangel Lead, beams beams beams."

Twin lasers lanced out from the fighter as they flashed past the destroyer, raking the flank of the warship viciously from stem to stern. Vapor exploded out from the ship, chunks of armor blowing away from the destroyer where the hull was weakened by the beams.

Tyke twisted the fighter hard about as they passed the stern of the destroyer, angling in on the next as he noted that Alex had a bit of a trajectory edge on him due to the course shift.

"Next one is yours, Noire," he said. "I'll follow you in."

"Roger, Lead, *Two* has tone . . . beams beams beams."

———

Berkan Fal

Hirik grabbed a nearby console to steady himself as shudders ran through the ship, shock running through him even as it did through the *Fal* itself.

131

"Destroy them!" he ordered as the unknown ships ripped past his destroyer squadron at high speed, twisting through space faster than anything he'd ever seen.

It wasn't their closing rates that were so impressive, he realized quickly, but the shifts in acceleration as they made evasive actions. The smaller vessels were proving damn near impossible for his defense grid to lock onto and, even worse, when they *did* get a lock, the damn things moved out of position before lasers could travel the intervening space.

They aren't Imperials, that's certain, he thought grimly as another shudder tore through his ship. Imperials weren't this fast. They didn't need to be. They had the power and armor to just slug it out at close range if anyone was stupid enough to engage them there.

"Break formation! Change course," he ordered. "Scatter the enemy ships, hunt them down individually! As small as they are, they won't be able to take much punishment."

The destroyer squadron broke formation on orders, each twisting in pursuit of one of the fighters they'd been assaulted by.

Hirik pointed to the lead ship, the one from which the original signal had come. "That one, follow that one."

"The *Selka* is already assigned—"

"I don't care. Two ships on him is fine; that one is the leader," Hirik snapped.

"As you command."

The destroyer twisted in space, warping the fabric of the universe violently to change directions as swiftly as possible. All lasers were firing, trying to bracket the speeding target that was staying out ahead of them.

"The enemy ships are holding in pairs," his second observed. "Interesting doctrine."

"We'll salvage their computer systems to determine why once they've been defeated," Hirik growled. "Worry about the present in the present, leave the future to care for itself."

"Yes my commander."

The whine of laser capacitors discharging managed to filter in through the armor and insulation surrounding the crew as dozens of powerful beams erupted from the *Fal* and lanced through space toward their targets.

———

Archangel One

"We've got three on our tail," Tyke said, grinning. "And *man* they're pissed!"

"Two on us," Steph corrected from behind him. "One chasing Noire. They've split the squadron individually. We just drew the short straw and got the attention of the enemy commander."

"You think that had something to do with your little speech?" Tyke asked as he guided the fighter through space, glancing over his shoulder to keep track of the enemy ships.

"Who knows?" Steph asked. "Teach them why you don't chase an Archangel."

Tyke nodded. "You might catch him. Hold on! *Archangel Two*, turn the tables!"

Steph pushed himself back into the bolstered seat in the rear of the flight deck, pulling restraints down around himself, as he knew what was coming. Tyke threw the acceleration *hard* in direct reverse of their course, bleeding velocity viciously fast. That didn't have any effect on those inside the ship, thankfully, as he did so by warping space, which neatly counteracted any effects of inertia that might have otherwise splattered them across the deck.

When he abruptly flipped the vessel end for end a hundred and eighty degrees to wind up pointing right back where they came from, however, a very real effect was felt. Steph's stomach lurched and he saw red as the gyroscopic motion pushed all the blood into his head and made his eyes feel like they were about to pop.

He tightened his muscles, clenching hard to keep the blood as low in his body as he could manage until, a moment later, it was over and everything returned to normal.

The abrupt flip had been within the already existing space-warping of their drive system, which meant that they were, once again, pointing in the direction of travel as the distance between them and the pursuing destroyers began to vanish at high speed. In the computer-enhanced display that was wrapped around the pilot of the fighter-gunboat, the gleaming white hull of the enemy destroyer loomed massively as Tyke once more called out the signal that he was firing.

The powerful beams of the fighter-gunboat again raked the underside of the destroyer as they ducked low and sped through the beams, their combined closing velocity far exceeding the capacity of *any* imaginable guidance system to track.

Archangel One and *Two* ripped past, already twisting in space as they did so in order to prep for the next pass.

In the back of the flight deck, Steph kept half his attention on the fight Tyke was managing while he split the rest with the remains of the squadron.

The enemy destroyers were considerably less powerful than the Imperial cruisers they were used to tangling with, but his gunboats were intentionally fighting well below their maximum capacity as well. He was annoyed that the fight had dragged on as long as it had, mostly because he was well aware that his team could have ended it in the opening barrage if they'd truly wanted to.

That would have exposed their technology, however, and done so in such a way that an Imperial analyst might be able to connect the mysterious new squadron in their space with the Terran fleet they'd just ended a war with months earlier.

That left him with beams at two hundred light-seconds or less, unfortunately, as those were the sorts of weapons that the locals knew and understood and wouldn't be overly curious about.

He'd even been forced to forgo the best aspects of Terran multispectral lasers, though they'd done a few tweaks there before the battle based on hyperspectral scans of the enemy destroyers.

It wouldn't be as effective as real time adaptation of the beams, but it would do the job.

"*Archangel Three*," he signalled Samuels. "Advise split right, engage enemy flanks when they chase."

"Roger, Lead," Cardsharp responded instantly. "*Archangel Three, Four*, split right, engage on return loop."

Steph watched the maneuver as Cardsharp and her wingman abruptly split formation, arcing away from one another. The two destroyers in pursuit did the same, predictably, not recognizing the trap that had been laid.

The Archangel fighter-gunboats maneuvered in tight arcs, completely unnecessary by the laws of physics of space travel, specifically to draw the enemy destroyers away from one another as they arced back around.

Cardsharp took the destroyer chasing her wingman, as did her wingman in turn, as they crossed the enemy's lateral hulls on a perpendicular course.

In ancient wet Navy combat, it was a maneuver called crossing the enemy's *T*, though in reverse. Originally, when dealing with sailing ships, being able to catch the enemy when their broadsides were pointed away from you was an advantage. In modern design, however, that was drastically less important. What mattered was exposing the enemy ships where they had far weaker armor by necessity of design while maximizing your own weapons' impact.

The two fighters opened fire from dagger range, striking midships of both targets and holding their fire for several seconds.

Explosions of flame erupted from the destroyers, blowing out what had to be several decks as Steph watched.

"Enemy ships are no longer turning to pursue, weapons are not tracking," Cardsharp reported. "Do we finish them off?"

"Negative. Let them go," Steph ordered. "We're not here for a body count, and the more people to spread our legend, the better."

"Roger, Lead. *Three* and *Four*, moving to reinforce *One* and *Two*."

Berkan Fal

Smoke filled the air of the bridge as Hirik stumbled forward, peering through the gray to where the weapons station screamed alarms that managed to pierce the sounds caused by every *other* alarm.

"Destroy them!" he snapped.

"We cannot! They're too fast and too close to track!"

Hirik snarled, baring his teeth at that response, but there was nothing more to be said.

"Commander! We've lost the *Caf* and the *Jarran*!"

Hirik turned, eyes falling on the squadron status report, scanning it in an instant. The two ships in question were still intact, more or less, but they'd suffered extreme damage and were breaking off the fight. He bit down on an urge to signal the commanders back, noting that both were currently fighting just to keep their drives from collapsing and could hardly spare anyone to repair weapons.

He glared at the screens for a few more seconds, flinching as the ship shuddered again, then turned back.

"Fine! All vessels, break off contact!" he ordered. "We've undoubtedly accomplished our primary mission anyway. Cease tracking and make for the outer system at best speed!"

A few tense moments later, it became clear that whoever the enemy was, they were not interested in pursuing their targets once the fighting was over. Hirik glared at the signals of the enemy vessels as they receded from his ships' scanners.

I do not know who you are, but I will not forget this. I have your profiles now. We will find out who you are, and you'll regret crossing the Belj Empire.

Berine Gael

Auran stared numbly at the displays as the Belj destroyers broke contact and began to climb out of stellar gravity, heading out on clear escape courses that would give them reasonably direct courses back to the Belj Empire. They were not his primary interest, however, and his eyes kept focusing on the glittering hulls of the small ships that had routed the Belj squadron.

"Do we have *anything* on them?" he asked, looking over to where his second in command was working furiously.

"Nothing," the man said, shaking his head. "They're not like anything on record, not in the Free Stars, not in the Empire, nowhere. I've even scanned the unconfirmed records with no results."

Auran shot his second an amused look, though it passed quickly. Checking the unconfirmed records was something only Tarman would have thought of. Most of those were reports by crackpots and other less than trustworthy sorts. Still, if a match had come up, it would have been something at least.

"They speak Imperial, but with an accent I'm unfamiliar with," he murmured. "Their ships don't present with a particularly strong power curve, yet they outfight a squadron of far more massive vessels with little to no damage to themselves—and we've never heard of them before."

He straightened, looking around.

"Does this seem as crazy to everyone else as it does to myself?"

No one bothered to answer the question, not that he'd expected a reply.

Auran didn't know what to think about what had just occurred, and worse, he wasn't sure what he could do if it turned out that this was some type of trap. The unknown ships had just flown into the teeth of the Belj—not the greatest force in the Free Stars, but certainly no slouches either—and come out unscathed.

If they turned out to be hostile, he was under no illusions, or delusions, of just how long he and the *Gael* would last.

Still, he had to be ready to try.

"Maintain combat positions," he ordered. "We don't know who these people are, but we can't trust that they're not hostile either. Have every weapon primed, just in—"

"Commander," the communications officer cut him off. "Open signal on the same channel they used before. They're contacting us."

Auran stared intently for a moment before he gestured. "Open the frequency. Let me hear it."

"Inbound destroyer, this is Captain Teach of the Emissary squadron," the voice said in that same accented Imperial. "We are standing down our weapons and awaiting contact."

Auran looked around, his thoughts clearly echoed on the faces and in the minds of everyone in earshot.

What just happened?

Chapter 12

Archangel One

"Really? Captain Teach? That's the best you could come up with?"

Steph chuckled at the look he received from Tyke, shrugging. "What can I say? I always wanted to be a pirate. In all seriousness, though, we know that the Empire captured Priminae and Terran ships, likely with their computers intact. They might have personnel files on some of our people, including myself."

"I suppose that makes this the *Revenge* instead of the oh-so-proper *Archangel One*?" Tyke asked.

Steph considered that. "I think I like it. Not Queen Anne's, mind you, but we can work the details out later."

Tyke nodded. "I suppose we can. What's the plan now?"

"Offer our services to the locals, for a time and a price," Steph said. "Then we fly under their flag for a while and work our way closer toward the Empire."

Tyke nodded as he stepped out of the control circle of the flight deck, pulling the NICS sensor off his neck. "You think we can trust the locals?"

"No more than I'd have trusted any of the various groups we had to throw in with during the war," Steph admitted. "Or than they could trust us, I suppose, if I'm honest."

Steph pulled his own NICS interface from a mount on the wall and slipped it over his neck as Tyke stepped away to secure his own gear. He'd take tactical command of the *Revenge*, as it were, while they were negotiating the status of the squadron within this system.

"Grab some coffee," he told Tyke. "and let Milla know to do the same. She gets tied up with her machines and systems."

Tyke nodded. "Wilco. Good luck."

"Thanks," Steph said as Tyke walked to the back of the flight deck and pushed the access door open.

Tyke pulled back, surprised by a figure in the door.

"Mind if I enter?" Seamus Gordon asked.

"No skin off my nose," Tyke said, slipping past him.

Gordon looked in without crossing the door. "Commander? Permission to enter?"

"Come on in, Mr. Gordon," Steph called as he worked at the holographic interface.

"Thank you," Gordon said, stepping in and letting the door slide shut behind him.

The intelligence agent looked around at the interior of the flight deck as he walked in, nodding in appreciation.

"First time I've been in here with all the systems up," Gordon admitted. "Very impressive."

"I'll give your compliments to Milla," Steph said, not looking around. "Do you have something specific to bring up, or just here to sightsee?"

"Well, you are about to enter into my territory, Commander," Gordon said with an inoffensive smile that somehow managed to send a shiver down Steph's spine. "I'd like to sit in, if you don't mind."

Steph gestured warily to one of the seats at the back of the room. "Feel free. I'll be broadcasting both sides here, but transmitting only from my own induction mic. Anything you say won't reach the locals, but it will distract me, so think before you speak."

"I've done this dance a few times in the past, Commander," Gordon promised. "I'll keep quiet unless I have something to offer."

Steph nodded, eyes tracing the telemetry of the destroyer as it surreptitiously placed itself between the squadron and the planet.

A brave thing to do, he supposed, but not terribly effective or intelligent on the surface. If he wanted to get to the planet, going through the destroyer wouldn't be a challenge, and the other captain had to know it.

"I wonder." He turned, eyes narrowing as he examined the augmented view that existed around them.

"What is it, Commander?" Gordon asked.

"Either our friend over there"—Steph gestured to the icon of the destroyer in the distance—"is brave but not too bright, or he's distracting us from reinforcements."

"Excuse me?" Gordon asked. "I don't understand."

"Putting his destroyer between us and the planet is symbolic, and he knows it," Steph said. "We could go through him in a heartbeat."

"Seems like something your Commodore Weston might do," Gordon suggested mildly.

"Eric would only do that if he thought he had a chance, or if he had no other choice, neither of which fits the current situation," Steph said as he tapped in a few commands. "In this situation, gravity is your friend. I'd park myself upwell of the potential enemy, just in case I needed to use the added potential energy of the star as one last arrow in my quiver."

"What good would . . ." Gordon blinked. "You'd ram them?"

"As a last resort, yes, but potential energy converts very quickly into kinetic energy in space for whatever use you might have. So what I'm wondering is whether our friend out there is gutsy but stupid, or . . ." Steph trailed off, smiling as he spotted something on the visual scanners. "Maybe he has backup approaching from the shadow of the gas giant right there."

Gordon leaned forward and looked at where Steph was gesturing. "All I see are glints of light. Are you sure?"

"Three more destroyers," Steph said. "Not enough to take us based on what we've scanned of the locals, but I'm glad to see that our potential employers aren't stupid."

Gordon nodded. "Interesting play, that, by the way. I wouldn't have thought of it, I have to admit. But then I cut my teeth on intelligence operations leading up to the Block War, not in the age of sail and pirates."

Steph chuckled. "Unfortunately, everything I know about modern intelligence work, which is limited, I have to admit, is useless in this case. We don't have any sort of exchange with the Imperial worlds, which makes classic infiltration impossible. We need a legend if we're to gain access to the Empire without them being overly suspicious of us."

"A merchant group might be lower key," Gordon said.

"It might," Steph agreed. "But we'll learn more this way, even if we don't actually gain access to the Empire itself."

Gordon had to concede the point. "It will be interesting, I'll say that."

"That it will," Steph said, pausing as an alarm sounded, announcing the approach of the destroyer. "I think we're on. Game faces."

"I'm always in my game face, Commander."

Berine Gael

Auran shook his head as he leaned over the communications display. "No My Lord, I do not have any idea who they are. We have nothing that matches on our computers. I was rather hoping that the central systems in the capital might have more."

"I'm afraid not," the man on the screen said seriously. "I've ordered a complete scan through all of our systems, including the ones that don't exist, if you understand my meaning . . ."

Auran nodded slowly.

"I understand," he said finally. "What are my orders?"

"Find out what they want," Lord Peruma told him firmly. "His Majesty is interested in why an unknown squadron of starships would intervene on our behalf. Possibly they have something against the Belj. However, they didn't pursue when the destroyers fled, so that seems unlikely. At the moment, we want to know why above all else."

"Assuming I determine the cause is in keeping with Kingdom security?"

"Then we'll have something to discuss with them, I suppose, Commander. First, however, see to the current needs of state."

Auran nodded. "Very well, My Lord."

The signal went dead, leaving Auran to stare at the display for a moment before turning around and walking to the front of his overwatch position.

"Very well," he repeated, but louder for the rest of the crew, "Signal the unknown squadron and Mr. . . . . Teach."

Archangel One

"Captain Teach, I presume."

Steph ignored the strangled snort behind him while he examined the man on the projected image before he responded. "That's correct. Commander Auran?"

The man nodded curtly. "I have been instructed to thank you for your intervention with the Belj starships, Captain. I would be remiss if I didn't wonder exactly what made you choose to do so?"

"Call it . . . a job interview," Steph said. "We've recently found ourselves at a bit of loose ends, and steady employment would go a long way to keeping the lights on."

Auran looked quizzical at his choice of words but didn't comment immediately.

"You are mercenaries, then," he murmured after a time.

"I prefer the term 'privateer,' personally," Steph said with a wide smile.

"That word means little to me," Auran admitted, puzzled.

"Local turn of phrase. No matter, 'mercenary' will do, I suppose."

Steph noted that the commander killed the audio as he turned to speak with someone offscreen, and quickly did the same.

"Thoughts?" he asked over his shoulder.

"He's perplexed, probably as much by your bluntness as your odd word choice," Gordon said, "but there's interest there."

"I'd be surprised if there weren't," Steph said. "The *Auto* and her crew did some decent probes of the nonaffiliated star colonies out here, and this one is the weakest of the bunch. They're really only independent because the others keep fighting over the scraps, as best Passer's people could tell. They need every running gun they can get."

"Agreed. That doesn't mean they can be trusted."

Steph snorted, finding the very idea hilarious. "I can't say that I've ever met a government that could be, including my own. Too many moving parts, as a rule."

Gordon couldn't exactly gainsay that statement, as much as he'd have liked to. The commander was right, sadly. A large, multiperson entity like a government might be filled with ninety-nine percent trustworthy people, but that remaining one percent would screw you every time.

The sound came back, bringing Steph's attention forward once more.

"Assuming we were interested in such services as you might provide"—Auran hedged around the statement, making it hard for Steph not to smile—"what might your expected fees be?"

"I'm certain we would be able to work something out, Commander," Steph said. "I—"

A sound of a throat clearing behind him caused Steph to glance over his shoulder as Gordon stepped into the range of the communications system.

"And who might you be?" Auran demanded, looking at the new figure.

"Gordon," the spook said firmly. "Squadron purser. And I believe you know what our fee would consist of."

It was everything Steph could do not to look at the other man in consternation as he tried to figure out what fee the man was talking about.

Auran, however, seemed to relax slightly at those words, though he also became somewhat more somber.

"You are speaking of a valuable commodity, Mr. Gordon. How can we be certain that your *services* are truly worth that?"

"I believe we've proven our mettle here today," Gordon said. "We can handle any duties you might expect of a squadron massing far more than our tonnage."

Auran nodded slowly. "A moment."

He cut the audio again, and Steph instantly did the same.

"What was that?" he demanded, turning to hide his face from the alien commander.

"Every small principality has *some* product that they're particularly proud of, generally something that functions as a tent pole to the local economy," Gordon said. "It's easier to let them do both sides of the negotiation as much as possible, given that we don't know enough to make demands."

Steph couldn't exactly argue with that, at least not until he saw the outcome of the negotiations.

"A little heads-up next time would be appreciated," Steph said. "Clear, *Purser* Gordon?"

The spook smiled thinly. "Clear, Commander."

———

Berine Gael

"Are you following the discussion, My Lord?" Auran asked as he watched the supposed mercenaries on his display out of the corner of his eye. Even without audio, their interactions made some things about them clear.

"Indeed, if they are what they claim, this could be a much-needed respite," Peruma said.

"And if they're not, this is likely a trap intended to cost us greatly. Mercenaries are rarely trustworthy."

"Engage them for a short-term mission," Peruma ordered. "The assault here was likely a distraction as much as anything else. Our analysts indicate that the crystal mines are most likely the true target."

"No one knows where those are," Auran said sharply. "Surely you're not suggesting that we allow these mercenaries to learn of the location."

"Of course not," Peruma said. "This is what I want you to do . . ."

———

It took a while before the audio came back. When it did Steph turned forward as he returned pickups on his side as well.

"Yes, Commander Auran?" he asked respectfully.

"We *do* have a short-term operation that you may be able to help us with," Auran said stiffly.

Gordon stepped forward smoothly, smiling pleasantly as he did so. "Then why don't we discuss details, Commander?"

Chapter 13

"All systems clear from transition, Commodore. Squadron has reported in, all accounted for."

Eric nodded to the report. "Thank you, Commander. Any signs of enemy presence?"

Miram shook her head. "Nothing to this point, sir, but we're still gathering data."

"Understood, as you were, then," Eric said as he looked over some of the incoming scans on his own, briefly skimming the results.

There was nothing there, of course—well, not beyond the normal sorts of things they'd expect to see upon transitioning into a new system. Gravity signals were already filtering in from across the system, locking down the location of large objects with relative precision. None were making any odd changes in orbit that might indicate a ship in motion, which meant practically nothing unfortunately.

Hiding a ship, or even many ships, in the area of space that your average solar system occupied was both challenging and easy, depending on the situation. If you had no particular tactical concerns, you could hide a fleet without concern. Just stay off the system's ecliptic by a decent degree, away from the path of the planets as they orbited the star, and it would be all but impossible for anything but the most intense and obvious scanning attempt to pick you up.

You would also be, inevitably, so far out of position from any object of strategic value that mounting an intercept would require an act of God.

So the *Odysseus* task group was largely ignoring those sections of space for the moment, and focusing on places that would present a strategic or tactical problem as they continued forward in their examination of the system.

Even so, it was an immense section of space, and all but a tiny fraction of a percentage of it would be inevitably empty.

If nothing else, we'll get excellent survey scans of the system, I suppose, Eric thought wearily.

This was the third system they'd transitioned into since leaving Ranquil, hunting the presumed Imperial group that was harassing Priminae sectors. The first two had turned up empty, and that was fine by him. The crew was still working up to full efficiency, and he'd rather not test them to destruction before absolute necessity forced his hand.

Even as that thought crossed his mind an alarm sounded, and Eric started cursing himself.

Goddamn you, Murphy, you Irish bastard.

"What is it?" he demanded, striding across the deck.

"Emergency transponder signal, Commodore," Miram said tersely. "Priminae encoding."

"Signal general quarters, bring the squadron to combat readiness."

"Aye sir," Miram answered instantly, turning her head just slightly. "Sound general quarters!"

"General quarters, aye!"

The alarm began to ring through the ship and the squadron beyond as Eric focused his attention on the scans of the system before them, wondering where . . . and if, the enemy was present.

Imperial Eighth Fleet Command

A soft alarm brought Helena to the command deck at a brusque pace. "Report."

Her executive officers stiffened at her voice, the senior present automatically turning.

"We detected a gravity shift near the edge of the system, Fleet Commander," he told her. "Normally, we would have considered it likely to be an outer planet, unlikely to be of any concern; however, there were . . . anomalies."

Helena strode over. "Explain."

She listened as he spoke, but her eyes were locked onto the scans coming in through the fleet's long-range scanning systems. The data was intriguing, to say the least.

"The gravity source came from nowhere on our sensors, ma'am," he said, sounding confused. "It flagged as a likely sensor failure, but when we did a systems check, everything tested as functional."

"Where did it come from?" she asked, now confused herself. She could see what he was referring to on the data stream, and there was definitely something there that made no sense at all.

"Uncertain. We're running the scans back, trying to determine that, but the only thing we can think of is some sort of stealth system."

That was a worrying thought.

If these anomalous people have the ability to fully stealth their gravity signature, that would go a long way in explaining the fleet commander's failure at subjugating them in the last incursion.

The problem with that idea was, of course, that stealthing a gravity signature was supposedly impossible. Gravity could be twisted and tamed, otherwise a ship the likes of an Imperial cruiser could never approach a populated planet. The gravity of her singularity core would utterly disrupt any populace with tidal forces the likes of which no one wanted to live through. However, it was quite impossible—supposedly—to disguise the quantum signature of any universal mass.

You could make the universe treat mass in different ways, similar to how one might convert matter to energy and vice versa, but that did not in any way *negate* the fact that the mass existed.

"Figure it out," she ordered, eyes tracking the course of the objects they'd detected. So far they appeared to be on a ballistic trajectory, making for what would likely be a deep pass through the system.

Nowhere near our position, damn it all.

She honestly would have been surprised if the two forces had been on a converging approach, of course, but it would have made things easier. Given the sheer scope of space, that was all but a fantasy.

"Signal the fleet, have them stand to for combat operations."

"At your orders, Fleet Commander!"

———

Belj Fleet, Deep Space Within the Free Stars

"Commander Hirik, what in the abyss happened to your squadron? Our intelligence indicated that the Star Kingdom destroyers were all out of position to intercept."

Hirik nodded cheerlessly in response to the admiral's words. "They were. However, a squadron of unknown vessels performed a fast intercept using the local star to disguise their approach from our visual scanners."

"That would hardly have impacted gravity sensors."

"No, Admiral. However, they were extremely low visibility on those scanners. We missed them in the interference of the multiple planetary bodies near their position," Hirik admitted. "They were small, fast, and extremely powerful."

The Belj admiral, one Sudecki Mir, scowled deeply as he considered that statement and looked over the computer records.

"This does not sound like the Star Kingdom," Mir said. "They should not have resources of this nature. They're *generations* behind our technical capacity, Commander."

"I have read the intelligence brief, Admiral. I cannot explain it," Hirik said.

Mir growled but waved the commander's screen off, leaving his deck in silence for a moment as he considered the situation.

"Sub-Commander."

"Yes, Admiral?"

"What are the indicators showing?" Mir asked, walking across the command deck to the strategic display.

"All signs show that the plan did precisely what we intended," the sub-commander confirmed. "The Kingdom recalled the available destroyers in an attempt to cover the capital planet, as predicted. We had pickets monitoring the withdrawal. Everything appears to be in order."

"And yet," the admiral muttered grimly, "our vanguard squadron has returned with barely two of the destroyers at full capacity, and two nearly destroyed. That was not in the calculations."

"There are unknown variables," the sub-commander admitted. "However, everything we can monitor is effectively at the expected optimum outcome."

"And yet, *should* it be?" The admiral examined the data, eyes flicking from point to point on the displays.

That was the question he had to answer. Should the indicators be as expected given the unknown variables? It didn't seem like they should, but if they were just dealing with one set of unknowns, it was possible, he supposed. The issue was that he didn't have enough to tell him if that was the case.

Mir had to make a call, but didn't have the information he needed to do so. He hated such situations. However, he was aware of just how badly they needed the computational crystals that only the Kingdom could produce in high enough quality to compete with Imperial technology. Without those crystals, the Belj Empire would soon lose influence and assets to their enemies.

"Send to all ships," he decided finally. "Operation is cleared to proceed."

"Yes Admiral. Sending now."

Mir sighed. *I hope this wasn't a mistake.*

———

Berine Gael

I hope this is not a mistake.

Auran found very little to like in the current situation, though he saw few options more palatable than the one on which they'd embarked. The mercenary squadron had agreed to the trial employment, and after a negotiation that still left him feeling slightly dirty and wrung out like he'd been physically beaten, he had put Lord Peruma's plan into action.

"Sir, the lead mercenary vessel *Gaia's Revenge* is signalling," his communications officer announced.

"Put Captain Teach through here," he ordered, frowning slightly. *Who, or what, is Gaia, I wonder?*

It was a name that spoke of a past story, one that he hoped to hear sometime if the current situation worked out in his favor.

In the meantime, however . . .

He turned to the display as it came to life. "Captain Teach, is everything in position?"

"According to the plan as laid out, yes Commander," Teach said. "My squadron is at your service."

"Thank you for that, Captain. If you are being honest with us, the Star Kingdom is in your debt," Auran said before his expression turned to stone. "If, however, this is a planned betrayal, my final act will be to see that you join us in the abyss."

Teach just smiled at him.

"I believe that you and I, Commander, are going to get along just fine."

The display went dead a moment later, leaving Auran staring at it blankly for a long moment. He didn't know if he liked the man who had been on the other end of the discussion or was beginning to loathe him. In either case, Auran supposed it didn't matter.

They had a task to accomplish.

All else would have to wait.

———

The galaxy is a massive place by any human scale imaginable.

Within a fifty-light-year sphere, there are roughly two thousand stars that contain around three hundred potentially habitable planets. Actual habitation varies wildly, of course, depending on factors impossible to predict without detailed surveys of practically every star within the sphere.

In areas such as the Empire, where populations had grown up and expanded out of their homeworlds, factors like terraforming and general geo-genesis technology resulted in a considerably higher-than-average population density. People expanded, pushing through boundaries, by their nature.

The Empire encompassed a mere two hundred habitable worlds, but it was considerably higher in population density than the average section of stars in the galaxy. Instead of occupying fifty light-years in diameter, the Empire occupied a section of the galaxy barely twenty-five across.

The section of space containing the pocket empires that had attempted to break away from the Empire had fewer methods for maximizing use of resources, however, and actually occupied a larger section of space than the Empire itself. Across almost forty light-years, sprawling worlds of multiple stellar polities made up the loosely associated worlds of the Free Stars.

Thousands of stars, hundreds of planets, and—one would *think*—more than sufficient resources for a hundred times the population that existed there.

One would think.

Over more generations than most could count, the Empire had been pitting the so-called Free Stars against one another. The pressurized nature of the wars the Empire fed from one side to another ate away at the resources of the polities within the Free Stars, and century after century of wars slowly left each successive generation with just a little less than their birthright.

As each generation began to realize that they would inherit less than their fathers had, they inevitably grew angry. Angry at their fathers, angry at the Empire, and angry at each other—most of all, at each other. Their fathers were gone, and the Empire was too big to truly comprehend, but everyone understood that when their neighbors got a little more, it meant a little less for them.

The cycle of war had casualties well beyond those who merely died.

_____

Belj Fleet

"Telemetry from our pickets confirm that the Star Kingdom destroyers are departing their capital system as expected, Admiral."

Mir nodded. "What of the unidentified squadron reported by Hirik?"

"No sign of them at all, Admiral."

"I do not like this," Hirik replied. "Continue tracking the Kingdom's destroyers, and *find* those unidentified vessels!"

"Yes Admiral."

So far, Mir had to admit that the plan was running almost exactly to expectations. He just wished they had more information on the unknown squadron. They bothered him. They were something new. He'd not seen anything new in a long, long time.

Mir examined the data that had been sent over from Hirik's squadron, trying to learn more about the enemy. They fit the expected in some ways, defied it in others. The strange mix bugged him.

No one is building smaller and faster like this. Everyone is following the Imperial standard. Larger, more powerful vessels are the standard. There's nothing in any reports that match this. No one is fielding ships even close to what Hirik ran into.

In his experience, keeping a secret on the scale of a Navy construction project was impossible. With so many people involved, *someone* would leak the secret, or some aspect of it at least.

And yet he had *nothing* on this squadron.

It makes no sense. Who are they? Where have they come from? Combat ships of this power do not appear fully formed from the emptiness of the abyss. Someone had to have built them.

Mir shook his head.

"Maybe Hirik was fooled," he muttered. "Maybe they are not what they seem."

That made more sense. Perhaps the Kingdom was running some sort of bluff, or perhaps they had managed to refit some smaller ships with military specification reactors and weapons.

It made more sense than an entire squadron of unknown ships coming out of nowhere.

That idiot Hirik walked into a trap. It's the only answer that makes sense.

――――

Gaia's Revenge *(Formerly* Archangel One*)*

"We are prepared for battle, Stephan."

Steph nodded. "Thank you, Milla. How has everything been going?"

Milla took a seat at the small table in the ship's miniscule cafeteria space. "It is . . . a very different experience. I built these ships, designed them, but I did not realize how small they really were, I believe."

Steph looked around. "It's a monster compared to my original Archangel, but that was an air superiority fighter. This is really more of a gunboat."

"I am not certain I really understand the difference," Milla confessed.

"Honestly? Not much, really," Steph said. "It used to be about maneuverability and speed. Smaller was faster, and speed is life. Technology has put paid to that rule, though, so now we have this."

He looked around the small, cramped quarters of the cafeteria.

"It's an older concept than we're used to," he said. "But it was effective in its day, and I think its day has come again."

"Tell me more about 'its day,'" Milla said.

"The best version I can think of was World War Two," Steph said. "PT boats were powerful heavy hitters for their size. They were used in all theaters but were really famous in the Pacific. Fast, obscenely powerful for their size, but vulnerable too because they were so lightly armored."

He laughed. "Back in the day, you wouldn't believe how often a PT boat would fight a battle and then just bob around afterward, hoping their side won, because they were out of fuel and needed a tow back to port."

Milla grimaced slightly. "I believe I can promise that, at least, will not happen to us."

"I've seen the reactor specs. I believe you." Steph laughed briefly before sobering somewhat. "We're pretty lightly armored compared to what we're likely to run into, though, especially as we get closer to the Empire."

"There is little that can be done to stand up against the energy of a warship's lasers," Milla said, "especially not on a vessel this size."

"Which is why we try not to get hit."

That, Steph was aware, would be easier said than done, but so far the tactic had worked well in their favor. It seemed like the influence of the Empire on the region had been much as the brass had predicted. He was certainly relieved that they'd gotten that much right, the nature of things being what they were.

The Empire, like the Priminae, favored big and powerful ships. They didn't have anything that matched the new-generation Archangels, let alone the space superiority version that his original fighter had been converted to. They didn't have the doctrine to counter that sort of tactic, and for as long as that held, Steph was fully planning on using every advantage it gave him.

Sooner or later, though, they would adapt. Humans always did. It was what made them human.

I wonder what Eric will do when that happens? Steph wondered briefly, thinking about how quickly his mentor had been able to improvise new tactics when thrown into the situations that demanded them. *I suppose I'm going to find out if I can walk the walk as well as he did.*

"Commander Michaels to the flight deck. Commander Michaels, please report to the flight deck."

Steph looked up sharply, pushing his coffee away as he got up.

"Time to go to work."

Milla nodded, following him out and splitting off to head for the engineering section of the small craft as he headed forward to the flight control deck.

———

"What is it?" Steph asked, swinging himself into the rounded room that housed the gunboat's flight control system.

"Contact," Tyke said from where he was monitoring the systems.

Steph saw that Tyke hadn't activated the tactical control system yet and relaxed marginally; that meant they weren't looking at instant action, for the moment at least. He stepped up behind the other pilot and looked over his shoulder at the telemetry.

"Hmm," he murmured. "Eight signals, light destroyers, all trailing far enough back that I'm surprised we spotted them. Do the locals have them on scopes?"

"I doubt it," Tyke said. "They're not giving any sign of it, and you'd think they'd at least contact us."

"Maybe. Either way, looks like they were right," Steph said, sweeping his finger across the telemetry map and highlighting all the enemy signals. "The attack was probably designed to make them panic and reveal the location of their strategic reserves. Not a bad plan, I suppose. Leaves a bit much to chance, or to the enemy, but I've seen worse."

"You've pulled off worse, Crown," Tyke said.

Steph grinned. "We all did. Beam the others, tell them to stay on plan. Let them close the trap, for now at least."

Tyke nodded. "Wilco. Should we warn the locals?"

Steph shook his head. "Not yet. Not in the contract anyway, and better for us if they react naturally when they do cotton on to the situation."

"Cold-blooded, Commander."

"We're *pirates* now, Tyke," Steph said, winking. "Cold-blooded is the name of the game, until it turns hot. Then damn the torpedoes and full steam ahead."

"I think you're mixing your metaphors. Pick a time period and stick to it, boss."

"You're just jealous that I get to be a pirate, Captain."

"Until you get a cool old-timey naval hat, you're just Crown to me, Crown."

"Don't you think I won't make one."

Tyke burst out laughing.

"What?" Steph protested. "I can sew!"

――――――

Berine Gael

"Commander, we're detecting echoes in the gravity trap scans."

Auran walked over to the scanner technician, looking down from the command bridge to the pit where the system display was located.

"Our . . . friends?" he asked.

"No Commander." The scanner officer shook her head. "Wrong location, and the signature matches Belj destroyers shadowing in the comet shield."

Auran nodded, unsurprised by the revelation.

"Orders, Commander?"

"Increase scrutiny of the echoes. Inform me when you confirm their identity," Auran ordered.

"Yes Commander."

Now, I suppose, there is little left to do but to wait.

――――――

Belj Fleet

"We're tracking the Kingdom's destroyers. They're approaching a small asteroid cluster."

"Refocus our scanners on the cluster," Mir ordered.

"Yes Admiral."

If the plan had worked, which it appeared to have, that cluster would be the target the Kingdom thought his fleet had actually been after, the initial attack intended to draw away forces from the primary target.

Now they just needed confirmation.

"Initial scans compiling, Admiral. We're detecting significant operations around the asteroid cluster. Communications intercepts, highly encrypted, are sourcing from the area."

That was promising. High comms traffic meant that there was some heavy activity in the area.

Governments among the Free Stars jealously guarded their resource discoveries from one another. Space being as big as it was, that was generally a fairly easy task to accomplish. *Finding* a competing polity's little nest egg of resources—now, that was tough. Aside from truly ludicrous levels of luck, the only real possible way to track down those resources was via the various types of statecraft that had become part of the way of life in the Free Stars.

The Belj Empire needs those crystals, far more than the Kingdom has been willing to sell us, if we're to gain an edge in the current conflict.

"We're scanning significant activity, Admiral. It looks like a harvesting site, no question any longer."

"Excellent. Order the fleet to close on the cluster."

Chapter 14

Berine Gael

"Enemy drive signatures showing on long-range scans!"

Auran strode across the bridge deck, looking down on the pit where the crew were working. "Signal all ships to ready for combat."

"Yes, Commander."

The alarms started in the distance as Auran examined the telemetry of the enemy ships now that they were running their drives fully in the open. The shadows detected earlier had been confirmed, of course, as the ships slipped out of the cover of the comet cloud and began accelerating down system toward the Kingdom's destroyers.

"Eight squadrons." He whistled, a chill running down his spine. "The Belj are apparently quite serious about this effort."

His own defense fleet consisted of considerably less, and Auran knew without question that the Belj had more than enough to walk through what he had on tap with barely any effort.

It is a good thing we were expecting this, he supposed, but even with all factors considered he was far from certain that he had sufficient advantages to win the day. It would be a close fight.

That left only one unknown set of factors.

I suppose we will see just how good these "privateers" truly are, and if they're worth the promised fee.

Gaia's Revenge

"That's it, this fight is kicking off," Tyke said over his shoulder as Steph strode back into the flight control deck, coffee steaming in his hand. "We have what looks like eight full squadrons, assuming they hold to their earlier convention."

Steph winced. "That's forty destroyers?"

"Confirmed so far, aye."

"That's asking a bit much, even for Archangels," Steph said idly as he called up a hard-light holo-projection and examined the data being scanned. "Hope the locals have a good plan, or this might be the shortest pirating career in history."

Tyke rolled his eyes as he watched the system shrink when Steph widened the display parameters. "What are you looking for?"

"Anything, really," Steph said. "We have hours before we're in the fight, and I'm curious."

"We are in an alien system, so I guess I can understand that."

"That's sort of what has me curious," Steph admitted. "It's a boring system. No habitable worlds, average star, nothing unusual in the scans at all. All very humdrum."

Tyke shot a dark look at his old friend. "You've spent too much time with Eric, you know that, right? I swear, that man could get used to *anything*."

Steph chuckled. "Yeah, well, there are worse things." He paused. "Huh. That's funny."

"What?" Tyke looked over.

"I don't know," Steph said. "Some of the numbers are a little off. I think there's something else out here."

"Such as?" Tyke gave in to his curiosity and came over, looking at the telemetry himself.

"If I knew, I would tell you," Steph said as he tapped one of the floating hard-light interface switches. "Milla?"

"Yes, Stephan." Milla's inquiring tone came through almost immediately.

"I want you to look at the telemetry here. Something is off."

There was a brief pause. "I will be right there."

The connection closed and Tyke paused, raising an eyebrow. "Doesn't have root access where she is?"

"Sure, but we're up here. Why wouldn't she want to come hang out with us?" Steph asked blithely.

"Right."

It didn't take long for Milla to appear, the gunboat being as small as it was.

"What is it?" she asked, approaching the center of the flight control deck, walking through the projections to where the pair were standing.

"I'm seeing what looks like echoes on the gravity scanners," Steph said. "I just want to confirm that the enemy doesn't have more backup than we're aware of."

Milla frowned, moving to his side as she examined the display.

"Echoes?" she asked. "Oh, I see. That is . . . odd."

"Enemy ships?" Tyke asked.

"Not certain. If they are, then they would appear to be quite far out of position," Milla said, sounding confused. "These would be well beyond the comet shield, Stephan. Likely at the very edge of the system's gravity influence."

"Could they be rogue planetoids?" Steph asked, thinking about the small rogue system they'd hidden in when approaching the stellar neighborhood.

"Perhaps. However . . ." Milla made some adjustments and ran the telemetry scans backward. "No. We can track their approach in our records. No, Stephan, they are most certainly vessels of some sort.

However, they are well beyond the range by which they could provide support to the Belj destroyer squadrons."

"Huh." Steph frowned.

"What are you thinking, Crown?" Tyke asked, eyes now scanning the display intently as he looked for any further anomalies.

"Observers," Steph said after a moment. "Someone wants to know what happens here but doesn't really care who wins."

"That's a bit of a stretch," Tyke said uncertainly.

"Maybe, but I don't think so," Steph said, pointing out a few of the sensor shadows. "They moved into the system right behind the Belj destroyers but appear content to hang back. From there they'll be able to follow all actions in the system, and I'll lay good money that the Kingdom and Belj destroyers don't have the scanners to even note that they're there. Milla, can we tell what class those are?"

"Possibly," Milla said as she worked out a few calculations, setting the computer to crunching the numbers. "They are larger than the destroyers, of that I am certain. We would not be able to scan even the shadows at this range if they were not."

"Cruisers, then," Steph said firmly. "And not locals, at least not Belj or Star Kingdom."

"How do you know that?" Tyke asked, exasperated.

"If either of those two had them, they'd have used them."

"I can think of a dozen other reasons they might not deploy larger ships here," Tyke countered.

"None that fit the intelligence we and the *Auto* gathered, I'll bet," Steph said.

Tyke grimaced, but finally shrugged. "It does seem odd that the Kingdom would hold back forces like that, I'll admit. We don't know much about the Belj, however."

"We know enough. They've invested too much in this to just leave their biggest guns sitting out the fight," Steph said. "No, that's someone else. How many are out there, Milla?"

Milla hummed softly to herself as she worked. "We've spotted at least a dozen, Stephan. I expect there are more we've missed."

"A dozen cruisers." Steph shook his head. "We need a bugout plan, just in case they're not content to watch. We're not a match for that kind of firepower."

"Well, I ain't arguing with you about that," Tyke said with feeling. "I'll start running multiple escape vectors." He paused, thinking. "Should we tell our new friends?"

Steph considered it, expression grim, before he finally shook his head.

"No. We still need to hide our capabilities," he decided. "Worst case, assuming they're not somehow behind this despite what I think, we'll advise them on escape vectors when the boom comes down. We should have a few hours' warning, no matter what."

Tyke nodded, his own visage as weary as that of his friends.

It sucked to do that to allies, no matter how new they might be, but mission parameters often sucked one way or another. The situation could be a lot worse, and had been for the pair of them more than once in the past.

"Meantime, make sure everyone is locked and loaded for the immediate threat," Steph ordered. "We have a role to play in this little drama. Make sure we nail the performance. We need them to want an encore."

Belj Fleet

The destroyer squadrons spread formation as they descended into the gravity well of the system, vectoring for the asteroid cluster as they continued to accelerate to combat velocities. Weapons charging, the eight squadrons assumed diamond formations as they dove.

On board the fleet command vessel, the *Belgra*, Mir watched the scenario unfold in what felt like slow motion as the ships under his command rapidly approached large percentages of light-speed and yet still managed to barely crawl across the soon-to-be battle space.

Odd, he thought, how much of his life was spent at velocities that most people couldn't even begin to comprehend, and yet how very *slow* it all was in reality.

Most combat was held deep within a system's gravity and, while it was technically possible to engage sufficient warping of space and time to exceed light-speed even within powerful gravity fields, it was not recommended. Even successful ventures past light-speed inside a solar gravity were almost certain to massively damage most vessels, as the stellar density of debris was considerably higher there on average.

Space-warping could only do so much to protect a ship from debris. Smaller chunks, gasses, dust, and the like were absorbed easily enough by the powerful twisting of space and time that squeezed a vessel through the void at high speed, but past a certain mass there was no amount of warp that would save you.

Striking an even slightly massive asteroid at better than light-speed, for example, would end in one way: with your atoms and charged particles scattered across the system in question with enough energy to radiate anything in your previous path, friend or foe.

When one factored in the general lack of responsiveness of average ship systems, quality of faster-than-light scanners, and such—well, it was generally not considered a good idea to attempt.

———

Belj Empire Destroyer Belgra

"Closing on enemy positions, Admiral. The Kingdom destroyers are racing for the asteroid cluster."

Mir nodded. "Calculate their expected turnover point. Ready firing sequences to my commands."

"Yes Admiral. Turnover expected within the next few minutes."

Mir tapped in a few commands as he stood over his command crew. "Prepare all banks for firing."

"All banks, all ships, standing by for your command, Admiral."

The admiral nodded, satisfied with the progression of the mission thus far and with the performance of his squadron. The end result, of course, would be the deciding factor, but that would soon be known.

"Enemy vessels have hit turnover, Admiral."

"Analyze acceleration, extrapolate course vectors, and fire when you have a solution calculated," he ordered firmly.

"On your command, Admiral!"

In a few moments the whine of laser capacitors discharging could be faintly felt more than heard, vibrating through the decks of the destroyers as they continued to accelerate down system toward their target.

"Weapon estimated time to contact is thirteen minutes."

———

Berine Gael

"Asteroid cluster dead ahead, Commander."

"Reverse thrust, bring us to a zero/zero velocity relative to the cluster by one light-second."

"As you command, zero/zero trajectory entered."

The destroyer rumbled around him slightly as the stress of the space-time warp shifting vectors made itself known. Auran winced slightly, knowing that was a sign of his drives being slightly out of alignment with the rest of the ship, but there was little he could do about it. Correcting drive alignment was a shipyard task, and there weren't remotely enough of those work slots to go around in the Star Kingdom.

"Enemy squadrons continuing to accelerate."

Auran didn't bother to acknowledge that announcement as it echoed around the bridge, more a perfunctory notice than anything else. No one expected them to do anything other than keep coming.

The Belj have committed a significant portion of their fleet to this. I suppose we should be flattered.

Eight squadrons, forty destroyers: a formidable force in the Free Stars. Short of attacking one of the capital worlds of a major power, the Belj could be forgiven for assuming it was enough of a force to handle practically any mission they chose.

Certainly, he knew that they could easily have taken the orbitals of his own homeworld with no problem. The only reason they hadn't was that taking the orbitals was one thing, but actually pacifying the citizenry of a planet below? That was something else entirely. It was rare, in fact, for any of the polities of the Free Stars to actually capture an enemy world, because the costs associated with annexing an independent population were almost always far in excess of the value of the world itself.

It had been tried, and often, early in their history.

The Kingdom had done so, capturing many worlds during an imperial phase of its own. Holding those worlds became a nightmare as the Kingdom was forced to continue expanding, gaining resources only to pour them into the endless pit of malcontent planets, while new ones demanded even more.

Eventually the expansion became unsustainable and the Kingdom's empire collapsed, dropping them from the premier polity in the Free Stars to the very bottom almost overnight.

A harsh lesson for a prideful people.

Over the centuries many had learned the same lesson, which led to the way things were now. Steal resources, not lands. Occupy valuable territory, not people. A grim reality, in his opinion, that made thieves of every citizen of every polity, as their governments stole from whoever had what they wanted.

"Arrival at cluster in three minutes."

Auran nodded. "All ships are to prepare for immediate combat action."

This is just the way the game is played.

———

The Aerin Star Kingdom destroyers decelerated at maximum power as they approached equilibrium with the asteroid cluster, warping fields twisting space-time intensely to bring the massive hulls to heel. Visually, the asteroids were barely noticeable without significant augmentation by the scanners, the light from the local sun being mostly absorbed by the solid masses clustered in the point of stable gravity on the leading edge of the closest gas giant's orbit.

Decelerating took time, and even with a powerful warping of space, it took more time the more massive the object being affected was. Destroyers were not particularly massive as far as starships went, but neither did they have the same power of much larger vessels. The Aerin squadron swung into orbit at high military power and were within several light-seconds of the cluster when the Belj lasers crossed their position.

Fire and destruction raged as metal hull and armor were vaporized in a flash of light and explosive power, throwing the small ships around violently as parts of their own construction became explosive jetting material streaming into space.

The battle had officially begun.

Chapter 15

Imperial Third Fleet Command Vessel

"So this is what the rabble were gathering all those ships for," Jesan Mich said as he looked over the telemetry they were scanning from the system, idle curiosity guiding him more than anything else.

The battle that was shaping up was of little interest other than learning what was being fought over.

The remote possibility that there was something out there worth the temporary interest of the Empire struck him, though he rather doubted that was the case.

The so-called Free Stars were in a constant state of warfare, as Imperial edict demanded, and they'd learned to kill one another for the slightest of excuses. He expected this was much the same, but at least while they were killing one another, he wouldn't be forced to sully his forces with the deed.

His fleet had crossed the warp trail of the fleet belonging to the laughably named Belj Empire, and he'd diverted them from their previous course to see if the matter might warrant his attention. As it turned out, the answer seemed likely to be no. By the time the battle was over, his analysts had calculated that very little would be left of the Belj and nothing would be remaining of their foes.

He shook his head, amused at the trap the Belj were flying into.

The asteroid cluster was undoubtedly supposed to be some resource-harvesting location, but the scanners on his fleet told a very different story.

"Fleet Commander, do you have orders?"

Jesan glanced aside at his second, considering for a moment, then shrugged.

"Enjoy the show?" he asked with a casual gesture. "This might be amusing, if nothing else. Let the crews watch the rabble fight."

"Ah, yes Commander."

Jesan returned his focus to the scans. The augmented screens were tagging each of the ships with identification markers and tracking them, making the entire affair more interesting and informative. His crews were due some entertainment after the fighting they'd been tasked with of late.

On the large display, the eight aggressor squadrons plunged into the system, their lasers firing near constantly according to the luminosity his sensors could detect from stray space particulate. An aggressive opening move, one he normally would have approved of, in fact.

Pity they didn't properly scout their battle space, Jesan thought sourly as he recalled his last, and all too similar, mistake in that regard. *It will be an expensive error.*

Gaia's Revenge

"Laser strikes on allied targets." Milla's voice carried over the communication system as Steph locked himself into the flight control deck and activated the NICS interface on the back of his neck.

"Roger that," he said, feeling the heat of the lasers wash over him as the bidirectional feedback from the interface fully initialized. "Archangels, *Revenge*. Hold your positions. Let them come."

"Roger, *Revenge*," Cardsharp said from *Archangel Three*, tension and eagerness in her voice. "By the way, when do the rest of us get cool pirate names?"

"Have one in mind, *Three*?" Steph asked, laughing softly.

"I'll get back to you on that," Cardsharp responded. "But the rest of us have been wondering something."

"Why do I get the feeling I don't want to know?"

"No idea," Cardsharp said, keeping her tone serious momentarily. "We just want to know when you're going to stop shaving, Commander."

Steph rolled his eyes. "Of course you are. Tell you what, I'll stop when you do, Sharp."

"Who says I haven't?" Jennifer "Cardsharp" Samuels riposted instantly.

Steph winced. "More information than I needed, Sharp."

"Don't start what you can't finish, Stephanos."

Steph killed the audio.

"I swear I cut myself every time I speak with that woman," he muttered.

"She does seem to be aptly named, Crown," Tyke answered from behind him, amused by the exchange.

"We called her that when she fleeced us at cards before a mission," Steph said. "Didn't know her well enough then to check that I had all my fingers after shaking hands with the woman."

Tyke just laughed.

"I get no response," Steph bemoaned before putting the audio back up and grinning. "Enemy positions?"

"Closing on predicted trajectories, Stephan," Milla responded instantly. "Fifty-three light-seconds and dropping."

"Showtime," Steph said over the squadron channel. "You all know your roles. Wait for the moment, then slice them up."

"Roger, Commander," the squadron pilots responded nearly as one.

Steph let out a happy sigh.

This was the way things were meant to be.

Belj Fleet

"Direct strikes, Admiral."

Mir nodded, pleased with the results of the initial moves against the Kingdom's destroyers. They'd achieved a respectable hit ratio according to the long-range scans, and that would be certain to increase as they continued to close the distance.

With the enemy only minutes away now, less than one light-minute, the odds of them being able to evade laser fire diminished with every passing second.

"Enemy destroyers are coming around!"

"Continue firing," Mir ordered. "Be ready for maneuvering orders."

"As you command, Admiral. All ships report ready."

Thus far, the enemy hadn't had the opportunity to return fire, but that would change shortly, assuming that ship hadn't sailed already. It would be a short while before any return beams could have made it back, after all. Mir was an old hand at space combat, and he expected he knew the rules as well as any man alive.

"Split formation," he ordered. "Shift pattern three."

"Pattern three, as you command!"

Berine Gael

"Return fire as the beams align!" Auran ordered sharply, a hint of smoke in the air of the command deck as he strode forward.

"As you order, Commander!"

The whine of laser capacitors charging filled his ears, the old banks loud enough to penetrate the interior insulation of the destroyer as the ship came around to align the beam cannons with the approaching enemy. A loud click followed by silence was the only evidence of a beam firing its hellish payload off into the vacuum of space.

His squadron were taking hits, but Auran held their space as the plan called for. It was paramount that the enemy come closer, and that meant giving them cause to feel they were gaining ground.

The story was easy enough to sell for two reasons. First, it was what the enemy wanted to believe—and second, it was true.

Auran gritted his teeth as another barrage of strikes turned the armor of his destroyers into expanding gasses, sending shudders through his *Gael* that could be felt through the decks as the whine-click of their laser discharges filled the air alongside the smoke of fires burning *somewhere*.

He hoped that the repair squads were on the job, otherwise he suspected that victory or defeat would end the same for him this time.

"Enemy squadrons passing thirty light-seconds, Commander!"

"Hold the line!" Auran ordered. "Let them come!"

Archangel Three

Jennifer "Cardsharp" Samuels shivered slightly in anticipation as she locked in her NICS interface and secured herself into the flight controls system of the fighter wrapped around her.

As the interface came to life, she *became* the fighter.

Heat washed over her from the lasers reflecting off Aerin destroyers, an almost cool breeze of cosmic wind at her back coming up from the local star. She could smell smoke and metallic odors in the space around her.

The enhancement of her senses was addictive, one she reveled in as it fully wrapped around her in a way she'd never be able to describe to someone who'd not experienced the feeling. Adrenaline coursed through her as she anticipated the coming battle.

"Archangels, enemy at twenty light-seconds and falling." Stephanos' voice sounded calm, cool, his previous humor gone as though it never existed. "Stand by to unmask."

"Roger," Cardsharp said, struggling to rein in her excitement and sound as calm as the boss. "*Archangel Three*, standing by."

———

Hiding a ship in space was easy and impossible at the same time, a particularly twisted paradox. Any enemy looking at the right place was simply going to see you, and there was almost no way to stop them. Ships simply couldn't mask their radiation effectively in space. Heat was the killer. It had to be disposed of in *some way* and, ultimately, in a closed system like a starship, the only option was to radiate heat outward.

You could direct the radiation away from a target, to a degree. You could contain the radiation for a *time*, but that was ultimately a short-term solution if it worked at all. Dying of heat stroke in the cold of space might seem contradictory, but it would kill you just as dead as anywhere else in the universe.

Ultimately, if an enemy was looking in the right direction, you were going to be seen.

It was even worse in the case of ships powered by Priminae or Imperial gravity singularities, or those that were actively warping space. Significant changes in space-time, such as those that created noticeable gravity fields, actively *called* out for notice.

On the other side of the equation, space was thankfully *huge*. Figuring out in what direction to look was, in fact, an almost impossible task. When a ship wanted to hide, it could do so by lowering its active attempts at garnering attraction and just hope to go unnoticed.

The strategy wasn't entirely reliable, but the odds were in favor of the hider rather than the seeker.

Of course, to skilled space hands like the pilots of the Archangels, that just made hiding a challenge worth putting some thought into, especially when you were forced to hide in the one place the enemy was *certain* to be looking.

———

Beams crossed back and forth as the small squadron doggedly exchanged fire with the fleet bearing down through the intervening space. Powerful weapons exceeding the terawatt range vaporized anything they touched while the vacuum of space sucked it all eagerly away.

The Belj ships had closed the range, warping space in reverse as they decelerated while keeping their weapons trained on the enemy ships, crossing to less than ten light-seconds when the ships within the asteroid cluster opened fire.

———

Belj Fleet

Mir cursed, recognizing the profile of the new ships the instant they revealed themselves on the scanners.

"It appears we know where the rest of the Kingdom's destroyers had gone," his second said grimly as the barrage of beams bracketed their position with hellish heat and destruction.

"That," Mir growled, "and one more place where the Kingdom's harvest location is *not*."

He left the tactical situation to his captains for the moment, quickly analyzing the situation to try to determine his best response. The scene was ugly, there was no question, but it took little more than a glance to confirm that the odds were still well in the favor of his fleet.

I would not have come this close had I known it was a trap, Mir thought sourly to himself, *but the Kingdom didn't have enough ships to threaten my fleet with destruction. Now I will merely have to ensure we take at least some of them intact, because we need that location.*

"Press the assault," he ordered. "Close ranks with the enemy!"

There was no response, but in the chaos of those working around him, Mir could see his orders being followed all the same.

He settled in to grimly oversee the battle, knowing it would be bloody and costly no matter how it turned out.

Gaia's Revenge

"They are committed, Stephan."

Steph nodded firmly, recognizing what Milla was telling him. The Belj squadrons could no longer evade close contact. They were committed to engaging the Kingdom's destroyers up close and personal. He and his had been waiting for just that moment.

"Archangels, unmask and engage the enemy. Watch your flight trajectories, do *not* get between the enemy and the Kingdom destroyers. I don't know them well enough to trust them to avoid shooting us, and even if I did, there are still a few light-seconds' delay to deal with. Accidents happen, so don't taunt Murphy!"

He barely heard the response as he was powering the drive reactors with a thought, throwing that power to the *Revenge*'s space-warp system and lifting the ship out of the shadow of the Kingdom destroyer he had been hiding behind.

The sleek gray hulls of the Archangels unmasked from behind their cover in near unison, each throwing off power curves that easily matched those of the much larger destroyers they had been hiding behind as they flung themselves through space and into the battle with an eager fervor.

The six fighter-gunboats blasted away from cover at massive levels of acceleration, crossing the intervening space between themselves and the Belj destroyers in mere seconds, fast enough that the shock of their charge left no time for reaction as the command rang out from the *Revenge* to open fire.

———

Priminae Space, **Odysseus** *Task Group*

"System appears clear, Commodore," Miram said into the quiet of the command deck as they stood over the second watch since the declaration of general quarters. "Shall we stand down?"

Eric didn't respond. He was standing in the center of the deck with hands clasped behind his back as he stared at the large display showing the augmented view of the system beyond the ship. The planets and sun were glowing. Faint traces of lines through space showed their ballistic trajectory through the universe, along with other items of interest the computers had been instructed to highlight.

He bit his lip, considering the scene, trying to figure out what was bothering him.

The commander was right. There was no sign of any enemy ships, let alone the Imperial Fleet that they had been looking for. The only thing out of the ordinary in the system, as best any of them could tell, was a single Priminae emergency transponder.

Not even a military transponder.

"Sir?" Miram spoke up, repeating her question. "Should we stand down?"

Eric frowned, thinking about that transponder.

Why is a civilian signal here? There hasn't been a colony in this system since the Drasin incursion, and there's nothing reported of value here worth coming this close to the edge of Priminae patrolled space.

"Sir . . ."

"No."

"Sir?" Miram questioned, not sure if he was speaking to her.

"No," Eric said again. "Maintain general quarters. They're out here. Issue orders to the squadron. I want interception drones deployed and the Vorpals at the ready launch position."

Miram stared for a moment before she nodded slowly. "Aye sir."

Eric tilted his head slightly, eyes falling on the spot where Odysseus stood in his modern composite armor. The commodore smiled slightly.

"Reverse acceleration, slow our transit through the system."

"Sir?" Miram looked confused.

"You heard the order, Commander."

"Aye Skipper. Helm reverse acceleration curve!"

"Reversing acceleration. Aye, aye, ma'am!"

Imperial Eighth Fleet Command Vessel

"Enemy squadron is approaching at one-third light, Fleet Commander."

Helena nodded somberly to herself, considering that. She had set her fleet moving, and now they were almost in range to force an engagement with them, but the enemy's closing speed was fast. *Too fast.*

At that rate, the engagement would last only seconds, leaving too much chance for failure.

She hissed, irritated, but there was nothing she could do. This time, the enemy would proceed unimpeded. Helena shifted, readying to give the order to stand down, when another call cut her off.

"Enemy squadron is slowing!"

Helena came to her feet, eyes wide. "Why? Have they spotted us?"

"No sign of that, Fleet Commander. They've just . . . begun slowing."

Is it a trap? Helena hesitated, an uncharacteristic concern filling her. None of her fellows would hesitate. The enemy had just made a fatal mistake, but she didn't command the First through Seventh Fleets.

She commanded the *Eighth*.

"Kill the drives," Helena ordered, her tone snapping across the deck.

"Ma'am?" her senior officer started to ask, but shook himself quickly and turned around. "Kill the drives! Ballistic course only!"

With the order relayed, he quickly walked over to her.

"Trap, Fleet Commander?"

"I don't know, but these . . ." Helena shook her head. "These *beings* are not behaving like the Oathers. I believe we have found our . . . anomalies."

"Yes, Fleet Commander. Should we not engage?"

"Orders are to gather intelligence. We do that first," she ordered decisively. "Our enemies will fall on *our* schedule, not theirs."

Chapter 16

Odysseus *Task Group,* **Odysseus** *Command*

"There!"

Eric turned, heading for the scanner station. "What did you find, Lieutenant?"

The young officer flushed slightly as his CO leaned over his shoulder, but pointed to the screen. "We picked up a stray signal as we crossed this space. Faint but modulated. Couldn't identify it, but we could track it, sir. Took a while, which left us with too much space to scan, but we got lucky."

Eric noted the glint of light from the system primary reflecting off a metal hull and nodded grimly. "We know where they are now. Track them back along their course through the archives."

"Yes sir."

The massive sensor arrays of the Odysseus Class cruisers scanned far more than even the enormous computers on board could hope to process. Not quite everything, but huge swaths of space were scanned and recorded onto fractal cores until the point that the computer finally got around to examining them. That meant that there was a good chance that the ships they'd located could be tracked back over hours, or even days or more, of recordings.

Eric eyed the trajectories involved and spotted the pattern before the computer even did. He barked out a laugh as he straightened up.

"I don't believe it," he said, shaking his head.

"Sir?" Miram asked, approaching. "What is it?"

"They could have forced an engagement, but they let us pass," he said, eyes following the departing track of the enemy ships, the count growing quickly as the computer ran deep pattern-recognition searches.

"That doesn't seem like the Empire," Miram noted. "Are you sure?"

"Look for yourself. The computer has the plot coming up." Eric stepped back.

He let her examine the data, walking out to the center of the command deck as thoughts whirled in his mind.

"You are surprised," Odysseus said gently, appearing beside him.

"I am," Eric confirmed.

"Why?"

Eric thought about it. "Because that isn't like the Empire. They should have believed they had us cold."

"Did they not? We did not know they were there," Odysseus suggested. "And your deceleration opened our flank to . . ." The entity paused, blinking. "You wanted them to attack. You . . . knew they were there, but how? Nothing showed their location until just now."

"I could feel it," Eric said, his tone serious. "What I didn't feel was the nature of the enemy commander. This one, he's patient. That's new."

"Commodore," Miram said, coming back to him, "you were right. Stranger still, sir, they were on an intercept course until you slowed the squadron. They'd only have been able to get a couple beams off in our direction, but they were *trying* to get us locked in."

Eric nodded, mentally tipping an imaginary hat to the enemy commander.

"Well played," he said to no one.

Until we meet again, Commander.

Belj Fleet, Free Stars

Mir was set back on his heels, shock reverberating through him as the small ships appeared from nowhere, charging with blinding speed, and tore into his squadrons with lasers that were at least on destroyer level, well beyond what ships of their size should have had.

"What in the abyss are—"

He cut himself off, his mind returning to the report from Commander Hirik.

The unknown ships. The commander wasn't as much a fool as I thought, clearly.

In the few moments of his shock at the ships' sudden charge, the six small ships had closed the distance to insanely close ranges, ducking in under his vessel's fire-control aiming systems and crossing their beams at far beyond the tracking rating of *any* of his weapons.

Mir could feel shudders running through the destroyer's deck below his feet as lasers raked her armor, vaporizing sections with vicious effectiveness and venting atmosphere to the void.

"Target the new vessels before they tear us apart," the destroyer's captain called, clutching at a rail as the ship again shuddered.

"We can't," the weapon's officer responded. "They're too close and too fast. Our computers barely even register that they *exist*, Captain."

The captain glared at the display for a moment, glancing back only briefly in Mir's direction before returning to his task.

"Shift to manual control," he ordered. "Try to anticipate the trajectories."

That got him a strange look, but the man at the weapons station swallowed hard and nodded.

"On your command, Captain," he said, turning to his controls as he opened a communications channel. "Weapon stations, shift to manual firing."

The captain pushed back, worry on his face as he turned and approached Mir's position.

"Will that work, Captain?" Mir asked softly once he was in earshot.

The captain shook his head. "Possibly we'll be fortunate, but with the computers we would not even have that. They literally were not able to detect the vessels quickly enough to project a likely trajectory."

"I see."

That put a spin on the situation, and Mir knew he had only seconds to make a decision. The small ships had timed their assault to near perfection. His squadrons were committed to a close engagement with the Kingdom's destroyers. That would be bad enough without the fast-moving vessels, as the outnumbered destroyers had the advantage of fortified positions in the asteroid cluster.

With the addition of the small, high-speed vessels, the scales of battle had changed without question.

"Full power to the drives," he ordered. "Bore on through."

"As you command," the captain said quickly, spinning back. "All squadrons to full acceleration! Fight our way through!"

Gaia's Revenge

"The enemy destroyers have returned to full acceleration, Stephan."

Milla's announcement came as little surprise to Steph as he twisted the fighter-gunboat around, instinctively flinching away from a near sweep of an enemy laser that scorched his skin through the NICS interface. The fighter flinched with him, skipping a few dozen meters farther from the laser's passage as his involuntary response was translated into reaction for the ship as a whole.

"Understood," Steph said.

The enemy had been put in a position where they had two real choices. Stay and fight, or use their kinetic motion to their advantage to escape the trap as best they could. If they'd picked the first, Steph was reasonably certain that his squadron and the Kingdom destroyers would have been able to win the day, but the losses would have been extreme on both sides.

By running, the Belj had given themselves a chance to fight another day. Since the asteroid cluster was clearly *not* what they had been hunting for, it was the intelligent play on their part and it suited Steph's purposes just as well. He was a little impressed that they'd made the call so quickly, but really, the decision was inevitable.

"Archangels, harry and drive them on," he ordered. "Stay close, stay fast, until they clear the Kingdom's line, then break off and let them go."

Keeping his own orders in mind, Steph dove in for the closest destroyer formation with Black's *Archangel Two* following tight on his six.

The two fighter-gunboats raked the enemy destroyers with short beams from their forward lasers, tearing up the armor of the vessels with vicious strokes of directed energy, but largely moving too quickly to do much serious damage even as they used that speed to prevent the enemy from achieving a lock on them in turn.

An explosion of vapor and dust ahead of him as he crossed close to the center beam of the Belj destroyer served notice that the Kingdom wasn't inclined to simply allow the enemy to pass unmolested. Steph pulled his fighter out of the pass prematurely to avoid flying right through superheated plasma and armor shards blown off into space right.

"Watch your flight paths," he ordered. "This area is downright hostile flying space."

Archangel Three

"No kidding, boss," Cardsharp swore as she twisted her fighter-gunboat hard in a tight corkscrew roll, evading the panicked evasive maneuvers of the destroyer she had been engaging.

She didn't know who was in charge or if they'd ordered such a maneuver, but she cringed as the ship *collided* with one of its fellows. She led her fighter into a gap between them, accelerating to safety with *Archangel Four* on her tail, neither able to get off any shots in the process, as they were too focused on keeping their own hides intact.

Probably not going to matter, Jennifer thought with a cringe, *I don't think we could have done nearly that much damage if we had.*

Fires were burning in the vacuum of space, glowing balls of plasma that clearly wanted to take on the spherical form that zero gravity would prefer but marred by the kinetic push given by the jets of fuel streaming from the hulls of the damaged warships.

"Who taught these idiots to fly?" her wingman, Lieutenant Erik "Viking" Skar, bitched as he guided his fighter through the growing debris field in her wake.

"Stay focused. Ask useless questions after the fight," she growled, bringing her fighter around in a tight turn to survey the situation, keeping her speed as high as she dared while flying close to so much debris. "They're panicking, and that makes them more of a threat at this range, not less!"

"Roger that."

Belj Fleet

"Captains, get your ships under control!" Mir snarled out the order over the squadron frequency, furious at the error he was seeing play out before his eyes.

It was, of course, one of the risks of flying tighter formations this close to a fight. Normally, he would never have asked that of his captains in the first place, but as the range to targets decreased, so too did the effective coverage area one could spread ships over without weakening their own fire density.

They weren't, however, supposed to be *that* close.

They weren't supposed to be dealing with small, high-speed attack vessels blasting through so close as to have their gravity fields interfering with one another either.

Mir actually thought that was likely the problem as much as anything else. He would have to examine the telemetry readings later, but it seemed probable that the gravity interactions with the enemy's fast-moving vessels had thrown off internal navigation.

"Spread formation," he ordered.

It was pointless trying to run a close formation for the attack now that it was clear they were running into a trap.

He glanced aside at one of his assistants. "Determine if those ships are able to maneuver, please."

"Yes Admiral."

It didn't matter, he supposed, whether they could or not. There was no possibility of stopping to put them under warp, as the rest of his squadrons were already accelerating away.

This is a minor disaster.

Now he just had to keep it from becoming a major one.

————

Imperial Third Fleet

"Well, now," Jesan said softly as he watched the fighting play out, "isn't that interesting."

He was pleased to have stumbled on the fleet a little too late to intercept them. Watching the battle in the lower part of the star's gravity well was proving to be informative.

"Someone out here is *innovating*," Jesan said, checking that every possible aspect of the fight was being recorded.

The Empire would want those scans.

"Yes, Fleet Commander," his second replied. "But who? And why would they be using such small ships?"

Not a bad question, Jesan knew. Normally, any vessel below the mass of a destroyer was considered too vulnerable and ineffective for combat. The Empire didn't field anything below the cruiser range, in fact.

"Do we have mass specifications on the unknown class?" he asked, pitching his voice to reach the signals and scanner stations.

"Still analyzing, Commander," the scanner officer replied. "We're estimating right now less than ten percent the mass of the local destroyers."

That was small.

The local destroyers were not the largest of the class he'd encountered either. Once, when the Empire still put such things in space, the largest Imperial destroyers were easily twenty to thirty percent larger than what the locals currently used. Those numbers put the unknown ships well below the active-duty requirements for any Imperial warship within the entire history of the Empire.

This conclusion nagged at him, however, because Jesan had seen smaller craft in action not all that long ago.

He walked over to the closest computer station and called up the records of the invasion into Oather space, comparing the silhouettes of the unknown ships with those put into space by the anomalous species.

Not even a close match. These are considerably larger, of course, he noted with a mild sense of mixed relief and disappointment. *Those small ships used by the anomalies were surprisingly powerful, but not truly a threat to a warship. These appear to be a threat, judging from the data we're scanning from here.*

On a whim he ran a signals comparison, looking for any sign of either Oather or anomalous transmissions, but those came up negative as well. They were only reading Free Star transmission protocols from the battle below them.

Jesan nodded slightly to himself.

"Just getting desperate, then," he murmured.

"Commander?" his second asked, walking over. "I'm afraid I didn't hear that."

Jesan shook his head. "Nothing important, Sub-Commander. I was merely commenting that the locals are showing more signs of desperation. They're building smaller, likely much cheaper ships in an attempt to field more power for lesser cost."

The sub-commander nodded thoughtfully. "They appear to have succeeded."

"Yes, and that is bothersome," Jesan confirmed. "But not a particular concern. What is the result of the battle?"

"The Belj have gone to full acceleration and have adjusted their course to evade contact as best they can. They won't entirely succeed, by our analysis, but they will preserve most of the fleet in the process."

Jesan grimaced. "Pity. Very well, full power to our drives. Take us into the system, signal fleet-wide, prepare for battle."

"As you command!"

Gaia's Revenge

Three of the enemy destroyers were burning in space, drifting without warps as they continued on their paths through the asteroid cluster.

Most of the rest were arcing away from the Aerin Star Kingdom destroyers as best they could while being raked by laser fire incessantly.

The commander of the local squadrons was intent on making the Belj pay as dearly as possible for their attempt on the Aerin homeworld as well as for this assault.

Not that I blame him, Steph thought as he eased back on his own fighter-gunboat's acceleration, letting the enemy gain some distance as he signalled the rest of his squadron to do the same.

Body count wasn't his goal; reputation was. The more of them that got away, the better it would be for the short- to mid-term. He was a little concerned about the long-term results of that; leaving living enemies at your back was a questionable move at the best of times, but Steph would play that out as it came. For the moment, they needed the legend. Anything else, well, they'd deal with it. The Archangels always did.

"Stephan!"

Steph twisted in place, feeling the ship jump in response to his surprise, and quickly got himself under control lest he do something stupid while in control of a warship.

"What is it, Milla?" he asked, recognizing that it wasn't in her personality to yell without due cause.

"We have a problem. Look to the long-range scanners!"

Steph refocused his attention, unmasking the long-range overlay that he'd had hidden so it wouldn't distract him during the fight.

He saw what she was excited about almost instantly and viciously suppressed the urge to start swearing and yelling himself.

"Archangels, *Revenge,*" he called automatically. "Break contact and fall back, let them go. We have bigger problems. Look to your long-range scanners and stand by for orders."

The others immediately signalled their acknowledgment of the order, but Steph was already opening a signal to the locals.

"*Gael, Revenge,*" he said. "We have an issue."

"Why are you not pursuing the enemy, *Revenge?*" Auran responded almost immediately. "We have a deal."

"Deal is still on, but if we all want to live to enjoy it, we might want to pay attention. I strongly advise you evacuate the system along one of the following trajectories."

He sent a range of courses over the signal to complement his words.

"What? Why?"

"Unless I miss my guess, those are *Imperial* cruisers coming our way, and I doubt they're just being friendly," Steph said. "Our contract did not include mixing it up with the Empire."

"What?!"

The channel went dead, but Steph left it open anyway as he shifted his focus and started running the numbers. The Imperial ships were hours out still, but that didn't mean that he and his were in the clear. There was a lot going on, and just bugging out wasn't a possibility.

We have time, and we have better acceleration than they do, Steph thought grimly as he ran the calculations. *We've got it. Just wish it hadn't happened this soon.*

"*Revenge,* we confirm your scans," the shaken Auran came back. "We are breaking off contact and fleeing the system. Thank you for the advisement."

"Not a problem. We'll leave on a different path, meet you back in the Kingdom," Steph said. "Acceptable?"

"Eminently."

"Good luck. *Revenge* out."

———

Imperial Third Fleet

Jesan grunted in mixed amusement and annoyance as the pests began to scatter as soon as his fleet signals reached them.

They noticed us slightly quicker than expected, he noted with mild interest.

The Belj fleet that he had tracked to this system were already fleeing, of course, but he could see the signs that the remaining vessels had also begun preparations for withdrawal from the system with some degree of urgency.

"There goes the first of them," his sub-commander announced.

Jesan nodded as he watched the first of the destroyer squadrons break contact with the Belj, accelerating away from his fleet on a course he knew they would not be able to intercept.

A mild irritation, but really, just sending them scattering like the pests they were was a mission win based on his current orders.

"Track them, standard procedure," he said. "What of the damaged vessels?"

"Several will not be able to evade us, Fleet Commander."

Jesan nodded. "Good. Vector as ordered."

"Yes, Fleet Commander."

———

Gaia's Revenge

Tyke paused as he looked over to where Steph was standing, staring at the telemetry data with an odd look in his eye.

"You okay, Crown?"

With no response forthcoming, Tyke walked across the flight control deck to where Steph had the holographic displays focused not on the Imperial ships but on the disabled Belj destroyers.

"Crown."

"Huh?" Steph half turned. "What?"

"You okay?"

"Yeah, I'm fine," Steph said, sounding bothered by something as he reached out and accessed the shipboard comm channels. "Hey Milla?"

"Yes Stephan?" she answered immediately.

"Full scan, active sensors, target the disabled Belj destroyers," he ordered simply.

"Roger, Stephan. Pulse out."

At their current range, the pulse return was almost instantaneous, and soon the screens were filled with more information than Tyke could decipher as he looked over Steph's shoulder.

"Can you make heads or tails of that?" he asked.

Steph nodded, gesturing. "Those two are dead in space—they've lost drive mass. This one over here is still under power, but they're drifting just the same. They've lost scanners and comms, see there? The instrumentation clusters were burned out, probably by our lasers. They're blind and deaf, but probably mostly intact beyond that."

"Alright, so?"

"So those are Imperial cruisers coming downwell, Tyke," Steph said grimly.

"I'm not following, sorry."

"Imperials don't take prisoners," Steph said, toggling the squadron-wide communications. "Archangels, stand by to offer rescue to the Belj destroyer crews. We have seven hours before the cruisers get here, considerably less if we want to entirely evade contact. Do this by the numbers, do not overly risk yourselves, but if we can get those people out of here, I want it done. *Archangel* Actual out."

Chapter 17

Belj Destroyer Baphon

Smoke filled the bridge, the ship's filtration system whining and rasping as it tried to clear the contaminants from the air. But those sounds were drowned out entirely by the alarms screaming for everyone's attention from all sides.

At least the fires have been extinguished, the ship's second in command thought grimly as he kicked aside a broken chunk of seating and slid into the free communications console.

The strike that took out the scanners and communications had caused a back channel burst to feed through the armor at its weakest point. The conduits that brought data back from those systems had served well enough to funnel energy of a different sort. Buffers designed to limit such events were entirely incapable of standing up to the sheer power of a warship's lasers. No one had ever really thought they might need to. The target was so small that it was impossible to reliably strike at such a point across conventional fighting ranges, after all.

The new ships had either proven that wrong or, more likely, just gotten incredibly lucky.

The explosions of energy blew out systems all across the deck, overloading buffers intended to protect against stray cosmic energies that weren't specifically directed at the ship.

"Primary scanners and communications are entirely off, Sub-Commander."

Jerich Mas glowered at the young crewman who was spouting the obvious.

"I find myself entirely aware of that, crewman," he barked. "Try to route to the backups."

"We can't." The crewman shook his head. "The lines are all melted to scrap. There're puddles of silicate cooling on every deck from here to the forward plates. We have nothing to route signals *through*."

Jerich swore under his breath but couldn't say he was entirely surprised.

"Pull lines from storage. We'll have to run a bypass," he ordered.

The crewman looked pained.

"What?"

"We don't have enough in storage, Sub-Commander. Logistics didn't assign us sufficient replacement parts during the last resupply. They said we didn't need them."

Abyss be damned bureaucrats.

"Fine, gather up what we do have and get it to the forward deck," Jerich ordered. "I'll meet you there."

"Yes Sub-Commander!"

Jerich ignored the man as he left the deck, pushing himself away from the useless communications terminal. The *Baphon* was deaf and blind. For all they knew, the battle was won or lost. By the abyss, they might be on a direct course for an asteroid twice the size of the ship. They couldn't tell.

He had to get as much back in running order as he could, as quickly as possible.

The fact that we're not being shot at is a plus, he thought, though he was fully aware it could just as likely mean that the enemy currently had other concerns than that they'd won the battle.

He was about to grab some more crew to start hauling gear forward when the entire ship abruptly rang like a bell. The deck shuddered under him.

"What in the abyss was that?" he snarled, grabbing a rail to steady himself.

No one seemed to have the slightest idea, which seemed about as expected given the current state of things. Jerich grabbed at a ship-wide communication system, thankful that those at least were still intact.

"All decks, report. Does anyone know what that was?"

Gaia's Revenge

"Saddle up, Marines!"

Master Sergeant Buckler marched down between the row of men and women, looking over their armor and arms with a fast professional glance. He was less than happy with what he was seeing, but it wasn't the fault of the men.

The gear they had was supposedly top-of-the-line, but it was all new and all distinctly nonstandard. He paused at the end of the row and sighed, but refrained from saying what he wanted to, knowing there was nothing to be done.

Why do they all have to look like rejects from a sci-fi film, though?

For obvious reasons, standard firearms were not an option. Those had been used enough against the Empire that they'd be tracked back to Earth instantly by even a cursory examination and analysis through Imperial Systems. Unfortunately, that requirement also left out the Priminae gravity cannons, as those were distinctly Priminae in nature, and leaving a trail back to them was almost as bad.

Instead, they got death rays.

The sergeant had just *barely* managed to keep from rubbing his palm across his face when he'd heard that. The weapons were close enough to Imperial standard that they would look like some offshoot, something developed by a particularly creative or desperate group based on known technology. Technically, they were called pulse rifles, but to his mind there was no way in hell he was going to give them the credit of being called a rifle.

The pulse aspect was true enough, however. They fired a burst of amplified electromagnetic energy, powerful enough to scramble everything from electronics to brains, but also delivering enough energy to boil water in an instant. The resulting impact was nasty enough that he wasn't embarrassed to be carrying one himself, but Buckler still wanted his battle rifle.

"Sergeant, are we ready to go?"

Buckler turned, eyes widening as he recognized the commander stepping down onto the deck.

"We, sir?" he asked with trepidation.

"We, Sergeant," Steph said. "The ship is in good hands. I'll be handling this myself."

Buckler bit his tongue.

Literally bit his tongue.

It was someone's job to tell the ship's commander that they had no business on a boarding party to an enemy ship, but it wasn't *his* job.

"Yes sir," he strangled out finally.

The commander just smirked at him, clearly knowing what was going through Buckler's head and enjoying the sergeant's discomfort. From a rack on the wall he pulled a rifle, also a completely new and nonstandard model, and casually cleared the breach before slapping a magazine home and clipping it to a sling on his armor.

"Everyone knows the job?" the commander asked, looking around.

"Oorah, sir!" the Marines called in unison.

"Yeah, we're gonna have to work on that," he muttered, shaking his head. "But that'll do for now. This is technically a boarding operation to provide succor, but the crew doesn't know we're coming, and they probably won't be too happy to see us."

He looked around. "What I'm saying, Marines, is start no trouble, but take no shit. Clear?"

"Clear sir!"

"Alright," Steph said, nodding to the lock where a couple Marines were cutting through the hull of the destroyer they were docked with. "Let's take that ship."

———

Baphon

Gira Mai was walking down an access corridor, looking for the source of some rather odd sounds that had been echoing through the ship after the loud ringing had shaken everything up. Orders had come down the pipe to find the source, as if he and the crew didn't have enough on their hands at the moment, and so he and others had been dispatched in all directions.

The smell of smoke had been the first sign that really worried him. Fires on board ship were *bad* things, and they already had more than their fill of that kind of bad. He heard a sizzling sound ahead of him and broke into a run, hoping to find the problem before it became something he couldn't handle easily on his own.

The smoke grew thicker ahead of him, though only just enough to begin obscuring his vision. Gira was still running when he saw sparks erupting into the deck from a hull access lock and skidded to a stop in fear as two massive spikes abruptly tore through the center and suddenly *wrenched* the doors open with a scream of metal tearing.

He fell on his backside, scrambling to crawl backward away from the hull breach as every nightmare he'd ever had about being blown into space flashed across his eyes. No howl of wind rushed past him, however, as instead a figure in dark gray leapt in through the breach and landed heavily on the deck.

The man was covered in smooth armor unlike anything he'd ever seen. The suit was glossy and refracted light as it moved. The person paused briefly to look around before he moved to clear the way for the next figure. More poured through the breach as Gira watched, but the first one was on his position before he could even process what he was seeing.

A boot planted in the center of his chest sent him flat on his back as a big, ugly weapon that he didn't recognize was pushed in his face.

"Move and you *die*."

The language was heavily accented Imperial, but the message was clear. Gira carefully kept very still as his eyes flicked past the man holding him down. More men were clearing the corridor, weapons sweeping for targets as they moved.

Behind them, one in identical armor was moving with a more casual gait. It was impossible to see features in the armor, but his stance as he walked seemed almost relaxed. He ambled to where Gira was being held and looked him over where he lay for a moment before tapping the man holding Gira down on his shoulder.

"Good work," the man said in that same accented Imperial. "As you were."

"Sir," the man said, pulling the weapon back and straightening up.

Gira stared up in fear as the man who seemed to be in charge offered him a hand.

"Well, are you going to take it, or should I give you back to the corporal?" the man asked, seemingly holding back an urge to laugh.

Gira didn't know what a corporal was, or who exactly, but from the context he could make a decent enough guess. He clasped the hand quickly, not wanting to be slammed back into the deck with the ugly weapon in his face yet again.

On his feet, he risked a trembling question.

"Wh . . . who are you?"

"Not important," the leader said. "Call us rescuers, if you like, or boarders. Either way, I need to speak with whoever is in charge."

Gira blinked. "The sub-commander is on the bridge."

The leader nodded, looking around as he settled one hand on a weapon secured at his hip. "Thank you. Now, which way would that be?"

———

Steph was pleased with how things were going, which worried him a little more than the unknown elements of the action did, if he were entirely honest.

The man they'd captured initially seemed to have no problem directing him and his Marines to the bridge and the ship's commander, and this bothered Steph deeply because the man didn't strike him as either a straight-up coward or a turncoat type. Rather, it didn't seem to occur to him that he might want to try slowing down the progress of hostile boarding elements on his ship. He was too free with information for Steph's liking, but he didn't appear to be lying either.

There's a story there, but I just don't have the time to work it out, Steph thought, filing it away to worry about later as he checked the time and furthered the countdown clock accordingly.

With the Empire bearing down on them, he couldn't afford to indulge his curiosity.

"Secure him," he ordered, pushing the man back to the Marine waiting behind him. "We need to take the bridge and end this cleanly and quickly."

"Yes sir."

With the crewman secured, Steph moved forward, checking the corridor layout as the Marines moved ahead to secure the path as they advanced.

"Sergeant." Steph called the squad leader over. "We're only a couple decks from the bridge, and apparently no one uses these ships for boarding operations, so there's not much in the way of an armory on board."

"Assuming the man was telling the truth, sir."

"Assuming that, yes," Steph conceded, frowning under his breathing unit. "But he seemed to be honest."

Buckler just grunted noncommittally.

"Keep your eyes roving," Steph ordered. "But we don't have time to second-guess. We're going to lance straight through, take the bridge, and secure the command staff. Hopefully that will end this."

"And if it doesn't?"

Steph considered that, sighing finally. "Best bring up the chems and TB systems, just in case."

Buckler's eyes widened under his breather. The very idea of using thermobaric explosives on board a ship he was *standing on* seemed to terrify him—as it should any sane person—but he nodded firmly.

"Yes sir. We'll be ready."

"I have no doubts, Sergeant. Be about it," Steph ordered.

Archangel Three

Jennifer Samuels grimaced as she edged the fighter-gunboat in closer to the stricken vessel just ahead of them.

"Alright, I've got them dead to rights," she said over the ship's comm. "Give me an open line to the enemy ship."

"Roger, Commander. Channel open."

"Destroyer of the Belj Empire," she called, wrapping her tongue around the Imperial language everyone on the crew had been required to learn as part of their assignment. "Please respond."

There was no immediate response, though she didn't really expect much. Jennifer kept an eye on the ship's power systems through her scanners, looking for any hint that it was about to try to fire on them, but that was a pretty low probability judging from the damage the ship had clearly taken and the lack of reactor mass registering on her gravity scans.

After a few seconds, she repeated the call.

On the third time, she finally got an answer.

"This is the Belj destroyer *Hirim Ja*," a frustrated-sounding voice said. "What do you want?"

Well, that's direct if nothing else.

"*Hirim Ja*, we are offering succor," she said. "How many crew do you have to be removed?"

There was a long pause.

"What?"

"How many crewmembers require evacuation?" Jennifer said again. "The Imperial cruisers are closing. In our experience, the Empire does not take prisoners. This is the only offer you're going to get. Stand by for evacuation, or we're leaving without you."

Several more seconds passed.

"Fine," she growled. "Good luck to you, we're lea—"

"Wait!" the voice had an edge of panic. "Wait, please wait!"

"How many crew do you have to evacuate?" Jennifer repeated.

The voice stammered over his words, clearly unsure but trying to respond.

"We . . . we have almost three hundred. I don't know how many are still alive. C-can you hold that many?"

"Roger. Gather all hands to your ventral docking ports," she ordered. "You *will* be supervised, you *will* be checked for weapons, and you *will* comply with our directives or you *will* be left behind. Am I understood?"

The shaken voice came back quickly.

"Y-yes. I understand."

Archangel Two

The two stricken destroyers were flanked by Archangels three through six, two of the fighter-gunboats each taking a destroyer and delivering the same ultimatum, while *Archangel Two* flew overwatch and tried to guard the five remaining ones as best they could.

Alexandra Black didn't much enjoy the job, but it had to be done.

The distant but rapidly approaching Imperial cruisers were the only active threat on her board for the moment, and the main source of the tension tightening down on the muscles in her neck as she constantly checked over the long-range scans to see if anything had changed.

Nothing had, of course. There were only so many things a ship could do on approach, and the Imperial cruisers were pretty much already doing them.

They were building high acceleration into the system, but mostly keeping within what the Priminae and Terran ships would consider safe military speed. They undoubtedly had more on tap, if needed, but the danger of pushing closer to, or through, light-speed within the powerful gravity of a star wasn't insignificant.

Disruption of a ship's warp field by opposing gravity waves became more likely as one entered into a significant gravity well. That disruption at high levels of acceleration could result in the ship's drives being unbalanced, at least briefly. On its own, that would be a minor issue at most, but losing your space-warp while traveling through a star's gravity well at high portions of light-speed could easily result in slamming headlong into all sorts of nastiness.

Even grains of dust at near light-speed would tear a ship to shreds in short order without the shielding of a space-warp.

So, for the moment, the Imperial ships were playing it safe, at least by military standards. That was still one hell of a lot of power and acceleration, however, and with the Archangels holding to a steady speed, that was acceleration they would have to make up if they wanted to avoid contact with the fleet of cruisers bearing down on them.

Alexandra was keeping one eye on *that* particular clock, hoping that Stephanos didn't push all of their luck.

Chapter 18

Now this is a curious change.

Jesan watched the enemy operations as they apparently paused to board the stricken destroyers for some reason he didn't understand. It made him wonder if there weren't something of value on the ships, though he could not imagine what that might be.

In the Free Stars, the definition of valuable wasn't always in line with that of the Empire, of course, so whatever they were after might be a trifle by his estimation. It was clearly worth risking their lives for, however, and that piqued Jesan's attention.

"Increase acceleration to maximum imperial power," he ordered. "Double the shifts on the warp systems."

"As you order, Commander."

That would put them close to the Imperial redline for ships' acceleration within a stellar gravity well, a line that was generally not to be crossed unless destruction of your vessel was the consequence of not crossing it. As it was, he knew he would have to report to the Admiralty of Lords for his order to increase acceleration, but it seemed warranted.

"What could possibly be so important in those destroyers that they would risk contact with us to acquire it?" he wondered idly as the hum of the ship's drives increased in the background.

Whatever it was, he aimed to discover the treasure for himself.

"Revised contact numbers being calculated now, Commander."

"Thank you, Sub-Commander."

———

Baphon

"Commander! We've been boarded!"

Jerich looked up sharply from where he was struggling to shift a large console that was still partially connected to the conduits that ran under the deck plates of the bridge. He blinked, staring owlishly at the man who'd just rushed in, unable to quite believe he'd heard what he thought he'd heard.

"What?" he managed to ask.

"We've been boarded, Commander."

Apparently I did hear correctly, Jerich thought as he let the console thump back into place and rose from where he was crouched, wiping his hands off on his already sweat-stained uniform. "By who?"

"We don't know, Commander. Reports speak of uniform armor unlike anything we've ever encountered," the crewman stammered out. "They're marching this way. Nothing is slowing them down."

"Lock the bulkheads," Jerich ordered sharply, crossing to one of the still-intact internal communications and systems control consoles.

"We tried, Commander. They cut through them in seconds."

That's impossible, Jerich thought, shocked. Certainly internal bulkheads weren't armored, exactly, but they weren't that easy to cut either. "Break out the arms. Issue to all crew with orders to secure against boarders."

"Commander, they'll be here before we can even start. You need to leave."

"I can't *leave*," Jerich snarled. "This is still the central control section for the entire ship. If we lose the bridge, we lose the ship!"

He crossed to a lockbox on the wall and palmed it open using his biometric signature, revealing a half dozen shipboard sidearms. Securing one for himself, Jerich passed out the rest to the closest crewmen.

"Secure the access corridor," he ordered. "We have to hold until the crew can rally from the armory."

"Yes Commander!"

Jerich crossed back to the communications terminal and began to issue orders as the men began to tear up materials to both block the access to the bridge and to use as cover.

What in the abyss is going on out there? Who boards a destroyer in the middle of battle?

Something had gone horribly wrong.

Now he just had to find out what it was, and whether he could do anything about it. Jerich had a sinking sensation about the answer to the latter, unfortunately, but for the moment he would focus on the first.

————

"Encountering resistance ahead, Commander."

Steph walked to the corner of the corridor, glancing around to where the Marines were exchanging fire with what looked like an entrenched formation located at a bulkhead passage just ahead. He raised an eyebrow, taking in the scene.

"Are they using computer consoles for cover?" he asked incredulously.

"That is what it looks like," the master sergeant admitted, shaking his head.

A whine and spattering sound echoed down the corridor, making Steph flinch back automatically before he registered it properly.

"What was that?" he asked, confused.

"Enemy fire, sir. They're using lightweight, high-velocity fléchettes, or whatever the local equivalent is."

"Fléchettes? Seriously?"

"Yes sir," Buckler said, shrugging. "I assume the logic is that having heavier arms might penetrate the hull."

"Fat lot of good that's going to do them in this situation," Steph said, pushing his rifle behind his back on the sling as he stepped around the corridor into the open and drew his service pistol from his hip holster.

"Sir! What are you—!"

Steph ignored the Marine as he started walking down the hallway, the hand cannon he wielded roaring as he fired semirandomly and return fire spattered uselessly against his armor. He strode past the Marine lines toward the fortifications, firing steadily to force heads down and keep people too freaked out to think straight.

Enemy fire doubled briefly as they tried to rally between his shots, but by the time he reached the fortifications, the density of fire had all but stopped entirely. Steph planted one foot on the upturned computer console and hopped up, pointing his pistol down at the shocked and cowering men behind it.

"Drop your weapons, or I stop missing," he barked in Imperial.

As the small weapons clattered to the deck, the sergeant and his Marines caught up, Buckler nearly apoplectic.

"What the *hell* was that, sir?" The sergeant would have been pulling his hair out if he wasn't wearing a sealed helmet rig.

"Stop thinking like Marines," Steph said, dropping the partially empty mag from his weapon and replacing it fresh before holstering the pistol. "Start thinking like pirates. Secure their weapons, then we take the bridge."

He hopped past the barricades, moving forward and forcing the Marines to scramble to keep up as some of them remained behind to secure the scene. The rest chased after the lunatic of a commander who had, apparently, lost his Goddamned mind.

———

Jerich flinched automatically as he heard a series of small explosions from just down the corridor, rising from his position and twisting toward the hatch as he looked to see just what had blown up.

Before he could open his mouth to demand information, however, one of his men was thrown back into the bridge and sent sprawling across the damaged gear they'd been getting ready to move. A man in dark gray armor stepped into the bridge and took up the entire hatch like some hulking, moving *wall*.

Jerich drew his weapon instinctively, arm sweeping up to target the invader. His motion must have been noted, though, because even as he began to draw a sight line down the ridge of his weapon, the figure was echoing his motion with lightning speed.

The weapon in Jerich's hand whined as it fired off a slew of high-speed shredders designed to tear apart flesh and the light body armor common on ships, but he barely noticed it over the echoing *boom* that filled the bridge.

A hammer blow struck him, spinning Jerich around and throwing his weapon clear as the world went insane. He blacked out briefly, or so he thought, and found himself on the ground, blinking in shock. The figure wasn't at the door anymore, he noticed dimly as his eyes rolled about and caught sight of the gray-armored man halfway to his position with more gray-clad figures appearing behind him.

The world went black again, and when it came back, Jerich found himself propped up on a computer station with the man crouching a short distance away, holding Jerich's own weapon in his grip as he idly examined it.

"Interesting weapon." The voice that came from the armor was distorted, inhuman.

The sound made Jerich shudder, though he supposed absently that might be caused by something else. Another armored figure was wrapping blood-soaked fabric around his arm and spraying something about the resulting mess. Jerich felt the fabric stiffen quickly, growing warm as something changed.

"Let the corpsman treat you," the first man said calmly when Jerich tried to move. "Otherwise you'll likely lose the arm."

"Who *are* you?" Jerich mumbled, feeling waves of burning pain assaulting him from his arm now, a sick feeling building in him.

"Doesn't matter," the man said. "What matters is why I'm here."

———

Steph looked down at the injured officer, wondering if the man was going to pass out.

"Can you keep him awake?" he asked the corpsman. "He seems to be the guy in charge of the rest of this rabble."

"For a while," the woman in armor beside him affirmed. "But he's lost a lot of blood. He'll need transfusions soon, or at least some synth."

Steph nodded, reaching out to lightly slap the man's face.

"Hey, pay attention," he said, holding a pair of fingers up between his eyes and the officer's. "You have a problem."

The man laughed weakly. "I believe that I can see that, yes."

"Not me," Steph said, shaking his head. "Your problem is that your ship is disabled and you have an Imperial *Fleet* bearing down on you. They'll be here in a few hours."

The man turned so white that Steph thought for a moment he was about to go into shock from blood loss.

"The Empire?" the officer croaked out. "Are you sure?"

"Sure enough. The rest of your squadrons ran like every demon in hell was chasing them, as have the Kingdom destroyers," Steph answered.

"Why are you still here?" the officer asked, eyes narrowing suspiciously.

"Not overly fond of leaving people to be killed in cold blood," Steph answered honestly. "Taking a life or dying in battle, that has some honor to it, though sometimes precious little. Watching the Empire just use your lot for target practice or, maybe worse, leaving you out here to die slowly if they decide you're not worth the effort—that's not really my way of doing things."

The man looked around the deck, noting that most of his people were being covered on one side of the bridge by two of the armored men while a few others were helping reconnect the systems he had been intending to move.

"Who are you people?"

"You can call me Teach," Steph answered, "but that's the wrong question. The right question is, how can we help you get out of this?"

"Get us off this ship and run," the man said simply. "We'll never be able to get the *Baphon* repaired in time."

"What's your name?" Steph asked from where he crouched, eyes boring into the man.

The officer sighed. "I am Jerich. Sub-commander of the *Baphon*."

"Sub-commander? What happened to the commander? Captain?"

"Captain," Jerich said. "He was injured in the blast that destroyed our scanners and communications systems. He did not last long afterward."

Steph nodded slowly. "Well, my apologies for that. Was likely as not one of my shots that did it."

"It was battle." Jerich seemed oddly unconcerned.

Steph wasn't quite sure what to make of the men he'd found on board the destroyer. All men so far, interestingly, and few seemed to care about who gave the orders. He looked down at the alien weapon in his grip, unsurprised that it fit his hand well despite its odd looks. Human forms meant human ergonomics, after all.

It wasn't the fit of the weapon that he found curious, though, it was the capabilities.

As he crouched there, a realization hit him, and Steph simply nodded in understanding.

"This isn't intended to fight off boarders, is it?" he asked rhetorically.

"Pardon?" Jerich asked, confused.

"Don't worry about it," Steph said, rising to his feet. "Corpsman, look after him."

She nodded as Steph turned away, making his way over to where the Marines and local crewmen were working to reattach consoles that had been taken apart for moving.

"How are the repairs going?" he asked in Imperial, eyes falling on a crewman who seemed to be in command after the bleeding man in the corpsman's care.

"Fine," the man responded instantly. "However, without more fiber lines, we cannot connect the navigation systems to replacement scanners or communications."

"We don't need to, don't worry about it. What's your name, son?" Steph asked, noting that the young man couldn't be much out of his teens.

"Derri, Commander."

"Well, Derri, just keep up the good work. Which one of these connects to the ship-wide communications?" Steph asked, gesturing around him.

Derri pointed. "That one."

"Thanks, kid." Steph nodded, patting him on the shoulder before heading over.

He was intercepted by Master Sergeant Buckler just as he got to the console.

"Bridge secured, and we've locked down much of the ship with the help of the crew here," Buckler said, frowning. "Damned if I can work out why they're so helpful."

Steph chuckled dryly, though there was little humor in it. "I can help you out there, Sergeant."

Buckler frowned, but before he could ask, Steph tossed him the officer's sidearm underhanded, causing him to snatch the weapon out of the air reflexively.

"Sir?"

"Figured it out a few minutes ago," Steph said, shaking his head. "That weapon, none of their weapons, were designed to hold off boarders, Sergeant."

"I don't understand?"

"They're designed to put down mutinies."

The master sergeant looked down at the alien weapon in his hand and let out a vile oath that left the commander again chuckling.

"Exactly," Steph said as he began to tinker with the console, thanking whoever was watching that it appeared to be a close match to Imperial and Priminae designs. "I would guess that there isn't a man on this bastard of a ship that isn't a conscript, barring a few of the officers."

"Well, that explains a few things," Buckler admitted, glancing over Steph's shoulder. "What are you doing?"

"Talking to the conscripts," Steph said as he opened a ship-wide channel.

"Crew of the *Baphon*, you may call me Teach. I have control of your command deck and all associated systems. Do not attempt to take this from me; you do not have the time to waste. As we speak, an Imperial Fleet is bearing down on our position. Your squadron has fled, as have the Kingdom destroyers. If you wish to live, you will do as I order. If you do not, then feel free to try to take my position. I will withdraw my forces and leave you here to die, either at the hands of the Imperial forces or the tender mercies of the vacuum. Officers may approach to negotiate with my forces. Treachery will be met with force. Teach out."

Steph killed the channel and turned back to the master sergeant. "Inform the guards that they're to search anyone who approaches, then let them through."

"Yes sir," Buckler answered, then sent the order over the team channels. "What's the plan?"

"Honestly? Still playing this by ear," Steph admitted. "I'm waiting for news from the others in the squadron, but I think we save the ship."

"How do we get the eyes back?"

Steph smiled. "We don't."

Chapter 19

Archangel Two

Alexandra Black examined the data coming in as she flew overwatch patrol over the remaining fighter-gunboats, all of which were currently attached to the three stricken destroyers. *I really hope Stephanos knows what the hell he's doing. We're running out of time.*

The Imperial vessels had accelerated again, and they were pushing the limits of safety right to the edge by the numbers she was seeing. That meant that their own safety margin was growing slimmer by the passing minute.

"Archangel Actual," she called. "*Archangel Two.*"

"Go for Actual, *Two.*" Stephanos' voice came back quickly.

"Whatever you're going to do, you need to get it done," Alexandra said. "The Imps have cranked up their boilers and are steaming hard in this direction."

"How much time do we have?"

She glanced at the numbers. "At maximum acceleration . . . we have another two hours, at most, before they'll be able to force an engagement."

"How long if we're limited to the destroyer's acceleration?"

"What? I don't know. We don't have precise specifications on those heaps. Are you crazy? Just get the hell off that thing already!"

"I'll take that under advisement," he told her, amusement thick in his tone, making Alex want to bang her head into the hard-light projections in front of her. "How are the others doing?"

"Fine so far. A few tried to get uppity, sneak weapons in, you know the drill. Most of them didn't get a shot off when the Marines confronted them," she said.

"Most?" The humor was gone in an instant from his tone.

"Most," Alex sighed. "One got a few rounds off. Tore up his own people, but nothing got through the Marines' armor."

"No, it wouldn't," Steph said with some relief. "Make sure everyone is searched before unarmored people are allowed anywhere near them. Officers are to be considered potentially hostile in particular."

Alex frowned. "Something we missed?"

"They're mostly conscripts, Noire," he told her. "Most of the crewmen don't seem to give a damn if the officers live or die, though I'm sure we'll see exceptions on both sides."

"Damn. Alright, I'll pass that on."

"As soon as the others are loaded, have them disengage and get ready to run," Steph ordered. "I'm working on something over here."

"Why are you trying to save that ship?" she asked.

"Other than the fact that it's a mostly intact *starship*?" he asked. "Alex, we're basically on our own out here, and we're running a cover as a privateer force. Privateers take prizes, it's part of our cover. No merc group is going to let a fully armed, almost-intact ship slip from their grasp if they can help it."

Alex rolled her eyes. "You are enjoying this entirely too damn much, Steph."

Stephanos' laughter made clear what he thought of the accusation.

"Get back to me when everyone is ready to move," he said. "Archangel Actual out."

The channel closed and Alex swore into the silence.

That idiot is going to be the death of me. In combat, if I'm lucky.

216

Imperial Third Fleet

"Movement on the targets, Fleet Commander."

Jesan looked up. "Oh? What are they doing?"

"Shifting formation at the moment, no sign of any attempt to flee as of yet," his second said.

Jesan considered that, thinking it rather odd. They had to know that they stood no chance against the Third Fleet. He had truly expected them to run quite some time ago, not spend precious hours playing around with wrecked destroyers. The little data they had on the new ships indicated that they had exceptional acceleration capability, though the scans they had of the initial battle left few details on whether that was their maximum or if they could maintain it.

In any case, he knew they were running out of time, with only minutes now counting down before the Third could force engagement against a standard acceleration, and not much longer for the faster smaller vessels they were dealing with. They had to make a move soon or the game was his.

Once the Third was close enough to force an engagement, he was quite certain he could eliminate all of the enemy vessels with no problem.

Why are they risking so much over three destroyers?

The act made little sense to him and, of late, Jesan had grown to harbor a rather great deal of antipathy toward things that made no sense.

Even after all those thoughts, however, he merely nodded to his second in command.

"Continue as ordered. Inform me once we are close enough to force an engagement, or that they have begun acceleration."

"As you order, Fleet Commander."

Baphon

"Sir, please," the crewman stammered out as Steph continued to work on the navigation and helm. "Without scanners the ship is quite blind. Putting significant acceleration would be of extreme risk."

"More extreme than waiting for the Empire to arrive?" Steph asked rhetorically, a twist of his lip showing his amusement while he worked.

The crewman blanched at that, but didn't back down as some of the others had.

"You should evacuate," the man said miserably. "You have a ship, you can flee."

Steph smiled, seeming to consider that before shaking his head. "Nah. I like this baby, so I think I'll keep her."

He made a couple tweaks and the helm returned to life, all connections to the ship's engineering section rejoined. Steph opened a channel from his armor communication system.

"*Archangel One*, Archangel Actual."

"*One* here, Crown." Tyke's voice came back instantly. "I hope you have news. We're about to get a *lot* closer to those cruisers than we ever want to be."

"Detach from the ship," Steph ordered. "I have navigation up, and I'm about to put power to the drives."

"Roger that. *Archangel One* detaching."

The deck vibrated under his feet as Steph entered some commands. "I need eyes, Tyke. Give me course heading and velocity numbers."

"Roger, Crown."

The deck shuddered again as the destroyer's drives began to warp space around them. Steph grimaced, recognizing the feeling as an indication that the drives were slightly out of alignment. It wouldn't be enough to seriously affect the ship in the short-term, he thought, but it would wreak all holy hell with long-term maintenance.

"We're under power and accelerating," he announced in the open.

"You fool, we're flying blind!" The wounded officer cursed at him. "There is an asteroid cluster directly ahead, and debris from the battle is sure to be all about our position!"

"You're blind," Steph said. "I see everything."

He wasn't lying either, as his HUD was showing an augmented view piggybacking off the sensor data from *Archangel One*. He was looking ahead and through the bulkheads of the ship, directly into space as they flew.

"Adjusting course heading," he said as he worked the controls. "Increasing space-warp . . ."

The ship shuddered, and then suddenly all vibrations ceased as the hum died out. He checked a few things, then growled as he saw that their acceleration had stopped entirely.

"Crown, you okay? Ship just started coasting again."

"Roger, Tyke, I noticed. Give me a minute."

"You don't have too many of those left, boss."

"Don't I know it. Hold on, I'll get back to you."

Steph tapped the ship's controls, bringing up access to the onboard communications system and opening a channel.

"Engineering, this is the bridge."

He gave them a few seconds before signalling again.

"Engineering, this is the bridge. If you want to live, I suggest you talk to me before I send my men down there to have a chat with you."

Someone quickly got on the line.

"What do you want?"

The speaker was understandably a little snippy, but Steph didn't have time to put up with attitude.

"I want to make sure that the Imperial Fleet on our tail doesn't catch us," Steph replied. "And to do that I need you to do your job. If you can't, tell me now and I'll call my ship back and get the hell out of here. You can take your chances with the Empire."

There was a pause, stretching out the seconds before the voice responded at all.

"Imperial Fleet . . ." the speaker said, like he was half shocked and half remembering something. Steph snorted at the stricken tone the voice took on, irritated by the lost time.

"You heard me, now and earlier when I told everyone on this bucket what was coming. Now make your decision. I'm fine with leaving you to their mercies if that's what you want. I'm a big fan of freedom of choice, so make yours now."

There was a long, drawn-out silence before the voice finally came back.

"What do you need?"

"Stop playing games with me, do your job, and give me engine power *back*! After that, well, we're flying blinded up here while getting our navigation data from my ship. That's enough of a disadvantage as it is, so get the drives to full efficiency, and do it *now*."

"How do we know you're telling us the truth?"

Steph grimaced, growling under his breath before he responded.

"Do you really care?" he asked.

"W-what?"

"I asked, do you really *care* if I'm being honest?" he demanded of the voice. "You lost the battle, either way. Your ship is crippled, your squadron left you for dead. Do you honestly give a *damn* if I'm telling you the truth? What's really on your mind?"

Steph held his breath, knowing he was gambling.

On any Earth ship, or Priminae ship, or hell, even an Empire ship, he'd not have asked that. He'd have led with the Marines and taken solid control of engineering from the start.

If he were wrong about the status of the crew . . .

"How do we know you won't just kill us after we help you?"

Steph let out a soft breath, closing his eyes.

"You don't," he answered honestly, "but we don't have time for that sort of proof. I'll give my word right now: If you help me help you, if you follow my orders, then you're *my* men. And I don't leave my men to die."

He took a deep breath.

"Make your decision. All our lives are in your hands," he said.

He killed the comm channel and pushed for more acceleration as the ship's drives lay silent, hoping that the engineering crew would do what needed to be done. Seconds ticked off, each feeling like *hours*, and then suddenly the power surged and the ship leapt forward again. Steph breathed a sigh of relief before opening a ship-wide broadcast that included the Marines over his armor comm.

"Alright, we're moving. Hold on tight, because the Imperial Fleet has a big lead on us in speed. We're going to have to redline this baby or they're going to catch us. I don't think I need to tell anyone what happens if they do, now, do I?"

Silence was the only answer.

Archangel Two

"About damn time!" Black swore as she pushed the throttle of her fighter-gunboat forward, matching pace with the captured destroyer.

The acceleration curve started to back off from the danger zone it had been in, but as everything settled out she grimaced.

It's not enough. They're going to be able to close to engagement range at this rate.

"Archangel Actual, *Archangel Two*."

"Go for Actual," Steph's voice came back.

"You need to push that heap harder," Alex said. "The Imps are gaining on you, and you're just not putting enough kick in your pants to open the range."

"Tell me something I don't know. This heap needs a tuning, pronto. They've just let the poor baby rust from the inside out. I swear some people don't deserve nice things."

"It ain't nice enough to lose your life for, Steph."

"I'm too good-looking to die, Alex," Steph responded.

"Too damn stupid to know you're dead is more like it," she yelled in response.

She was getting really sick of hearing his laughter over the comms.

Baphon

Steph checked the numbers he was getting on the relay from *Archangel One*, grimacing despite his cheerful tone. They weren't great. The destroyer's acceleration was considerably lower than he had expected, and it didn't look like they'd be able to get clear of the fleet's beams before they were brought into effective engagement range.

He was also trying to fly a frigging *destroyer* through a combat HUD and a second set of eyes pacing from a quarter million kilometers away.

Frankly, it was making him dizzy and giving him a migraine.

He opened a comm to the Marines.

"Guys, it's not looking as good as I'd hoped," he said. "I'm not ready to give this up just yet, but I want you all back on the *Revenge*. No sense risking you here. I can deal with these people."

Buckler spoke up.

"Begging the officer's pardon, sir, but don't pull that self-sacrifice bullshit with us. We'll offload when you do."

"Goddamn it, you dumb leathernecks, I'm giving you an order," he growled. "There is no damn reason for you to be here right now."

"An order, you say?" Buckler asked, amused. "A good Marine would have to follow that, I suppose."

"You're damn right! Now, get off my ship."

"Too bad I don't see any Marines here, sir. Just us pirates. Har har."

Steph swore, earning him nothing but laughter from the Marines.

"Fine. Make yourselves useful, then. Check the prisoners, see if any of them can tune the drives. And someone get up here with me—I need a copilot."

That caught them up short, and it was several moments before the Marines stopped uncomfortably looking at each other and one of them reluctantly stepped forward. Steph barely seemed to notice as the Marine stepped up to the helm.

"You ever fly anything before?" Steph asked, not looking over at the man.

"Nothing bigger than a bush plane."

"Huh," Steph said. "Better than I expected. Okay, I'm sending you new codes for your HUD. Get them installed and active, then we'll see if you can fly this heap like a puddle jumper."

"Yes sir," the Marine said, sounding sick.

Steph glanced aside briefly. "What's your name?"

He could have looked up the man's IFF tag on his HUD, but right now it was busy doing something more important, and frankly, Steph preferred to ask the question face-to-face—or as close as he could manage.

"Corporal Harris, sir."

"Alright, Harris, relax. You'll do fine. There's not a lot to hit out here, and I'll handle any fancy flying," Steph said reassuringly. "I just need you to monitor flight telemetry when I'm busy with other stuff."

"Yes sir, got it," Harris said. "New program is up and running. I think I've got it."

"Good. See the acceleration curve in the top right?" Steph asked.

"Yes sir."

"Okay, we want to keep that in the green."

"Um . . . sir, it's in the red."

Steph laughed mirthlessly. "I know."

"Oh." Harris swallowed. "So how do we . . . ?"

"I'll let you know when I figure it out," Steph said as he reverted his HUD to normal settings and stepped back from the helm.

He glanced at the wounded officer on the ground. "How is he?"

The corpsman looked in his direction. "About as good as can be expected, given you shot him with a cannon."

"He shouldn't have brought a pea shooter to a gunfight. I take it he's not going to be of much use for a while?"

"Not if you want him to live for longer than a few minutes," she said with a shake of her armored head. "He's not going anywhere. Maybe I can wake him up if you want to ask questions."

"No, leave him," Steph said, looking around the room. He recognized one of the crewmen. "Hey Derri!"

The young man who'd helped put the consoles back in place looked up fearfully. "Y-yes Commander?"

"What's your job on ship?" Steph asked.

"Technical maintenance," Derri responded. "Primarily replacing fiber lines."

"Big job?"

"It has been," Derri said, eyes wary as he looked for the point of the questions. "The fiber overloads easily, especially when the systems aren't properly aligned."

Steph glanced around. "I'm guessing not much on this baby is aligned properly these days from the sound and feel of her."

Derri shook his head. "No, there's little time or resources available for ships in the repair slips. We are . . . some time overdue for repairs and slip maintenance."

Steph had no trouble believing that, though he was mildly surprised the vessel's state was as bad as it appeared. The Kingdom destroyers had shown similar signs, possibly a little worse, but Steph had put that down to the smaller polity being more hard-pressed.

Now we have two data points. He thought about the situation. *I wonder if we'll find it much the same through the entire region?*

He was becoming more convinced that was exactly what they would find, in fact. The interference of the Empire showed that they were not content to merely leave the region to its own devices. They were actively keeping the conflict burning, if he had to make a guess.

He expected the Empire was probably funding competing sides of the conflict. Pushing them to kill each other, keeping them from noticing that Imperial forces were likely stripping the region of anything of value.

I wonder how many of the locals even know the game is being played, and how many just take the Empire's dime when offered without questioning what the real price of their largesse is?

He sighed, gesturing to the Belj crewman.

"Come on, Derri, walk with me."

Steph started moving, not looking back as Derri looked around in confusion for a moment before scrambling to catch up. He smirked as he noticed a pair of Marines quietly dispatched to follow him by a subtle signal from Buckler, who was watching the scene out of one eye from where he was, trying to get some of the damage cleared so more could be repaired. The sergeant apparently didn't trust his commander not to do something stupid and get himself killed.

Smart man, Steph thought as he continued on without pause.

"Where are we going?" Derri asked fearfully.

"Engineering."

"What?"

"But first we have a stop to make," Steph said as he opened his comm. "*Archangel One*, Archangel Actual."

Behind him, but visible on his armor's command system, the two Marines glanced at each other, then quickly called for two more as they followed the commander out the door.

Imperial Third Fleet

"Enemy destroyer is under power, Fleet Commander."

Jesan frowned, walking over to the display as he did.

"Their acceleration is still low," he noted. "Are we on track to intercept?"

"Yes, Fleet Commander," his second confirmed. "As long as they don't increase acceleration much more we will intercept in just over an hour and should be able to maintain engagement with the destroyer, at least, for no less than twenty minutes."

More than enough time to see it obliterated.

He still wondered what value the enemy saw in that antiquated vessel, but for the moment it didn't matter. If he got a chance, he might ask them, but frankly he wasn't likely to get that chance, as his mission profile didn't call for such things.

For the moment, unfortunately, he really didn't have anything he could do or say. They were under the maximum acceleration permitted him by Imperial law, and given his current status with the empress, Jesan was not inclined to flout the law at the moment.

He could only watch—and wait.

Baphon

Milla nervously crossed the threshold that lay invisibly between the Archangel fighter-gunboat and the destroyer, the press of gravity changing as she transitioned from one field to the next with the practiced gait of a career spacer.

She instantly noted that the *Baphon* field was not properly aligned, however, the slight pitch of the deck making her feel like she was just barely standing on an incline. It was an irritating and slightly dizzying sensation that the young woman fought to push from her mind as she walked forward to meet the figures waiting her arrival.

"Stephan." She nodded to the commander. "I believe I can tell why you called for me already."

"That obvious?"

"If the rest of the ship is in as good a shape as the gravity, I am more surprised that we are still intact with every passing second. Let us go to the engineering section, no?"

"Yes." Steph gestured. "This way. Derri here is one of the maintenance crew. He knows the way."

"Excellent." She nodded to the unarmored man. "Please."

"O-oh, uh, right this way."

Milla and Steph fell into place behind him, their Marine escort taking positions on either side of Derri and behind the two commanders as they moved.

––––––––

Engineering was about as Steph imagined it, much to his disgust.

"Jesus, did they *ever* keep up maintenance on this thing?" he asked as they entered, the Marines leading the way and quickly locking down the immediate area as Steph and Milla both looked around the interior of the destroyer's reactor room.

The fact that they were in space was likely the only reason everything wasn't rusted, from what he could see, and Steph was making some personal bets that a lot of the systems exposed to space were likely seized via vacuum welding despite the lack of air to oxidize parts.

"This is too much of a job, Stephan," Milla said, shaking her head. "It will take *weeks* to put right, longer without proper infrastructure."

"Just get the warps aligned." Steph tried not to sound like he was begging. "We need the power."

She sighed. "I will do as I can."

Milla tossed her kit bag to the deck, eyes sweeping the floor as she took in the various uniformed men who were trying to hide from the gaze of the Marines and their weapons.

"Who is in charge here?" she asked.

After a moment, Steph growled.

"I'm getting real tired of being forced to repeat questions," he ground out. "The lady asked a question."

A man nervously rose up. "I am?"

Steph sighed, shaking his head. "Better, but still the wrong answer. Who is in charge here?"

The man looked confused before offering. "You are?"

"She is." He pointed to Milla. "We have an Imperial Fleet chasing us, and if she can't get the drives back in alignment, we're not going to make it. So you are going to do what she says or we're going to have a little *discussion*."

"She is in charge," the man said fearfully.

"Good." Steph turned to the Marines as Milla got to work, shifting to a private tactical channel. "Not a scratch on her, right Marine?"

"Oorah, Commander."

"I'm going back to the bridge. You four stay here, watch her back. I'll be fine."

The Marines nodded reluctantly, though they did radio ahead to the bridge before Steph was out of the room.

———

Milla was grumbling under her breath, already crawling over various bits of machinery and calling out orders and questions.

"What stores are available on board?" she demanded as she examined a coupler that looked like it should have fallen off sometime a decade or so earlier.

"We have a database here, but there is not much," the man who'd spoken with Steph said reluctantly.

Milla dropped down and checked the system she was directed to.

"This is what you've been working with?" she asked incredulously, looking over her shoulder at the men who just nodded with wide eyes. "I'm impressed. This ship should have fallen apart years ago. You have done wonders with what you have had available."

They appeared surprised, exchanging glances.

"Unfortunately, this will not do for the immediate circumstances," she went on. "We will have to get more creative. Thankfully, you all appear well used to that. Let us get to work."

Archangel Three

The six Archangels were pacing the accelerating destroyer, flying in fairly tight formation as they kept close to the ship the squadron commander was on, none of the pilots particularly happy about the situation.

Jennifer had known Steph for several years by this point and thought she understood the man well enough, but his decision to try to save the ship was beyond her. The crew she could understand, despite them being enemies just a few hours earlier. Leaving men to be killed in cold blood didn't sit well with her either, but saving the destroyer puzzled her.

For a fighter jock, the boss sure seems to spend a lot of time in bigger ships these days, she thought with some amusement.

She took a moment to examine the telemetry data, judging the rate of overtake by the Imperial Fleet, and mentally shivered. There was nothing they could do against that much firepower.

They'll be in engagement range soon. I hope Steph has a plan.

Baphon

It's creepy how quiet the corridors of the ship are, Steph decided as he stepped back into the bridge.

He'd barely encountered anyone on the way back from the reactor room, and those he did were quick to get out of his way, scattering like he was firing wildly with each step or some other equally ridiculous situation.

What struck him as more odd, honestly, was that they were so clearly practiced at getting out of the way of someone walking the halls of the ship.

"Where are we?" he asked, pushing the observation from his mind as he examined the state of affairs on the bridge by eye.

"Sir," Harris answered immediately. "Still in the red, sir."

"That's not a surprise," Steph said as he walked over to the helm and brought up the augmented view in his HUD with data supplied from the Archangels surrounding them. "We're not going to outrun them like this. Let's hope Milla can work some magic in the reactor and warp generators."

"And if she can't?" the Marine asked.

"Well, we have a few options," Steph said as he examined the composition of the system they were flying within.

They were currently on a downward trajectory, aiming to cut through the inner system before climbing out of the stellar gravity on the other side of the system from the Imperial's approach. Steph ran a few numbers in his head, deciding that was still the optimal plan, but he had a few tweaks to add.

"Archangel squadron, Archangel Actual," he said. "Be aware, I am adjusting course. Stand by for operational orders."

"What are you doing?"

"Bringing us a little closer to the gas giant whose orbit we're crossing," Steph said.

Harris blinked. "Are you aiming for a—what do they call it—a gravity assist?"

"Not specifically, no, though I'm not above giving it a shot," Steph responded. "For one thing, even if we made it work for us, the enemy would just follow us through. Wouldn't gain us much, I'm afraid. I mostly just want some cover and a distraction, and those moons and rings should do the job."

"Yes sir, if you say so."

"Relax. They don't have us yet." Steph grinned. "This is where things get *fun*."

"Sir, that's what I'm scared of."

Chapter 20

Imperial Third Fleet

"Enemy vessels are closing on the orbit of the gas giant, Fleet Commander."

"Follow them in," Jesan ordered, now paying full attention as the pursuit was entering its last legs.

His fleet's lead elements were almost within engagement range, and he'd ordered them to fire as soon as they had even a partial lock on the enemy vessels. For the moment, they were all aiming for the destroyer, simply because the smaller ships were considerably more difficult to target at range.

They would have to get much closer for those.

They are rather difficult to properly scan, he noted.

The power curves were visible, however, so they had a reasonable location for each within a certain margin of error; it was just too large a margin for precision targeting at special ranges.

"Lead vessels have opened fire, Fleet Commander."

"Finally," Jesan grumbled. "Show the telemetry."

An augmented view of the fleet came up on the main display, showing a beam emerging from three of the vanguard ships and moving slowly across the intervening space toward where the enemy destroyer was entering the gravity well of the gas giant.

An odd choice, ducking in closer to a significant gravity well, Jesan thought. They were limiting their own acceleration, or risking the collapse of their space-warp, not to mention picking up a massive amount of debris if the warp didn't collapse.

He cringed involuntarily at the thought of what would happen to a ship moving at that velocity through the planetary rings of dust and debris if its space-warp collapsed.

It would save us the power required to destroy them, I suppose.

"They have to cut power soon," his sub-commander said, also examining the telemetry.

"Perhaps." Jesan wasn't so certain.

"You do not believe so?"

"Desperation makes fools of wise men." He laughed mirthlessly. "And those Belj fools were not wise men at the best of times."

The sub-commander snorted. "As you say, Fleet Commander."

The beam had crossed half the distance while they talked, but something else had occurred as well.

"They've accelerated," the sub-commander said, surprised.

"What?" Jesan shifted his focus, noting that the destroyer had, indeed, *increased* power to the drives. He scoffed, shaking his head. "Fools indeed."

Baphou

Steph was amused to note that everyone around him was calm as the ship dove through the rings of the gas giant, warping space at higher and higher rates as they came into the planet incredibly steeply. Of course, that calm demeanor was because no one who might understand what he was doing had any idea he was doing it.

The Marines all had access to the ship's telemetry, but even Harris beside him had *no clue* just how dangerous the current maneuver was.

The destroyer was angled down into the planet, warping space ever more efficiently as Milla's work began to pay off. They were likewise being pulled into the planet by the gravity of the massive super-Jupiter, increasing their speed marginally by both the direct force of gravity and by the motion of the planet as it traveled around the local star.

"Milla, I'm going to need a custom warp geometry in a few minutes," he said measuredly, hoping not to alert her as the only person on the ship with both access to what he could see *and* the knowledge to recognize how crazy the stunt was.

"Are you out of your mind, Stephan?" The frustrated woman's accent was more pronounced under the pressure of the moment. "This is not the *Odysseus*, or even one of my Archangels. I cannot predict how this ship will react to such a change."

"Doesn't matter. I need it done. I'm sending you the specifications," he said, shooting off the details.

After he'd sent them, Steph knew instantly that he'd made a mistake. Alright, perhaps the word "mistake" was a bit much, since drastic action was necessary, but there was no way she wouldn't recognize what he'd sent.

Three . . . two . . . one . . .

"Stephan! Are you *insane*?! Why are we diving into the gas giant's upper atmosphere?!"

He was about to answer when an explosion behind the destroyer caused him to shift his focus. "Archangels, what the hell was that?"

Cardsharp came back a moment later. "Imperial laser just nailed the debris ring, burned up a hell of a lot of dust on your six, boss. Just FYI, I think you're in their range now."

"Yeah, got that. Alright, I need eyes close but not *too* close. You'll be harder to target. Don't go taking a shot meant for us."

"We haven't planned it, boss. Good luck."

Steph grinned, swapping over to Milla's channel. "Does that answer your question? We need time, and I'm going to buy it. Now, get me those custom geometries pronto, Milla!"

Her inarticulate barrage of frustration was all he heard before the channel went dead, causing him to grin widely as he adjusted the ship's vectors while they slipped past the super-Jupiter's magnetosphere and entered into the extreme edge of the planet's atmosphere.

"Sir?"

"What is it, Harris?" Steph asked, not glancing aside.

"I'm no expert, I know, but is a warp ship *supposed* to be this close to a large gravity source while under power?" the Marine asked.

"Nope."

"Okay, that's what I thought."

Apparently satisfied that his boss either knew what he was doing or was completely crazy, the Marine fell silent, seemingly fine with either outcome. Steph grinned.

He'd practically grown up with Marines, thanks to Eric, but had never actually signed up himself. The situation during the war got so desperate for a while that it just wasn't a good use of his time to bother with basic training or even the more advanced versions. He knew how to fly, and the newly born Confederation *needed* pilots in a desperate way, so he was dropped right into the cockpit with Eric as his wingman.

By the time the war was over, the idea that he might need to sign up with *any* unit never crossed his mind. He was an Archangel. No other unit could compare in his eyes.

Still, there were times when he just absolutely *loved* the almost-fatalistic loyalty inherent in Marines.

"Everyone, hang on," he said aloud. "It's about to get rough."

———

Evan Currie

Imperial Third Fleet

Jesan nodded in appreciation as he saw the maneuver for what it was.

"They are increasing their immediate acceleration while putting the planet and rings between us," he said. "Not entirely unimpressive, though the risk is rather extreme, I must say."

"Not compared to being caught by us," his sub-commander said quietly, a *hint* of grudging admiration in his tone.

"Truth," Jesan admitted.

He examined the telemetry, then gestured to the display. "Split the fleet around the planet. We'll intercept as they emerge."

"As you order, Fleet Commander."

Jesan didn't care how impressive the maneuver was, he wasn't taking his fleet into *that* mess.

"Commander, are they doing what I think they're doing?" the sub-commander asked, his head tilting slightly as he stared in shock at the display.

Jesan looked closer, blinking in shock as well.

The destroyer was turning over as it dove, going into the upper atmosphere of the planet, *inverted*, deep enough that on the Third Fleet's scans they could see the friction burn beginning despite the warping of space still being easily detectable.

"The commander of that ship is certifiably *insane*," Jesan said firmly.

His sub-commander had no inclination whatsoever to argue.

Archangel Two

The Belj destroyer *Baphon* continued to dive through the upper ionosphere of the gas giant, its warp field shimmering as it sucked up charged particles at dangerous rates. The ship was quickly masked from the visual scans of the trailing Archangels as the heat friction and charged particles combined to create a blast field that was all but entirely opaque.

Normally that field would have blinded the ship as well, making its pilot guess at tiny details like altitude and whether or not they were about to crash into something, but since the *Baphon* had been blind before the dive, little had changed on board.

Archangel Two skipped over the atmosphere, keeping under the rings of the planet as it accelerated to catch up with the *Baphon's* emergence point, continuously transmitting telemetry data on high-powered direct beam signals to the ship.

———

Alexandra Black shook her head as she noted the changes in the acceleration of the destroyer, amazed it was holding together. She was quite certain that, short of possibly Eric Weston, there wasn't a captain in the Terran forces who'd take a new cruiser in perfect shape through a maneuver like she was seeing, let alone a battered old destroyer whose best days were *long* past.

"Goddamn him if he isn't making it work," she said over the tactical link with the other pilots.

"That is the most annoying thing about him, Noire," Tyke said.

A flash of light made both of them flinch as another laser burst was wasted on the planet's rings.

"They're getting persistent," Cardsharp noted. "And closer."

"Too close," Black said. "We're cutting this whole thing too damn close. What the hell is he thinking?"

"He's getting into the cover," Tyke answered. "Maybe a little too much, maybe not. We'll be better able to evaluate after we get out of this."

"You mean *if* we get out of it?" Black asked dryly.

"Crown is Double A," Tyke said firmly. "We don't stop, we don't give up. Get used to it, Noire, you're in the family now."

"Why do you call him Crown, anyway?" Cardsharp interjected into the silence.

"That's his call sign."

"I thought it was Stephanos? Was that prick lying to us this whole time?" she demanded, irritated.

Tyke laughed. "He just doesn't like the story of how he got named. Stephanos is ancient Greek for, well, crown."

Sensing a story, Cardsharp's tone turned eager. "What's not to like about the call sign Crown?"

"I'll tell you later, when the boss is around to hear it, but you're assuming he got the name based on the royal symbol. Don't."

———

Baphon

Steph grimaced as the ship shook around him, the temperatures registering on board beginning to spike, and generally everything starting to feel like it was going to fall apart at any moment.

Why do I feel a chill down my spine while I'm sweating like a pig? he wondered absently as he kept making course corrections based on his best guess of the ship's location, as interpreted from the ball of *fire* that the Archangels could see that marked the *Baphon*'s passage through the atmosphere.

Everyone had an idea that something wasn't quite right at this point, but Steph ignored all of them as he worked.

"Milla, I need those new geometries," he gritted out.

"Stephan, with all respect," she screamed in his ear, "if you want a miracle, come down here and *do it yourself!*"

"Hard pass, bit busy up here."

"Yes, I am aware of what you are busy doing, you madman!"

"If this is going to work, we *need* those changes, Milla. No rush, though."

"Shut up and let me work!"

———

Milla snarled as she unsealed her helmet and angrily tossed the hardened shell aside, letting it clatter to the deck as she got back to work.

"Lieutenant Commander!"

One of the Marines had turned, blurting at her in shock.

"It was distracting me from my work," she growled, furiously working on the equipment.

"Ma'am, you should keep your helmet on." The Marine quickly surveyed the room for threats.

Milla snorted. "If any of them wish to die, they may shoot me in the head *now*. It will save me a great deal of pain if I fail, I suspect."

Not having an answer to that, the Marine fell silent as Milla continued to work. Beads of sweat formed on her forehead, where she was no longer protected by the climate-controlled system of the armor. But she ignored the discomfort as she set a new series of coded commands into the ship's reactor control.

"The commander, he is insane," she said, her tone almost conversational in nature. "You know that, right?"

The Marine shrugged in his armor. "Good combat commanders usually are, to one degree or another."

"You people never cease to intrigue me," she said, entering the last few commands. "Infuriate me as well, of course, but intrigue nonetheless."

With something of a flourish she entered the last command and executed the code, turning to the local crew who were struggling to keep the entire system from flying apart under the stresses they were flying through.

"Ready yourselves," Milla ordered. "Expect surges and new stressors. We need to keep the strain on the systems from blowing out anything until we get clear of the Imperial Fleet!"

Then she grabbed her helmet, not putting it back on but bringing it close enough to speak into.

"Stephan, changes implemented!"

———

"Grab on to something!" Steph ordered as he sent the ship deeper into the atmosphere of the gas giant, plunging through the ionosphere into the upper thermosphere.

The shaking of the *Baphon* intensified around them as the ship's space-time warp couldn't deal with the added stresses and began to transmit more and more of the forces into its hull.

"External heat is reaching dangerous levels," one of the crew called out from across the command deck.

Steph didn't know who it was, and didn't bother turning to see. He knew what the stresses were, far better than anyone else at the moment. The bow shock ahead of the ship was actually limiting the worst of the effects, but the heat and pressure were increasing as the *Baphon* plunged ever deeper.

Milla's alterations to the warping of space around them were coming into play, however, as the atmosphere thickened and the warp field began to have something to bite into.

He remembered pulling a similar move in his Archangel, near the end of the war. They'd been pushing the limits so much in those days, becoming legends in their own times—and in their own minds. He grinned as the ship began to shudder violently around him, as Steph took her down into the atmosphere of the gas giant, knowing they were trailing fire for a thousand kilometers in their wake.

Some days, I love my job.

Chapter 21

Archangel One

"Holy shit."

Tyke's whispered words were almost reverent as he watched the destroyer plunge through the atmosphere of the gas giant, accelerating the whole while as it used the bow shock of the space-warp to lower friction and increase the efficiency of the gravity assist the commander was running.

He didn't know if the maneuver was going to work, but it sure was spectacular.

The destroyer was trailing a wake of flames across the face of the planet. If it were a habitable world, he was sure it would be one hell of a show from the surface. As it was, it was a heck of a show from space.

Mind you, the light show above isn't half bad either.

He turned his head, looking at the augmented view through the holographic cockpit view around him as another laser bloom vaporized more dirt and dust in the rings above them while they passed close to the edge of the planet's atmosphere.

"Imps seem to be getting aggravated," Cardsharp said.

"Don't believe it," Noire cut in. "They've split their fleet, going around the planet. The light show is mostly just distraction, though I'm sure they wouldn't cry too hard if they got in a lucky shot."

"What, you're telling me that the Empire isn't stupid enough to take their cruisers into a steep gravity well while under hard warp? Shocking, I said, just shocking," Tyke responded. "It's almost like they want to keep their ships intact rather than risk blowing out their generators and crashing headlong into a gas giant."

The Archangels were skimming the upper atmosphere, their smaller mass making it far safer to warp space deeper in a gravity field, arcing around the face of the planet where they hoped to meet the boss' ship as it came out the other side.

The destroyer was running on ballistic calculations now, the interference having finally cut them off from their limited comms and with it access to the navigation computers on the Archangels, so there was nothing left to do but wait.

———

Baphon

"Good news," Steph said cheerfully. "The warp geometry Milla put together is holding up. We're probably not going to burn up in the atmosphere."

"Why does this sound like a good news/bad news situation, and you're holding back the bad news?" Harris asked dryly from beside him.

"Well, the slightest mistake now *will* send us plunging into the planet to be crushed into a small ball . . ."

"That would be the bad news, I take it?"

"No, that's *great* news," Steph told him.

Harris winced. "I'm going to regret asking this, but how is that great news?"

"Come on, Marine, what are the odds that *I* make a mistake?"

"Oh Christ, Sarge! We're all going to die!"

"Suck it up, Harris," Buckler growled, holding on to a rail as the ship shook around him. "At least if we go, we get to tell this bastard we told you so for the rest of eternity."

"That is *never* going to happen," Steph growled, a chill creeping up his spine at the thought of spending eternity with a bunch of pissed-off Marines.

Trust Marines to take all the fun out of this, he thought in annoyance as he opened a comm to Milla. "I'm going to need every bit of power you can give me."

"It is yours, try not to kill us with it."

"What is it with everyone doubting me all of a sudden?" Steph complained.

"Who said it was sudden?" Harris asked.

"Oh shut up, Marine," Steph said, putting all the power he could to the warp drive.

The shudders of the ship increased, and anything remotely loose clattering around them as dust and dirt from years past began to drift from every crevice. That continued for a few seconds before a sudden bang rang through the ship, and they were all thrown heavily into the air before the destroyer's gravity yanked them back down in heaps all over the deck.

"What the hell was that?!" Buckler demanded from where he was lying with his feet tangled in the rail over his head.

"We just skipped off the lower atmosphere," Steph said gleefully, as he was the only man in the room who managed to keep his feet. "Don't worry, I planned that!"

"With all respect, sir," the master sergeant growled out, "that's what worries me!"

Archangel Three

"Ow." Cardsharp winced as they watched the destroyer skip off the lower atmosphere of the planet hard enough that it shook its fireball for a moment and once more became visible before being engulfed again.

"Brilliant," Noire whispered over the communications line. "Assuming he doesn't get himself killed, of course."

"You know what the hell just happened, Noire?" Tyke asked, curiously.

"He must have used the ship's warping of space-time as an inverse aerofoil," she answered. "They briefly dug into the lower atmosphere, but skipped out of it to redirect the destroyer back into space. It let him keep far more of his velocity than a traditional escape vector. The maneuver is called an aerogravity assist, but I don't think anyone has ever thought to do it without a specially designed vehicle."

Noire paused, considering. "Usually an *unmanned* vehicle, if I'm being honest about it."

Tyke groaned, "Why does this not surprise me?"

"I can confirm, he's gained a lot of speed and isn't losing it as fast as expected," Cardsharp cut in as she checked the telemetry. "The destroyer is climbing out of the atmosphere and will be ahead of us unless we pick up the pace."

"Let's not keep him waiting," Tyke said, putting more power to his own drive.

"Roger that," Noire said as she and the rest increased their own warps to match, racing the fiery destroyer around the curve of the planet as they watched to see it climbing out of the atmosphere, a falling star in reverse.

Imperial Third Fleet

"We've lost contact. They've crossed the terminator of the planet. We will pick them up again momentarily," the sub-commander said as the telemetry scans they were watching went dead.

Jesan merely nodded. He knew what had happened. The enemy captain was not one he would care to meet in battle on even odds, he decided. Insanity in one's enemies was *not* a desirable situation to find oneself dealing with.

He had already faced that situation in the near past and had zero inclination to seek it out again.

It was, however, amusing and slightly exciting to observe in a completely outclassed foe. Jesan almost felt like cheering for the unknown captain. He had provided some rather impressive entertainment. They had even made the display available to the crews of the Third Fleet simply to raise morale.

May not even be a bad idea to simply let them go, Jesan thought. The destroyer at least, if he could manage to force the smaller vessels into an engagement. The crew would likely enjoy letting this one escape, if only to hunt the captain down another time to see if he could offer up as much entertainment again.

He would not do that, however. As amusing as the thought might be, he could not afford it under his current status with the Imperial House. Any sense of failure might be enough to see him, and his crew, censured.

In the Empire, some censures only happened once.

"Increase closing velocity," he growled.

"Commander," his second replied. "We are at the edge of allowable military—"

"Noted. Increase closing velocity."

Baphon

The *Baphon* exploded back into space, shedding flames and shimmering electrical cascades as the ionized particles were sequestered deep in the trough of the forward space-warp while others were expelled from the rear crest.

The ship plowed through the rings at high speed as the interference began to clear and Steph was once more able to check his telemetry against the information from the Archangels.

"So far so good," he said. "Nice of you lot to catch up. What kept you?"

The six gleaming fighter-gunboats dropped into formation from the rear, matching his new velocity and acceleration as the ship was now climbing hard out of the stellar gravity well with as much power behind it as the reactor room could manage.

"Watch it, smart guy," Noire answered. "None of us felt the need to light our butts on fire to get in the mood to run."

"Whatever works, Noire," Steph said, checking the Archangel scans for the Imperial Fleet. "Where are the Imps, anyway?"

"Coming around the planet," Tyke answered. "Seems that they weren't interested in following you down into a suicide run."

"Some people—just no adventure in their souls."

"Is that what you call it?" Cardsharp asked. "I thought it was shit in your brains."

"Is that really how you talk to your CO?" Steph complained.

"Yes!"

"I swear, I get no respect."

An alarm over the network cut off any reply the others might have had.

"Imperials just rejoined the party," Cardsharp said. "And they're looking to rock. Lasers are bracketing our position. They're going to get our range soon. How is the accel curve looking there, boss?"

"Well, we're not in the red anymore," Steph said. "But we're far from the green. They're going to have several minutes where they might just be able to get a hit."

"Well, fuck."

"Nothing much to do about it, I'm out of brilliant—"

"Lucky!"

"*Brilliant*," Steph stressed, "maneuvers. Just have to ride this one out and hope for the best now."

"Hoping for the best rarely seems to work in a combat situation, Steph," Cardsharp said seriously.

"Don't I know it," Steph responded wearily. "You have your orders."

"Roger that."

―――――

Imperial Third Fleet

"They survived," Jesan said, a little surprised.

His sub-commander hissed softly. "More than that, they're pulling away. We will only have a few minutes to engage at extreme range now."

Jesan shrugged. "Good training for the beam crews. Inform them to go to constant fire as quickly as the beams will charge."

"On your order, Fleet Commander."

Jesan nodded absently, eyes on the small dots that depicted the enemy ships. The fleet had lost time splitting around the planet compared to those that had plunged in close to the gravity well—enough to lose their quarry in a short period, but it was better than losing several of his vessels.

He heard the whine-click of his flagship firing along with the rest of the fleet, a barrage of beams showing on the displays as they calculated their passage through the intervening space.

His eyes remained on the visual scans, however, since Jesan was aware that the first sign of a strike would be a flash of visible light in the darkness.

Baphon

Milla wiped her brow, cleaning the sweat away as she slumped against the closest wall. She pulled the armored helmet over her head. Now that the work was done, she wanted to see what she had succeeded in doing.

What she found was that they were back in the void, climbing hard for interstellar space, with the Imperials still in pursuit but far enough behind that the *Baphon*'s crew now had a chance at survival.

Catching the tail end of Stephan's conversation with his fellow pilots was a little disheartening, however, as he seemed to be willing now to settle for the luck of the draw. She somehow felt wrong about that. Milla secured her helmet, linking into the telemetry from the Archangels, and mentally reviewed what she knew of their capacities.

She was hesitant to offer the idea that came to her mind. It seemed insane to her. However, after what they had just done . . .

"Stephan," she said hesitatingly. "I believe I have an idea."

"Wow."

"That's all you have to say?" Cardsharp demanded of Steph after they'd listened to Milla's suggestion. "You've obviously driven that poor girl as crazy as you are! I swear to God, Stephanos, you need a padded room and a nanny."

"I am sorry?" Milla said into the conversation. "I did not mean . . ."

"Don't apologize," Steph said. "I *love* it!"

"Of course you do," Cardsharp said, resigned.

"Thing is, I don't know if any of the others are pilots enough to pull it off," he went on as though she hadn't spoken.

"Hey," Alex growled, cutting in. "Don't think I don't know what you're doing there, Steph."

"Are you saying it's not working?"

The pilot of *Archangel Two* sighed deeply. "You know damn well it's working."

"Excellent," Steph said, his tone smug. "So I say we go with Milla's insane plan this time. Only pilots good enough to pull it off say aye."

"Aye," the six Archangel pilots ground out, some sounding like he was pulling teeth.

Genuine music to Stephanos' ears.

Chapter 22

Imperial Third Fleet

Jesan watched as the numbers slowly began to diverge again, the enemy ships now making up the disadvantage they'd earned early on when his fleet had been accelerating while they remained on a ballistic course. Shortly, he knew, they would be out of range entirely and would escape him.

It wasn't a critical miss on his part, but there was a frustrating element there just the same.

He would, he decided, loop back around once they were fully out of range, just to examine the disabled destroyers left behind, on the off chance that they had left something that might explain the actions of the unidentified ships. He didn't truly expect to find much, not without considerably more context than he had, but it would be required for his report.

The fleet was still firing and would continue to do so as they sought the range to the enemy ships. He expected to get a few solid strikes, simply by statistical averaging if nothing else, but at the extreme range they were dealing with, it would be easy for the enemy to evade the majority of the beams with only minor course changes.

Space was vast, and even a cruiser's beam had an infinitesimal focal diameter in comparison.

"Enemy vessels altering formation, Fleet Commander."

Jesan frowned, curious more than anything else. "Define that."

"Never seen anything like it. They're pushing into a *very* tight formation. Estimate cluster . . . Commander, they have to be overlapping their warp effects."

More and more curious, and reckless.

Jesan examined the formation on the display as the computers struggled to get scans clean enough to determine what in the abyss they were doing.

"Concentrate fire," he ordered. "They're grouped together, making our targeting easier."

"As you order, Fleet Commander."

What are they thinking?

It didn't matter, he supposed. They had just given his gunners the best opportunity yet, right as the vessels were about to escape.

Archangel One

Tyke cringed as he felt the gravity in the fighter-gunboat twist, trying to pluck him out of the secured control section of the deck. He was so close to the warp field of the destroyer that he could feel it through his interface, like a prickly sensation across his left side.

"Easy, easy," he said, mostly to himself though he was on the squadron channel as he murmured. "Don't think about how crazy this is . . ."

"Easy for you to say. I've been thinking of nothing else," Cardsharp responded, edging *Archangel Three* into position from the other side while Noire dropped in from the top. Archangels three through six were filling out the pattern on the ventral side of the destroyer, all seven ships overlapping their space-time warps as they did.

"Very good," Milla said over the network. "Bring the last ships into alignment . . . excellent. Hold position carefully. I will send calculations to each of you. We will need to synchronize our drive fields now."

"Roger that. It's your play, Milla," Steph said, tension thick in his voice as he struggled to control the destroyer without being able to see from the perspective of the warship itself. "The *Dutchman*'s drives are at your command."

"*Dutchman*? Really?" Alexandra complained.

"It's a good name," Steph protested.

"You are *such* a child."

"Fine, you can name the next prize we take," Steph countered.

"Next one? Why the hell did we take this one?"

"For the last time: We. Are. Pirates."

"Child," she repeated slowly, enunciating the word with precision and deliberation.

"You are all children," Milla cut in. "Now, please focus, or this will be the shortest maneuver any of you have ever attempted. *Bapho*—"

"*Dutchman!*"

She sighed. "Fine. *Dutchman* drive warps increasing. Set frequency, overlap gravity waves."

"Roger, Milla," Alexandra called for the team. "Drive warp oscillations rotating to match your frequency . . . We're showing wave cancellation here, losing acceleration."

"Rotate frequencies, slowly," Milla said. "I have sent each of you individual patterns to follow."

"Roger that. Archangels, initiate frequency rotation."

With six smaller ships forming tightly on the destroyer's aft section, their own drives overlapping with the space-time warp of the central vessel, the small convoy tore through space as it climbed for the edge of the local stars' gravity influence. Behind, a fleet of massively larger ships were still in pursuit, throwing everything imaginable at the fleeing vessels in an attempt to take at least a few of them out.

The overlapping gravity fields that warped space and time to provide propulsion for the ships operated largely like any other form of wave mechanics. At first, with the fields out of alignment, the interference largely canceled itself out or even negated the effectiveness of the drives, slowing their acceleration.

As the Archangels rotated their wave frequencies to match the destroyer's, however, the gravity waves began to reinforce one another, turning the crest of the wave behind the ships from a large source of power to a veritable rogue wave of gravity that surged in power and drove the seven ships ahead in a rush.

———

"Holy crap!" Steph screamed, hanging on to the console in front of him, desperately trying to keep the bow of the ship pointed in the right direction as the imbalance of forces attempted to steer the aft sections of the vessel ahead of the front.

An Alcubierre drive vessel, which the space-time warp designs were all in some manner related to, had often been compared to "surfing" waves through the universe. In theory, Steph had always understood that comparison, but in practice the process never really felt like that to him, and he had been known to do a little surfing in his time.

Under normal operation, an Alcubierre vessel was far more like a train running on tracks. You steered the ship by changing the tracks dynamically rather than by changing the point of travel the way you would in a conventional reaction craft. This was due to the balance of a space-warp, with a crest pushing the ship from behind and an equal but opposite trough for the vessel to "fall" into. To change directions, you shifted the vector of the crest and trough, and the ship would follow.

Steph was learning, however, that the surfing analogy wasn't as bad as he'd thought. When you massively unbalanced the rear "crest," things got . . . twitchy.

"I don't know if I can hold this damn thing," he warned, hugging the console as he fought the controls to keep the ship straight.

"What? Not *pilot* enough, Stephanos?" Noire said, her tone mocking.

Steph rolled his eyes. "You try steering this pig with this much power pushing you! Milla, are we holding together?"

———

Milla, in the engineering section, was in a similar position to that of Steph. Desperately gripping the console in front of her while everyone else around her had been thrown to the deck in the initial surge of power, she too was fighting the power imbalance generated by the synchronized space-warp to the rear of the ship.

"I believe so, Stephan," she gasped out, her stomach twisting around in her gut as the internal gravity seemed to *want* to shift, yet somehow didn't. "I am reading warp field increase of almost four times!"

"Great. Maybe we'll escape the Empire long enough to be splattered across the galaxy!" Steph responded.

A shudder ran through the ship, startling Milla, who looked around for what might have caused the disturbance.

"What was that?" Steph demanded.

"The Imperial Fleet is firing on us with everything they have."

———

Imperial Third Fleet

Jesan blinked in surprise as he watched the acceleration curve of the enemy ships suddenly increase.

"What is happening?" he demanded, looking around to similarly confused faces.

"I . . . I believe they're reinforcing the destroyer's drive warp with their own," a technician from one of the scanner pits said, sounding rather incredulous, as though he didn't believe what he was saying.

"Is that *possible?*" Jesan blurted.

"In concept? Yes. I have never heard of anyone *attempting* such, however," the technician said. "In order to even consider it, you would have to fly incredibly close. Closer than starships *ever* maneuver, Fleet Commander. The ranges would be practically touching hulls."

Jesan examined the data they were scanning, measuring it against the man's words.

They could be that close, he thought. The group's proximity was difficult to tell, however, because the interference from their drive warps directly from the rear made it nearly impossible to get clean scans.

"All beam stations are still firing?" he asked.

"Yes Fleet Commander, but there is something odd about that too," the same technician said, shaking his head as he bent over the console and stared at the data. "I . . . Fleet Commander, I believe we have their range and have been striking the target dead-on."

Jesan closed his eyes. "Then why are they still intact?"

Archangel One

Tyke flinched as the augmented display wrapped around him flashed with an aurora of light and crackling power that would have taken his breath away in the proverbial sense if he weren't afraid it was going to do so in the literal.

"I wish they'd *stop* that!" he growled, becoming more irritated than scared.

"The beams are being pushed aside by the gravity crest," Milla said. "Even what little makes it through has been attenuated enough to render the attack less than effective. We should be safe from the Imperial Fleet so long as we can maintain this formation."

"Pretty effective," Steph said, surprised.

He'd been aware that beams, and other weapons, were powerfully affected by the space-warping that larger vessels used for propulsion, but this was the first time they'd actually been able to *bend* lasers away from the target.

"Unfortunately," Milla spoke up, "this defense will only work while fleeing the enemy."

"Or decelerating into engagement range," Steph corrected. "This is a strong potential weapon, Milla, if we can make it work in a tactical scenario. We'll train on it. For now, however, how long until we're in the clear?"

"Shortly," Milla responded over the network. "Distance to FTL transit is three light-minutes for the Archangels. I would prefer at least five for the *Dutchman*, however."

"Five should be fine," Steph said. "Set your courses for our planetoid outside the Aerin Kingdom. We'll split up to scramble our direction and meet up there once we're certain we're in the clear. *Archangel One* and *Two*, I'll need your eyes."

"Roger," Tyke said. "With you to the end of the line, boss."

"Just don't make it seem too *close* next time," Noire countered.

"No promises." Steph grinned. "Don't you know, it's a pirate's life!"

Epilogue

Seamus Gordon stood with hands clasped in front of him as he supervised the loading of the second half of the squadron's payment for services rendered. The Star Kingdom had made good on their end of the bargain with what was, by all accounts, a king's ransom in naturally formed quantum computing cores.

He wasn't really sure what they were, but every bit of information he'd been able to gather confirmed that the crystals in the crates were valuable enough to warrant starting a war.

Or helping end one—for the time being, at least.

Gordon didn't give a damn about the cores. He was aware he might change his tune on that, but for the moment the only true value they had to him was the credit they established for the squadron legend.

Demanding a high price for their help made Stephanos' little privateer squadron more respectable in the eyes of the locals, and that had real value of its own. If the crystals were actually worth the effort, well, that would be a bonus. He had no doubt that the Confederation and the Priminae, as well as the Block he supposed (not that he particularly cared about them), would be highly interested in what passed for resources out in this sector of the galaxy.

He looked over to where the commander was speaking with their contact, Auran, now captain of the *Gael*, smiling as he considered the new assignment he'd wrangled himself.

It's good to be out in the field again, and this is the farthest in the field anyone has ever been.

"Congratulations on your promotion," Steph said to the Kingdom's captain while they allowed others to handle the exchange of payment.

He had been pleased that the Kingdom kept up their end of the bargain with minimal hassles. He had half expected them to try to pull a fast one. Lord knew he'd been the victim of that in the past, and then he hadn't been operating as an "independent" contractor.

"Thank you, Captain Teach," Auran said, his use of the name and rank forcing Steph to bury a grin. "Without your help, the events of the past few days would have turned out far differently."

"It was a pleasure, even if your politicians tried to steal my destroyer," Steph said with a bit of a smirk.

"Not so much steal, Captain, they merely questioned whether the rights of capture were included in our agreement," Auran corrected him with a glint in his eye.

"Potato, potahto," Steph said.

"Pardon? I am afraid I do not understand?"

"Don't worry about it."

"I have been instructed to inquire as to whether your services will be available in the future," Auran said, the humor draining from him.

Steph understood why a career military man wouldn't be happy asking a question like that, so he didn't let it bother him too much. They'd been dancing around this since he and his squadron had reappeared in Star Kingdom space with their captured destroyer in tow.

Negotiations had been such that he was fairly sure the inquiry was coming and had factored that expectation into things. Some of the former crew of the newly christened *Flying Dutchman* had opted, perhaps surprisingly, to continue serving with the pirates who'd taken the ship.

Frankly, he thought that was insane, but when the first had asked for permission to serve with him, Steph allowed it and unknowingly opened the floodgates. In retrospect, perhaps he should have realized that would happen and refused, but such a stance would have been out of character for the role he'd chosen. He had no desire to press-gang anyone into service, as some pirates had historically, but he didn't think it would look right to turn down volunteers.

Establishing clear lines would be essential in defining the recruits from his core force, but that would be simple enough. His people were soldiers, and they knew what flag they truly flew under. The rest? Well, they would be his as well, and he would treat them as such in every way—every way save one.

There was zero chance that any of them would ever be permitted to gain access to anything that even hinted at the squadron's true allegiance. Infiltrators were not just a possibility, going forward; Steph was well aware that they would become a certainty at some point. A mercenary group was something that local governments, to say nothing of the Empire itself, would want to keep tabs on, particularly a *successful* mercenary group.

Which works in our favor, as long as we keep them all in the dark.

The legend they were building needed to be bulletproof, able to survive *any* scrutiny. So he would make certain that was exactly what it was.

As for the rest of the captured or rescued crews, he'd arranged for repatriation through the Star Kingdom. Apparently, such events happened with some regularity, so a system was in place to facilitate the exchange of crews taken after battles.

I don't know if that's depressing or comforting. But at least they don't make a habit of taking no prisoners the way the Empire does.

"We will be available, depending on the case and prior commitments," Steph answered, "with the understanding that we have no interest in tangling with the Empire. I don't know what they were up to, but an Imperial Fleet is out of our weight class."

"Not only yours," Auran said with a heavy tone. "We do not know why, but the Empire has been raiding several of the larger polities in the region. Thankfully, I suppose, we here in the Kingdom have been considered beneath their notice this pass."

Steph nodded. He had a good idea what the Empire was doing. If he was right, the region was going to blow up with infighting in the very near future. Bad for local stability, but an excellent environment for a private contractor to make a reputation for himself.

"Well, aside from that limitation, we'll consider contracts with the Kingdom going into the future," Steph assured the captain.

"Elements within the government will be grateful to hear that," Auran confirmed. "And though I probably should not admit this, I am not as opposed to having your support on hand as I am supposed to be."

Steph chuckled. "I believe we will be able to work together well enough, Captain."

"And I, Captain."

———

NACS Odysseus, *Outer Priminae Space*

"Coded signal, Commodore. Archangel tags," the communications officer said. "Tight beam signal, sent from nearby."

Eric looked up. "Send it to my console. Don't look for the source."

"Aye, aye, sir."

Eric tagged the compressed folder as it hit his system, running it through his personal decryption key, and opened it up.

Most of the material he set aside, which would have to be examined in detail later. For the moment he was interested in the synopsis. That had been kept to a single page, written concisely in the manner he was used to from the war, complete with the little flourishes that Steph was prone to use.

He smiled as he read, memories of good times and bad accompanying the experience.

Well, it seems that Steph is getting into his new job, Eric thought, grinning as he finished. Gaia's Revenge *and the* Flying Dutchman. *Cute.*

He was struck by the fact that Steph had taken a prize ship, a decision that seemed a little reckless even for Steph, at least until he noted the last part of the report. One of the image files sent in the coded transmission was a complete core dump of the destroyer's computer system. The intelligence there would be damn near invaluable, even if it was tangential to the true target of interest in the area. A ship might or might not have been worth the risk, but that computer core certainly was.

Eric tagged all the files for immediate relay to the admiral and closed them down.

For the moment, he had more on his plate than whatever Steph was up to.

"Have we located any sign of the Imperial Fleet in this sector?"

"Negative, sir."

"Alright, move on to the next one."

"Aye, aye."

Eric looked out into the depths of space beyond the ship, his thoughts on the mysterious opponent waiting for him out there in the black.

This game has just gotten more interesting, and more complicated.

Imperial Capital, World Garisk

"Your Highness, you asked to be informed of former Lord Jesan's progress?"

Emilia Starsbane looked up. "Oh? Has he done something interesting? Or did he fail?"

"Neither, exactly, Your Majesty."

The aide frowned, hesitating, which irritated the empress to no end.

"Out with it, fool."

"Sorry, Your Majesty. The former lord . . . The fleet commander has reported an unknown contact within the so-called Free Stars."

Emilia stiffened, sucking in a breath. "The anomalies from the Priminae worlds?"

"Apparently not, Your Majesty. Likely merely a new class of vessel, much smaller than even the normal destroyers that are common in the region," the aide said. "Analysts suggest that the locals are likely growing more desperate for resources and have opted to build lighter, high-speed vessels to combat their fellows. They are quite fast and apparently a match for destroyers, but Jesan reports that they do not appear to have the power to handle even our cruisers, to say nothing of larger classes."

Emilia relaxed marginally, though she was still unhappy to hear of yet *another* new variable being added to what the Empire was dealing with.

"Thank you for the report. You may go."

The aide left, leaving her standing in the center of her reception room.

"What do you make of that, Father?"

"It will require more study, Daughter," he said as he walked in behind her. "But you know this."

"I know. I just . . ." She smiled wistfully. "I wish you were still here with me, Father."

"I am here always, child," the figure behind her said, wavering in the light before fading away, leaving only his voice. "Together, we will make the galaxy pure. Never forget."

"I won't," she promised in a whisper to the empty air where the figure had been, her eyes sparkling with fervor. "I will cleanse it with fire, for you, Father."

ABOUT THE AUTHOR

Bestselling Canadian author Evan Currie has an imagination that knows no limits, and he uses his talent and passion for storytelling to take readers everywhere from ancient Rome to the dark expanses of space. Although he started out dabbling in careers such as computer science and the local lobster industry, Currie quickly determined that writing the kinds of stories he grew up loving was his true life's calling. Beginning with the techno-thriller *Thermals*, Evan has expanded the universe within his mind with acclaimed series such as Warrior's Wings, the Scourwind Legacy, the Hayden War Cycle, and Odyssey One. He delights in pushing the boundaries of technology and culture, exploring the ways in which these forces intertwine and could shape the future of humanity—both on Earth and among the stars.